A MAN
FOR GLORY

BY

CAROLYN DAVIDSON

First published in Great Britain 2013
by Mills & Boon, an imprint of Harlequin (UK) Limited.
Large Print edition 2013
Harlequin (UK) Limited, Eton House,
18-24 Paradise Road, Richmond, Surrey TW9 1SR

© Carolyn Davidson 2013

ISBN: 978 0 263 24139 6

Ha
renewable and recyclable products and made from wood grown in sustainable forests. The logging and manufacturing process conform to the legal environmental regulations of the country of origin.

Printed and bound in Great Britain
by CPI Antony Rowe, Chippenham, Wiltshire

Reading, writing and research—**Carolyn Davidson**'s life in three simple words. At least that area of her life having to do with her career as a historical romance author. The rest of her time is divided among husband, family and travel—her husband, of course, holding top priority in her busy schedule. Then there is their church, and the church choir in which they participate. Their sons and daughters, along with assorted spouses, are spread across the eastern half of America, together with numerous grandchildren. Carolyn welcomes mail at her post office box, PO Box 2757, Goose Creek, SC 29445, USA.

Previous novels by the same author:

A MARRIAGE BY CHANCE
THE TEXAN
TEMPTING A TEXAN
STORMWALKER'S WOMAN
  (short story in *One Starry Christmas*)
TEXAS GOLD
THE MARRIAGE AGREEMENT
ABANDONED
  (short story in *Wed Under Western Skies*)
TEXAS LAWMAN
OKLAHOMA SWEETHEART
A CHRISTMAS CHILD
  (short story in *The Magic of Christmas*)
LONE STAR BRIDE
MARRIED IN MISSOURI
  (short story in *Mail-Order Marriages*)

and in Mills & Boon® Super Historical Romance:

REDEMPTION
HAVEN
THE OUTLAW'S BRIDE
THE BRIDE

A MAN FOR GLORY is dedicated to those women who found happiness in marriages of convenience—a common occurrence in the olden days. My own grandmother, at the age of fifteen, came from Austria to marry a man in Dearborn, Michigan, without ever seeing him. It was a marriage that produced seven children, one of whom was my father. I have a love for such relationships, and write about them often.

And, as always, this work in its entirety is dedicated to Mr. Ed, who loves me.

Prologue

Green River, Kansas
1847

The man who answered the door looked as if he'd seen better days. His hands were work-worn, his clothing no doubt soiled from toiling in the field out back of the barn. The pitchfork he'd apparently been using leaned against the side of the house, as if he'd left it there so it would be handy when he returned to the seemingly insurmountable job he'd left undone. Hay lay on the ground in neat rows, drying in the sun.

It looked as if he might be in need of help and so she offered. "I'm looking for a job, mister. My name is Glory Kennedy. I need a place to stay and work for my keep. I can cook and clean and I'm a hard worker."

Her gaze met his, and shadows beneath his

eyes told of long days and nights without enough sleep. And the words he spoke carried the ring of truth.

"Pleased to meet you. I can sure use some help here. But one thing we'll get straight right off. I won't be lookin' to get underneath your skirts, girl. I just want a woman to take care of my young'uns and keep things up around here. My name's Harvey Clark, a widow man with more work than I can handle. I'd be pleased should you give me a hand. There's an extra bedroom you can use."

The man's offer was far from what Glory had hoped to hear back during those days when she'd been a dreamer. But life had proved to be one set of failures after another, with the latest landing her on this man's doorstep, hearing him offer her a life of servitude and not much of a promise for a future.

She'd walked away from the wagon train after her parents were buried, lying side by side with many more from the group. Diphtheria was a powerful disease, and had it not been for Glory's mother sending her from the wagon when she and her father became ill, she'd have no doubt been buried along the trail with the dozen or so who'd been put to rest beneath the prairie grass.

Her unwillingness to choose a husband from any of the survivors who'd offered had left her on her own, for a woman unmarried could not travel with a wagon train. And so she'd run, across the open country where tall grasses grew in endless meadows, to where a small town cast its shadow on the horizon. And then the sight of a group of buildings, a tidy farm, had offered shelter of a sort.

Now the man who stood before her offered her more of the same future that had sent her fleeing just days since. Except that this one claimed he had no interest in lifting her skirts, only needing her to tend his children and keep them and their clothing clean.

Looking at it from that viewpoint, she was tempted to quit running and hiding and instead seize the opportunity to settle in one spot for longer than a day or two.

"How many children do you have?" she asked him, noting the rough beard, the shaggy hair, the fatigued eyes.

"Two. A boy past the age for startin' school,

and a girl, walkin' and talkin', but not much use to me yet."

She needed all the cards laid out on the table, so she prodded a bit more. "You want them cared for? And you want someone to cook and clean?"

His head had been bowed, but now he lifted weary eyes to her, and she saw beyond the wrinkled clothing, the lean body and the whiskered face. Saw a man at the end of his rope. A man who might be the means to an end for her. An end to running, a chance to catch her breath and find a new beginning.

"And you won't expect me to—" Unable to utter the words, she felt a blush cover her cheeks and heard a dry chuckle from the man who faced her on the narrow porch.

"No, I won't expect anything of you but that you treat my young'uns right, and see to it there's food on the table."

From behind him, a small face peered past his denim trousers. Wide blue eyes viewed her with suspicion and a small hand rose to press against a soft mouth. The child was probably two or three years old, if her father's words were to be believed, for she was obviously the one who walked and talked but wasn't of much use to the man.

Small for her age, but bright-eyed and dainty, she viewed this stranger as though she hoped for some small bit of attention.

"This is your daughter?" Glory asked quietly, venturing a smile at the child.

"Essie's her name. Her mama called her Esther, but she answers to most anything." His big hand touched the matted hair, resting there in a gesture Glory decided could pass for affection. And that small gesture decided her future.

A man couldn't be all bad when he touched a small child so kindly, when his first thought was for someone to tend her needs. And so she nodded briskly, sealing her fate for the days ahead.

"I'll take on your children, mister. I'll cook and keep things clean if you've told me the truth about having a room of my own where I won't be disturbed and food for me to cook. I'll need a washtub and a scrubbing board and a good supply of soap. I don't cook in a dirty kitchen, and from what I can see past you, yours isn't much to brag about."

Glory saw the look of hope that formed on his weathered face. "I'll provide what you need if you'll take on my young'uns and feed them some good meals and wash up their clothes."

"You've got a deal, mister," Glory said, recognizing that a better prospect might not be available should she keep on walking.

"Just one thing, missy." His eyes darkened as he gave her chapter and verse of his bargain. "You'll marry me, first chance we have to get to town. My kids won't be living in a house with a man and woman who don't share the same name. And if something happens to me, they need to know that there's somebody who'll look out for them."

Glory swallowed hard, taken aback by the words he spoke, and then she tilted her chin and spit out her own conditions. "The bargain will still remain, mister. I'll still have my own bed and you'll stay out of it."

His look was hard, but his brief smile gave consent to her words. "I give you my word, girl." His head jerked toward the interior of the house. "I had one woman up there in my bedroom. A mighty good woman. There ain't another alive can take her place. I don't want another one."

Glory nodded her agreement and stepped past him, her steps slow as she walked through the doorway into the farmhouse that would be her home.

And as she passed by the small girl, a tiny hand

reached up to touch her own, as a fragile smile appeared on the small, dirty face.

"Tell you what, Essie. Let's get you washed up and your hair combed. I'll warrant you're a pretty girl."

"Yes, ma'am," the child said quietly. And in that moment Glory's heart was touched and her courage strengthened by the choice she'd made.

Chapter One

Green River, Kansas
1850

"**Y**our papers seem to be in order, Mr. McAllister. What I want to know is why the bank sent a Pinkerton man out here to see me." The sheriff held the sheaf of paperwork in his hands, glancing once more at the first page of Cade McAllister's identification, the details certifying him a Pinkerton detective, in the employ of a large bank in St. Louis.

"You had a hanging here a month or so ago, sir. I was sent to verify the man's identity and begin a search on behalf of the bank for the money he took in a robbery ten years ago. The bank had a dandy time catching up with him. Pure luck they ran him down to ground here."

The sheriff nodded bruskly. "The man was

Harvey Clark and though it was a nasty business, I did just what I was ordered to do by the government. Clark was a bank robber, according to the details I was given. I was all set to send him back to St. Louis, and let the law there handle it, but my orders were clear. He was sentenced to death by hanging ten years ago, and when he escaped in a jailbreak, his sentence trailed right along behind him. They gave me the job of carrying it out here in Green River."

"Sounds like we're on the same page, Sheriff. Can't say I envy a lawman his job when it comes to such stuff, but my job now is to try locating the gold."

Joe Lawson chuckled. "More power to you, McAllister. There's been a dozen men digging around on the Clark farm in the last couple of weeks and no one's had any success yet. My guess is, it's in the house somewhere, but I've made it my business to take that place apart since the hanging and couldn't find hide nor hair of it. The cellar's an open book, the pantry the same. I went over the bedrooms with Mrs. Clark's permission. I think she'd like to have the gold located same as me. It'd save her a lot of frustration, should it come to light, for she fears the chance of strangers coming by and giving her a hassle over it."

"Well, I'm the next best fella for the job, it seems. The insurance company doesn't want Mrs. Clark to know who I am. They've given me a cover as a man looking for a farm to buy, with a nice nest egg in my pocket."

"Mrs. Clark isn't interested in selling her place, McAllister. Nor in getting married and giving the title to a husband. And that's what will happen should she marry again. The law don't do much for women, you know."

Cade grinned. "I know all about that. My mother was left a ranch when Pa died, and when she remarried, it all went to her new husband. Fortunately, he was a man of honor and he took care of her and raised me and my brothers the way my pa would have wanted."

Joe Clark nodded knowingly. "She's a lucky woman, then. Lots of men are looking to free-load. Glory Clark's been stung a couple times, had to use her shotgun to chase off a fella or two when they came courting. She's a good woman, McAllister, and I won't put up with any shenanigans where she's concerned. You'll be honest with her so far as you can."

"I won't tell her who I represent, Sheriff. My job is to find the gold that Harvey Clark hid somewhere. I'll get a reward for it, and keep my hands clean. I'm not a thief, nor a man to harm a woman in any way."

The sheriff placed the sheaf of paperwork on his desk with a flurry of pages scattering hither and yon. He gathered them up into a pile and opened his desk drawer, placing them inside. "Your job is your own business, McAllister. I'll introduce you to the widow lady as a man looking to buy a place in this area. I'll show her the stuff the bank sent that covers you, the letters from your minister in your hometown, and give you my recommendation as an honest man."

"How do we go about meeting this lady, Sheriff?" Cade asked, already looking ahead to the task he'd assumed. One way or another he'd find the gold, and in the process, leave the lady a bit to help her along in her struggles.

"Let's take a ride out there right now, McAllister. She's always at home, what with two youngsters to take care of."

And without further ado, the men rode west from Green River to where a holding sat several miles out of town. A sign over the lane leading to the house read, The Clark Farm, and near the unpainted house, a woman stood in the midst of a garden.

"That's Mrs. Clark, McAllister. She's young, but capable. Been raising those two young'uns by herself and running this farm alone. I won't stand for anyone giving her a hassle."

"I read you right, Sheriff," Cade said, taking in the small figure ahead of them. She was dark-haired and slender, a woman who appeared too small to be saddled with a farm and two children to raise. "There won't be any shenanigans on my part."

"If I didn't feel you were a man to be trusted, I wouldn't have brought you here, mister. Now let's introduce you and I'll leave you to it." The sheriff raised a hand in greeting and they halted their mounts near Glory Clark.

"Mrs. Clark," the sheriff said in greeting. "This here is a fella who's on the lookout for a piece of property to buy and run. I told him about your farm and he's mighty interested in making a deal with you."

"I'm not giving up my farm, Sheriff. I thought you were aware of that," Glory said firmly.

"Ma'am, I'd like a chance to talk to you and

meet your children. This place looks to be a fine setting for a horse-breeding and training ranch. I'd like to give you my credentials and introduce you to my thoughts for your place," Cade said with assurance.

"How would you know all that just from riding up my lane and taking a gander at the place, mister? I'm willing to sit down on the back porch and talk to you, but I'll tell you right now, I'm not willing to sell out to anyone."

The man nodded. "My name's Cade McAllister, from Oklahoma. I'm good with horses and know all the ins and outs of running a farm. I can put in a good day's work with the best of them, ma'am. Perhaps I can be of some use to you here. Anyway, can we sit and talk?"

There was about the man a look of honesty, Glory thought. He was sturdy, a man of strength, if she was any judge. Besides, the sheriff seemed to think he was to be trusted. His clothing was clean and a bit worn, but his saddle was well oiled and the horse he rode was a good one, a stallion of perhaps sixteen hands, held under control by the man's easy grip on the reins.

It wouldn't hurt to hear him out, she decided. She led the way to the porch and called into the screen door as she climbed the steps. "Essie, please bring out some lemonade, and a plate of the cookies we baked this morning."

Within minutes, a small child, pretty as a picture, appeared in the doorway, sidling past the threshold with a tray in her hands. "Here you go, Glory. I didn't know how many glasses you wanted, so I brought four." Small and delicate in stature, the child was fair-haired with eyes as blue as a summer sky, with a ready smile for the visitor.

Glory touched the girl on the shoulder and took the tray from her hands. "Thanks, Essie. Now, go find Buddy, then both of you come back here and sit with us."

"Yes, ma'am," she answered, and ran off across the yard to the barn.

"Won't you sit down, sir?" Glory asked the visitor.

"Yes, ma'am. I surely will. My name is Cade, ma'am. The sheriff said yours is Glory Clark."

She looked down the lane toward the town road, where the sheriff rode his horse at a steady trot. "Guess he's heading back to town. You know, I had a bad time with him, what with him robbing my young'uns of their pa the way he did. But he's been kind to us since then. He's a pretty sharp man, to tell the truth. If he trusts you, guess there isn't any reason for me not to do the same," Glory said. "Now, what are you wanting to offer me?"

Cade handed her a sheaf of papers and sat back on a rocker near the back door. "I'm a man of sufficient means, Mrs. Clark. I have a decent nest egg in the bank and a good knowledge of horses and such. I've been looking for a place to buy and I'm mighty interested in this one." His gaze rested for a moment on her face, then slid to encompass her entire body as he spoke again. "I'm an honest man and if you'll read the paperwork I gave you, I think you'll see that I'm on the up-and-up."

Glory nodded, admiring the man before her. And that in itself was a strange happening, for she had been made offers aplenty, both for her property and her hand in marriage, by a number of men from the surrounding countryside, and none of them had earned more than a wave of her shotgun for their trouble. Cade McAllister was different. He was tall and well-built, with eyes that looked at her squarely, and documents that might support his claims. He appealed to a part

of her that had long been cold and empty, bringing to life a warmth within her very being.

"Let me read this over, Mr. McAllister. If you
have the time, you can join us for supper. And
perhaps you'd like to bed down in the barn tonight. Tomorrow I'll hear you out, but I'll tell you
now, I'm not looking to sell my place. We'll talk
more, after I've had a chance to deal with this
raft of papers you've given me to read."

Cade nodded. "That makes sense to me, ma'am.
Can I wash up at the horse trough?"

"Either there or in the kitchen," Glory answered. She rose and went into the house, Essie
and Buddy following behind. Without instructions, the two children washed their hands and
faces and prepared to set the table. Glory watched
as her guest washed at the sink and then stood
by her table.

She nodded at a chair and he sat, speaking to
Buddy in a casual manner. Glory watched as
she prepared the food for the table, and a shiver
took her unaware as Cade glanced up at her and
smiled. Perhaps she'd been foolish, allowing
him into her home. And yet…she looked at him
again and met his gaze. Dark eyes seemed to
see her very thoughts and his mouth curved in a

warm smile. She could only hope she hadn't put her family in peril. She shook her head, a small movement that denied that idea.

Another glance at Cade found him grinning at Buddy, and then Buddy addressed Glory, his smile wide as he spoke of the man who sat beside him. "I sure do enjoy talking about books and such with Cade, Glory. He's read a whole lot of stuff, some that I've read, too. I'm gonna show him the ones the teacher from the school in town lent to me. Maybe after we eat, he can go in the parlor and look at my library."

Library. Glory thought of the six or seven books that comprised the boy's collection. Hopefully Cade would voice his approval of them and thus encourage Buddy. She considered the impact the man had made here already. She could only hope that his presence would not be a mistake that would cost her… And then she faced the truth of the matter as she recalled his words. I'm interested in this place. But his meaning was clear, for a good portion of his interest was focused on her, Glory Clark.

He might have already cost her more than she could afford.

Chapter Two

"Get out some bowls and small plates, Essie." Glory issued instructions as she brought a kettle of soup to the table, then sought out a ladle to use. Filling the bowls Essie provided her, she placed one before each chair and spoke again to the girl who watched her.

"Get some butter in the pantry, please, and bring out some jam," Glory said quietly, and Essie moved quickly to obey. A container of jam in one hand, the plate of butter in the other, she paused by Cade's chair and shot him a quick grin as she arranged the table. Glory sliced bread with a steady hand and filled a plate with the remains of a loaf she'd unwrapped from the kitchen dresser where she stored her bread.

A coffeepot sat on the back burner of the kitchen range and Essie ran to find a cup for

Cade, then brought it to him and placed it by his bowl. "I'll get you a glass for milk, Glory, and one for me and for Buddy, too."

Glory took a pan of biscuits from the oven and dumped them into a bowl, then put them in the warming oven. "We'll have the strawberries atop the biscuits for dessert, Mr. McAllister. We have lots of cream to serve with them, and we have them often thataway, for biscuits and strawberries are a favorite of the children."

They all took their places at the table, then Glory spoke words of thanksgiving for the food, the children folding their hands while she prayed. Buddy looked up at her as she buttered his bread and scooped honey from the dish and spread it atop the butter.

"Glory, my pa's not ever coming home, is he?" Buddy asked in a quiet voice.

Glory lifted her gaze to the boy. "Buddy, we've talked about this before, and as tough as the answer is, we have to move on with our lives. Your pa is dead and gone, buried in the churchyard. Now we can only do our best to go on as he would have wanted."

"I just feel like he should be here," the boy said quietly. "Every time I look out in the hay field, I think I should see him there. And when I come in the house, I expect to see him at the dinner table or washing up in the sink."

Glory nodded at his words. "I think you're just grieving for your pa, Buddy. It's all right to wish he were still with us, but the truth is that he'll never be back and we have to go on. We'll have to take up the slack and work hard to make him proud of us, won't we? And we won't forget to pray that he's in a better place now."

The boy tore his piece of bread in half and offered it to his sister, who took it with a smile that seemed to be thanks enough for the lad.

The meal was simple, but the four people around the table ate it with relish and then sat back while Glory prepared the strawberry dessert.

"Sure looks good, ma'am," Cade said with a grin.

"Glory cooks good for us," Essie told him, sucking a berry from her spoon, earning a quick look from Glory. "I think I kinda remember the day she came here, but I was pretty small back then."

"Well, I'll never forget that day," Buddy told them. "She was sure pretty, and she washed

Essie's hair and made her a braid and tied a red ribbon on it."

"I do remember that, after all," Essie said with a quick smile at her stepmother. "I'd forgotten the braid and the ribbon."

"I'd say you two have more good memories of Glory than you could ever count. Your pa sure was lucky to have her here with you."

"He married her so she could be our stepmother," Buddy said.

Glory looked at Cade squarely. "It was more to make certain that I would inherit and have this place should anything happen to him, I believe."

Cade nodded his agreement with her words and dug into his dessert. "The children were right. This is delicious, Miss Glory. I can't tell you how much I appreciate a home-cooked meal. I've been riding from town to town, kinda on a quest for a place that would appeal to me and hoping I'd feel a sign of sorts when I saw a spot that would be right for me. But I'll tell you true, any man would want to sit at this table once he'd had a sample of your cooking, Miss Glory."

Glory smiled at him, her gaze assessing. He was a man to be admired, for according to the papers he'd given her to review, he was not only honest and forthright, but had a fund of money available should she want to sell any portion of her farm to him. But if she was to be proven wrong, if this Cade McAllister was not all that he seemed to be, she could be making a big mistake. But then again, if she was right, if the sheriff was correct in his thinking, then Cade might be the salvation she sought, for she was weary of carrying this load alone. He might prove to be a mentor for Buddy, an older brother for Essie, perhaps a friend for herself. Maybe even a man to look out for her and the children on a permanent basis. A man who would be willing to take on the work here and make a success of Buddy's inheritance. Who might consider being a partner in the farm.

Cade helped clear up the table, then watched as she and Essie made short work of the dishwashing. Glory wiped up the table and hung the dish towels on the short line on the back porch, then shook the rug that lay by the back door. Essie put it back in place, a final chore that seemed to end the evening's ritual.

Cade stood and stretched, then pushed his chair back under the table. "I'll be heading for the barn, ma'am," he said. "I'll put my bedroll up in the loft if there's enough hay left up there."

"Enough for a man to sleep on," Glory assured him, watching as he made his way across the yard to the barn. Their usual bedtime came at dusk and tonight was no different, for the children were weary from a long day, and even Glory sought her bed as soon as darkness enveloped the farmhouse. She settled into the feather tick and closed her eyes, but found that sleep eluded her. The man in her barn appeared before her as if he were there in her bedroom, a vision she beheld as she thought of what might be in her future. It would surely be a blessing to have a man to do the chores and work the fields. After turning from one side of the bed to the other, the bedclothes tangling about her body, she rose to find her dressing gown. Tying it firmly at her waist, she slid into her house shoes, then descended the stairs and went out the back door, seeking the silence of the night and the familiar sight of the fruit trees in the orchard.

As she had in the past, she walked among the trees, admiring the blossoms that filled the air with a faint scent. She lifted her eyes to the sky, seeking some bit of wisdom perhaps in the stars that pierced the darkness. Change hovered in the air that surrounded her, and she stood as still as a statue, her gaze upward, thoughts of Cade McAllister filling her mind again. There was about him a sheen of honesty, and she was drawn to him, her body almost seeking out the warmth of his whenever she was near him.

The future loomed before her and she was fearful of what it held, for she was mighty tempted to accept the offer of the man who lay in her hayloft. It was a given that keeping the farm intact for Buddy to inherit one day involved seeking help. Perhaps Cade could be persuaded to work as a partner. She turned from her stargazing and headed back toward the house, hoping she would find Cade agreeable in the morning.

The barn was warm with the body heat given off by the animals, and in the hayloft Cade rolled up in a quilt and found a lush bed beneath the eaves. From below, the cow lowed contentedly, the horses nickering to each other from neighboring stalls. From the house, he heard the closing of the back door, and he quickly rolled to his feet and went to where the door swung easily open over the front of the barn.

Below him, in the moonlight, Glory walked toward the garden, and then beyond that to where a half dozen fruit trees bloomed. Her hair hung long against her back, freed now from the dark braid she'd confined it in during the day. It rippled in the moonlight, a cloud that reached her hips and swung with each step she took.

He watched her for perhaps a half hour, until she turned finally from her stargazing and pondering and made her way back past the fruit trees and through the garden to the back porch. As she turned toward the house, she looked at the barn, her gaze moving across its door, up to the roof and finally to the window in the loft where he stood, watching her.

"Mrs. Clark, wait up a minute. We need to talk." His voice was pitched low, but it apparently carried to where she stood, for she nodded, sliding her hands into the pockets of her dressing gown as she turned to sit on the edge of the porch, waiting silently.

He climbed down from the loft and approached across the yard to stand before her. Glory touched the porch beside her, a silent invitation for Cade to settle there. He sighed as he took a seat next to her, then cleared his throat.

"Glory, I hesitate to bring this up, but I'm gonna be blunt. I've heard the whole story from the sheriff, about Mr. Clark being in jail and sentenced to death. I know about the hanging in Green River and him leaving you with two children to raise on your own. The sheriff said you were married to the man a couple of years back when you were looking for a place to live and he needed someone to tend his house and family."

"That's all true, Cade. I was looking for a place to stay and he took me in."

"And now the positions are reversed, Glory, for I'm the one looking and you've given me a place in your hayloft to sleep for the night. Sound kinda familiar to you?"

She looked up at him for a long moment and then with a curt nod, agreed. "I can see what you mean, but I don't understand why you've chosen to settle in this area. What reason do you have for wanting to work a farm here in the middle of nowhere?"

He looked down at her, admiring the vision of loveliness before him. "I've been looking for a long spell for a place to settle. My family's in Oklahoma and I could go back there and find some land and live close to home, but there's something about Green River that appeals to me. I spoke to the sheriff about the available places hereabouts and he said yours was the best of the lot, but that you weren't interested in selling. But he did say that your place was needful of a man to work it, and you and the children were having a tough time keeping things going. I asked him to bring me out here to meet you, and maybe come to an agreement with you. This farm sounded like the sort of place I was looking for. Two hundred acres, a sturdy barn, a house that's been tended over the years and only needs a coat of paint to bring it up to snuff. A woman and two children who'd benefit from a man around the place to keep an eye on things and keep them safe."

"Sounds like you've got everything all sorted out, mister," Glory said sharply. "You sound like you're ready to settle in and be a part of the picture."

"I'd like to at least talk about it with you, Glory. You're a woman alone, and I'm a man looking to invest in a farm. I surely do admire you and respect you for the job you've done here. I don't expect you've looked at me and seen enough to warrant inviting me to stay for a spell but I think we might be able to make a go of it, and hold this place together. Make it into a prosperous holding for Buddy to inherit. I like a challenge, Glory, and this farm seems to be offering just such a challenge to me. I'm not trying to push you into making a decision right this minute, but I'm willing to give it a chance to work out. Should you take me up on my offer to invest here and help you make a success of the place, we'd have to present a united front. Between us, we'd be supplying a good home in which to raise these two young'uns you've been caring for. They deserve a family surrounding them, and you and I could give them that very thing."

Glory looked shocked by his words. "If you're talking about marriage, I'll tell you right now, I'm not ready for that, Cade. I know these children need a father figure in their lives, but for now, we're doing all right on our own. The question is, would a marriage be the best thing for them? Or for me? Might not a partnership work better?"

"Look. Glory, since you're not willing to sell your place outright, might you agree to me investing my money here and become half owner of the farm? I'll work hard in the fields and teach Buddy how to handle horses and give him a chance to become a horse trainer himself if he'd like to learn the trade."

"The children and I are used to working hard, Mr. McAllister. I've carried my share of the load over the years and done whatever I had to in order to provide for Buddy and Essie."

"You earned your way here, if I see things straight, ma'am. You're an intelligent woman, for you've had schooling beyond the ordinary, I'd say, from your speech and the ability you have to express yourself."

She nodded. "I went to college back home for two years. In fact, I have enough schooling to teach, should I ever want to. For now, just doing lessons with Buddy and Essie is satisfying enough for me."

Cade thought again of the man whose death had brought him here. "I can't help but think that Mr. Clark would be pleased to have me here, ma'am. He thought enough of you to marry you and leave you with this place. I'd say you both gained from your bargain. What I don't understand is why no one from town stepped up to offer for you after your husband died."

Glory pressed her lips together as if thinking of her reply. And then she sighed. "When the sheriff took Harvey in to jail, the story made its way around that he was a bank robber, and I had a couple of the hired hands from ranches west of here stop by and offer to look for the money Harvey was accused of stealing. I sent them off without much of an answer, just the shotgun in my hands. I don't know if Mr. Clark did what he was accused of doing or not. But I don't think there's any money around here, for it seems that in three years I'd have found some trace of the gold he was supposed to have stolen somewhere around this house. And he sure didn't seem to have any extra to spend. He was a thrifty man, but he took care of his own."

She looked up at him then, and her words were a warning. "If you've got any ideas about gold here, mister, I'll tell you right now, there won't be any digging around or searching my house for a treasure. The only thing worth having in this place is those two young'uns upstairs in bed. I don't believe that Mr. Clark left anything more precious than that. He'd have told me otherwise."

Cade nodded thoughtfully, preparing the lie he was about to speak. "That may very well be, ma'am. At any rate, I'm not looking to find any gold. I don't consider it important enough to be digging holes or searching through your attic in the hopes of finding a treasure. I'm looking for a place to work and make my way and maybe make something of what I've been offered."

Cade cleared his throat, considering the lie he'd just spoken so readily. He'd traveled the country in his job, for being a Pinkerton man paid well and he'd never come out empty handed at the end of a quest. Still, he felt guilty for lying to Glory.

He eyed the woman before him and knew that his plan was more tempting than it might have been had Glory Clark not been so lovely a woman, had she not appealed to him so much. Offering her the story he'd halfway conceived in his mind, he began, knowing he would be living a lie with every breath he took.

He doffed his hat, and his gaze on her face was hopeful. "I'm thinking if you marry me, we could kinda work things out for everyone's benefit, ma'am. I never planned on this sort of thing, And if it's any comfort to you, I'll make a vow to you that I won't be looking for gold while I'm here. I'll be too busy with working and fixing things up the way Mr. Clark would have wanted it.

"I'm changing topics here, ma'am, but I think

it's important to settle one thing. Did anyone ever come looking for your husband? Maybe strangers who might have known him from the past? It seems like he'd have been the object of a search of sorts over the years."

"Not that I know of," Glory said slowly, her thoughts scanning the years past, seeking answers to his questions. "We lived from one day to the next, not a lot of money to do with, but enough to get along. He didn't seem to have any secrets that I could tell. But he did seem to keep a good eye out, making sure no one was around that didn't belong in the area."

"Well, keep thinking about it, Glory. You may remember something that seemed unimportant at the time. And in the meantime, consider my plans for our future.

"My father died when I was but a child, about Buddy's age—ten, I think—and left my mother with a place to keep up and bills to pay and no cash coming in."

"I'd say that sounds familiar," Glory said softly.

"Yeah, well, it's what happened, and we were left in a tough spot. There was a neighbor man, a widower, who came by a few days after the funeral and spoke with my mother, told her he was willing to take on the job of husband and father if she was agreeable to it. To make a long story short, she took him at his word, and he became my stepfather. He didn't adopt me— my name is the same as my natural father's, but in every way that counted he was our dad, me and my brothers'. He raised us, took care of my mother and ran the farm for her. I don't know if he loved her to begin with—probably not—but he saw a need and knew he could fill it. So he did. He made a success out of the place, made good money, and best of all, they were happy together."

"And did you see the same sort of need here?" she asked, studying the ground beneath her feet.

"Yeah, you could say that, I suppose. I could almost hear my dad speaking in my ear. Telling me this was my chance to show my gratitude for what he'd done for my family all those long years ago. I won't tell you any tall tales, or make up a glowing picture of our future together. But I will tell you I'll be faithful and honest and do my best to help you and the children, just the way Harvey Clark would have wanted."

Glory looked up at him, admiring his height, the broad shoulders that pulled his shirt tight over his chest. He was a good-looking man, surely a man most women would admire, and she was no exception. But she needed to be sure that he was on the up-and-up before she made any drastic decisions.

"I'm not sure I want to be an object of charity, Cade, but I suspect I can see better why you're doing this. It made me wonder about you, why a man would take on a family and be responsible for two children the way you've said you would."

He grinned and shrugged his shoulders. "I'll admit that the idea of having a place of my own appeals to me. This is your farm, but if I stay here, it won't be just as a hired hand. There's the matter of marriage to be settled, Glory. It won't work any other way."

He lifted his hand to her face, tilting her chin up so that she met his gaze. His voice softened as he spoke. "I will tell you that you're a woman who'd appeal to any man with eyes in his head. I don't understand why half a dozen men haven't asked you to marry them." And then he hesitated.

"The town will no doubt look askance at me being here, living with you and the children, without a wedding taking place. I'll not cause you to fret about that part of it tonight, but we need to be making a decision right quick."

"I'll think about it, Cade. In fact, I probably won't be thinking of much else." With but a moment of hesitation, Glory slid from her seat on the edge of the porch, and then climbed the steps and went into the house.

The man took her breath. He made her tremble deep inside where her heart dwelt.

She made her way in the dark, through the kitchen and up the stairs, to where her bedroom was tucked beneath the eaves. She'd slept alone there for three years, dependent upon Harvey Clark for a place to live. He'd been good to her, and though he'd probably made mistakes aplenty in his life, he hadn't caused her any grief. He'd only done as he'd promised. She tossed her dressing gown over a chair and crawled into bed, clad in her long white nightgown. There to sleep fitfully, her dreams filled with visions of the man who slept in the barn. A man who tempted her as had no other.

Chapter Three

Cade walked slowly back to the barn, his thoughts filled with the prospects he might find here. Glory was the first woman he'd thought about with an eye to the future. But first, he'd have to find the gold he was certain was hidden somewhere in the house, and which he'd been contracted to find. But then…then he'd concentrate on Glory. The thought of marriage with the woman was more than appealing. Perhaps it was time to settle down, once this job was finished.

He climbed the ladder to the loft and sank down into the pile of hay where he'd tossed his bedroll. Settling in, he allowed sleep to overcome him, his body weary from a long day's labor.

Daybreak was announced by the rooster in the chicken coop and Cade awoke, refreshed and ready to look over his surroundings. The barn showed the hand of a good carpenter in its construction, the joists joined properly, the roof intact, the floor solid beneath him. He folded his bedroll, climbed down the ladder and opened the back door of the barn, looking out to where fields stretched almost to the horizon. Those near at hand were lush with grass, pastureland any farmer would hold dear.

Beyond the pasture, a field of hay gleamed in the sunshine, ready for cutting, a crop that would more than fill the hayloft where he'd slept. Harvey Clark had owned a farm worth having. The sheriff had said it comprised two hundred acres, and should the rest of his land show the promise that lay before Cade now, it was a dream come true for the roamer who surveyed it this morning.

Should the woman marry him, he would be the owner of a fine piece of land. The future took on a new look for the man who gazed out upon waving grasses and sunlit fields of hay. It seemed the trail he'd followed for the past few years had finally come to a halt at the end of the rainbow. He'd worked and saved his wages and been a success as a Pinkerton man.

The promise of a good reward for the gold he

sought was worth working for. He'd worked long years as a Pinkerton man and it was time to settle down and seek a future. A future that beckoned him and promised ample reward for the hard work he was willing to put into it. If things worked out as he hoped, his career as a Pinkerton man would be at an end and he would spend his life as a married man should Glory be agreeable. At that thought he grinned, for if Glory went along with his plans, she would be a prize worth having.

He closed his eyes for a moment, remembering the sight of her, dark hair a cloud about her as she walked in the orchard. The woman appealed to him in a mighty way, and he vowed to himself that he'd be in her bed within a week or so.

He heard the sound of Buddy's voice outside the barn, and the big door slid open, revealing him to Cade's sight. The boy headed for the first stall where the cow awaited his attention, and speaking softly, he soothed the animal, "Don't be scared, Daisy. It's just me, comin' to milk you and give you some hay."

"And I'll probably feed the chickens," Cade muttered beneath his breath as he walked from the back door of the barn to where the boy had begun his task.

"Morning, sir," Buddy said looking up with a quick grin, his dark hair still tousled from his pillow.

Cade's index finger rose to touch his hat brim. "Your stepmother fixing breakfast?" he asked.

"Yeah, Glory cooks real good, mister. My pa always said that her staying with us and taking care of us was the best thing that ever happened in our family. 'Course, the baddest thing was when my mama died."

"Was that a long time ago, Buddy?"

"Yeah, I was pretty little then, and Essie was just walking good. She was a bitty little thing, with her long yellow hair and big blue eyes. And then it seemed like a long time before Glory came to the door and she needed a place to live and my pa said she could stay with us if she married him."

Cade felt the hair on his nape quiver. "Your pa wanted to marry Glory?" he asked mildly, even as he felt like balling his fists at the thought.

"He told Glory when she came to stay that she couldn't live in the house with us without them being married. He said it wouldn't look right."

"So they got married?" Cade kept his tone mild, silently urging the boy to continue.

Buddy obliged as if he enjoyed Cade's company. "Yeah, but it didn't make a lot of difference to my pa. Just meant that Glory took care of us and did the cooking and stuff and taught me my letters on account of school is so far away in town. But she told me I could go to 'real' school after the harvest this year if we could afford a horse for me to ride back and forth. But that was before all the trouble with Pa, and now I don't know if I'll still be able to go. There's gonna be lots of work to do and Glory can't do all of it by herself."

"Can you read pretty good, Buddy? Do you have books?" Cade wondered privately just how accomplished a teacher Glory was, though two years in college would have given her a pretty good education. But Buddy left him in no doubt as to her prowess.

"Of course I can read," he said stoutly. "Glory got books from the real teacher in town and I can read all the way through the hardest one she's got. I know my numbers and I can multiply and everything. That guzinta stuff is hard, but I'm working at it."

"Guzinta stuff?" Cade searched his mind for what the boy spoke of but Buddy enlightened him promptly.

"Yeah, you know. Like four guzinta eight two times."

"Oh." A smile fought to appear on Cade's face, but he resisted it manfully. There was no way on God's green earth he would make the boy think he made sport of him. Still, the description of division struck his funny bone and he had to turn away lest he insult the lad.

Buddy propped the pail between his knees and reached for the cow's udders. "Reckon I'd better get busy with the milking. Glory was mixing biscuits when I left the house and she said she'd make rice pudding today 'cause we got lots of extra milk. And then I gotta put the horses out to graze." He muttered the last words, listing his chores and Glory's activities in a muddled rush. One Cade surprisingly found no difficulty in following.

The cow's tail swished, causing Buddy to duck, and he cautioned the animal with a stern word, causing Cade to laugh aloud as he made an offer of help to the boy.

"Tell you what, Buddy. I'll go stake the horses

in the field out back and then gather the eggs and feed the chickens while you milk. That way, we'll be done about the same time and we can go eat that breakfast your stepmother is putting together."

"Would you really, sir?" Buddy's grin was wide as he heard the offer of help, and he hastened to settle down to his chore.

Cade led the four horses out to the knee-high grass behind the corral and pounded stakes he'd found by the back door into the ground. They settled down to graze and he returned to the barn, brushing a quick hand over Buddy's hair as he passed by on his way toward the door and the path to the chicken coop.

The hens were hungry, and when he rattled the feed pan they deserted their nests and made their way with haste to the fenced-in yard. Cade spread the grain with a generous hand and gathered the eggs without event. He made his way to the house, egg pan in hand, and called out from the porch.

"Glory? I've got the eggs and I spread chicken feed for the hens. Buddy is about done with the milking and he said he's ready for breakfast." He opened the screen door and entered the kitchen.

"He told me you're a good cook and I'm willing to sample whatever you've made for us this morning."

Glory grinned, her blue eyes flashing as she shot him a quick look. "Well, come on in, Cade McAllister. Put the eggs in the pantry and wash up at the sink."

"You know, a good crop of hay, two perhaps, would ready this place for the winter, with plenty of feed for the animals. The corn is coming up well, and with some diligent hoeing and hilling, we could have a good crop for the corn crib," Cade said as he found his seat at the table.

"You've obviously learned how to garden well, Glory," Cade said. "Your patch near the house is certainly thriving. Hardly a weed to be seen," he said with a grin.

"I put in a good garden, Cade. And we'll put most everything into Mason jars for the winter. There's tomatoes and potatoes and carrots and all the rest. I planted corn and beans and onions and between Essie and me, we'll fill the pantry with enough to do us for the winter."

"I've spoken of marriage, Glory. The choice is up to you, but I'll admit I'm more than ready to move in and take care of the hay and all the rest before winter." His eyes were intent on her as he spoke. Even without considering the gold he'd contracted with the Pinkertons to find here, Glory was more than worth an offer of marriage. Things were looking up, Cade decided. It might take some time to woo Glory into a wedding, but he had a whole heap of that to spare.

"We having scrambled eggs to go along with that this morning?" he asked, peering over her shoulder as she stirred a pan of sausage gravy.

"I'll put them in the other skillet in just a few minutes, soon as the gravy is ready to put on the back burner," she answered. She glanced at him, a sharp look that gauged his mood and put him in his place. "Don't sneak up behind me, Mr. McAllister. I don't like surprises."

His grin was unrepentant, she noted, but his words made a stab at sincerity. "Yes, ma'am. I'm sure sorry. I'll make more noise next time I look over your shoulder."

She turned from the stove, the big spoon held before her, sausage gravy dripping from its bowl, and his long index finger was quick, catching the tasty drop before it could splash on the floor, and instead sliding it between his lips.

Buddy had followed him into the house, bearing a heavy bucket of milk. "This here's last night's milk, Glory. I'll put it in the pantry. I covered it good last night with a clean towel before I put it in the springhouse." He stowed the pail under a shelf, out of the way from straying feet, and returned to the kitchen, his eyes swerving directly to Cade.

"Like I was tellin' you out in the barn, Mr. McAllister, if I go to real school after the harvest and the last of the hay is cut, Glory says I should do good. She thinks I'm right smart."

"I wouldn't doubt that one little bit," Cade said agreeably. "While I'm thinking about it, son, I'd think you could call me Cade. My pa was Mr. McAllister and I ain't got used to the name yet. Been Cade all my life."

"Yessir, I can sure do that...can't I, Glory?" he asked when he caught a stray glance from his stepmother, who'd turned back to the skillets on the range. "If he says I can call him Cade, it's all right, ain't it? Makes him seem sorta like a friend, don't it?"

Glory nodded as she turned from the stove where she'd poured the bowl of beaten eggs into an iron skillet and faced the two males at her table. Buddy was grinning, and Cade looked right comfortable where he sat, watching the breakfast she cooked. "I'm thinking we'll eat better if there's plates under these eggs and gravy," she said sharply. "Would you see to it, Mr. McAllister?"

"Yes, ma'am, I surely will," he said as he stood and approached the dresser where he'd seen Essie finding dishes and silverware. Four plates and a like number of knives and forks appeared on the table in moments, and he stood behind his chair, waiting.

"Anything else I can do to help, ma'am?" And then, more softly, he said, "I'd like to talk to you after breakfast about what we discussed last night."

"I thought you'd already made up your mind," Glory told him, pouring the sausage gravy into a bowl, then scooping the eggs into another. She placed them on the table, then reached into the warming oven atop the range to pull out a pan of biscuits she'd stored there. In moments, she'd filled the glasses with milk, poured a cup of coffee and put it in front of Cade, and called out for Essie to come to the table.

The girl appeared from the direction of the hallway, a braid hanging ragtag down her back and a look of chagrin on her face. "I can't do my braid the way you make it, Glory. I tried three times already and it don't look right no matter what I do to it."

"Sit down and eat, Essie. I'll braid it up for you after breakfast. It just takes a bit more practice. You'll catch on."

The food smelled tasty, Cade decided, the eggs and gravy steaming in their bowls, the biscuits crusty on the outside, and when he broke one open the inside was light and looked to be tender.

"Mr. McAllister..."

He glanced at her. "Ma'am?" He looked askance, then noted the folded hands the children held before themselves, and bowed his head, holding his own palms together as he'd been silently directed.

Glory spoke a short prayer of blessing on the food and the family; her words were sincere, obviously used often. It was plain she was not displaying company manners, only performing a ritual common to this table.

After the children had chimed in on the "amen," Cade spoke up. "After my pa died, my mama used to always pray before we ate, and then when my stepfather moved in, she said he should take his place in the house as man of the family and he always did it from then on."

The children were silent, and Essie cast Cade a wondering glance, as if she sought out the truth of his position in this house. Glory simply smiled, her comment mild, but much what he would have expected of her.

"We're always thankful for our meals, Mr. McAllister. I know we work hard growing much of the food, but we're thankful for a place to put in a garden, and the rain that waters it for us, and a good well to take up the slack when the rain holds off too long. Sometimes we take turns saying a blessing. You're welcome to take a turn if you like."

The children grinned, and Essie kicked Buddy's ankle and snickered behind her hand, as if imagining the big man across the table doing such a thing. They'd only done it themselves at first to please Glory, for Pa had said that she ran the kitchen, since she cooked the meals, and they must do as she said.

"I'll take the job for supper at night, since I'm planning on being here—for a good while, anyway," Cade said, tossing a look of satisfaction at Glory. He pushed his plate away, the surface of it almost as clean as it had been when it came fresh from the cupboard shelf. "Good breakfast, ma'am."

"Thank you, sir. Now, if you'll put the dirty dishes in the sink, I'll take a few minutes to braid Essie's hair for her." The child moved to stand in front of Glory and in moments the braid was formed and Glory dropped a quick kiss on the smooth cheek as Essie whispered her thanks.

The child ran out the back door, calling for her brother as she went. Buddy left the table to run after Essie, and Glory's eyes touched the man who had cleared the table in barely a minute. His eyebrow twitched and a grin tilted the corner of his lips as he returned her appraising look.

As if he could see within her, his gaze narrowed and his dark eyes glowed. She felt a twinge of uneasiness, wondering at his thoughts. And then he answered her unspoken question before it could be asked.

"We'll work it out, you and me," he said softly, his eyes warm on her face.

"I told you, Mr. McAllister, I don't know if I'm ready for what you want."

"Well, the first thing you might do to prepare yourself is forget the Mr. McAllister thing and remember that my name is Cade. After all, I'm the lucky man you're going to be living with, one way or another."

She looked up at him and her smile was quick, deepening the dimples that dented her cheeks. "You've got a slick way of putting things, McAllister, quite a line of blarney. It sounds to me like you've got things all arranged in your mind."

He chuckled at her words. "Blarney, is it? You're sounding like a colleen from the old country, Glory."

She cast him a flirting glance. "I suspect I come by it honestly, Cade. My father came over on a boat from Ireland, met my mother in New York, who was fresh from England herself, and married her. I suppose I picked up a bit of his way of talking. I catch myself once in a while thinking in my mind, using his words."

"I thought as much. There's just a hint of Irish in your speech, not a lot, but enough to tease me as I listen. And your eyes are like the black Irish. They go with your dark hair."

"My father was dark haired and blue eyed. I suppose I take after him, for my mother was fair."

He hesitated for a moment and then pursued

the point. "Would I be out of line if I asked about your parents? Are they still alive or have you lost them?"

"I know where they are, for all the good it does me. I helped bury them both along the trail near Wichita when a good many on the wagon train sickened with diptheria. So many died in those few days. When my mother sickened, she sent me to a neighboring wagon and I wasn't allowed near my parents again. After they died, the wagon was burned and everything in it, and my parents were buried, along with a dozen or so others who didn't make it."

She spoke in a low voice, the words almost cold, as if she'd placed them so far back in her memory they were in a box named the *past*.

"You're all alone in the world, then," he asked quietly. "No brothers or sisters?"

"No, there was only ever me. Mama didn't have any more babies. But I'm not alone in the world. I have Buddy and Essie. They're my family. Harvey Clark gave them to me the day I moved into his house. They're mine like a small sister and brother would be, almost my own kin."

"You've done a fine job raising them, Glory.

Buddy is a strong boy, seems honest and upright. And Essie is a real sweetheart."

"She's a good girl, is what she is. And Buddy will own this place when he's grown and he'll farm it like his daddy. And Essie will learn to wash clothes and tend to women's work. Like scrubbing out a load of clothes before breakfast."

She left the kitchen then, stepping off the porch, bypassing the farm wagon parked near the house, to where a wash basket sat beneath clotheslines.

She reached into the laundry basket and pulled out a pair of denim pants. Glory snapped them in the air and hung them by the back of the waist, leaving the wind room to blow the legs dry. Three more pair of trousers followed, two of Buddy's and another worn pair, probably left from the children's father. Several shirts followed them onto the line and then Glory lifted the empty basket and placed it on the porch.

She bent to pick up the long pole that would prop the line high, catching the rope between the two nails on top, then standing it upright to allow the breeze access to the clothes that began to billow at the wind's bidding.

She looked up at the line, satisfied with her early morning's work. Tomorrow she would strip the sheets from the beds. Or perhaps the next day, depending on the weather. If it should rain, she would bake bread and churn butter, sweep the parlor and tidy up the bedrooms a bit.

Being settled in a place she could call home was a fine thing, she'd decided three years ago when she'd first come here to live. No one kept an eye on what she did, so she'd done what she pleased, and Harvey Clark had kept his peace, satisfied with the clean house and well-cooked food on his table.

This Cade McAllister looked to be a different kettle of fish. And yet, she felt a bit warmed by his wanting to look out for her. She prided herself on her ability to tend to things on her own, but maybe it would be nice to have someone around who might seek her comfort once in a while. Harvey had been a good man, but they'd lived in two separate worlds, him in the fields and the outbuildings, her in the house and garden. He'd expected her to hold up her end of the bargain they'd struck that first day, and she had done her best.

Cade spoke then. "I was thinking, if there were a fence around the pasture, it would eliminate a lot of hassle, what with staking the animals," he suggested.

"Harvey said he wanted to put up a fence, but he was saving up for it," Glory answered, looking up from the table where she sat, writing sums, a schoolbook in hand.

"Maybe we could do it now, get the fencing from the lumberyard and enough posts to do the job."

"I haven't the money for it," Glory said defensively.

"I have. And I don't mind doing the work. It'll be better in the long run if the animals are free to graze the whole pasture."

"I'd rather you didn't put a lot of money into the place until we decide…" Her voice trailed off as Glory looked beseechingly at Cade.

He smiled, a look of understanding etching his features. "We'll talk later, then. And in the meantime, I'll take a look at what's out there." She nodded her agreement.

Cade left the kitchen, stepping down from the porch, ducking to avoid the clothesline as he headed for the barn. In mere moments he'd gone out the back door and come back into view, walking along the fence line of the corral, a hammer hanging from his belt, a sack of what looked to be nails in his hand. He was checking out the wire to see if it was loosened anywhere, she suspected. One look at Cade McAllister and she'd have sworn he wasn't a farmer, yet there he was out walking the fence line and tending to the stock.

And she was lollygagging around paying mind to him instead of the work that awaited her in the house. She put away the schoolwork she was planning for Essie later on, folding the paper neatly and setting it aside.

She carried her empty basket to the clothesline, her mind busy with thinking of the dinner she was expected to have on the table at noontime. Taking the clothes from the line, she folded them loosely as she went, shaking out wrinkles and smoothing the fabric as she bent over the basket. A bit of care now made the ironing easier, she'd found. And the overalls would do as they were, only the shirts needing the touch of an iron.

The children were waiting for her, their chairs pulled up to the kitchen table, their books and papers neatly sorted. Essie was busy writing on her chalkboard. Buddy's nose was in a book, for he craved reading.

"I wrote a page of numbers for you to work on, Essie," she told the girl.

Essie grinned up at her. "I'm about done with them already," the child answered, finishing up a number nine with a flourish. "I added those you wrote down and did a whole line of take-aways on the bottom, just like you said I should yesterday."

Glory had a habit of writing out Essie's numbers to be added and subtracted every day right after breakfast and left them for Essie to work on. Now she bent over the table to check the little girl's adding and subtracting.

"You did it just right, Essie. I'm proud of you. I'll have to give you harder ones tomorrow. You're almost as good as your brother."

Buddy shot a conspirator's look at Glory, obviously secure in his advanced knowledge and willing to concede a bit to his little sister. "This here is a good book, Glory. It's about the country of France and the people rebelling."

"Is it one the teacher sent?" she asked

"Yes, ma'am. It's called *A Tale of Two Cities.* A man named Charles Dickens wrote it."

"I'm proud of you, Buddy. You'll be more than caught up with the rest of the children your age when you go to school in town after the harvest. You read as well as I do already. After you finish that book I want you to write a report on it for me."

His forehead wrinkled. "What sort of report, Glory?"

"We'll call it a book report. You can decide what you've learned from the story and what it meant to you. You'll have to name the main people in it and tell what happened to them. It'll help you get ready for writing such things in school. And it'll be something for us to show the teacher when you start your first day. Kinda let her see what you can do, so she'll know which grade to put you in."

He seemed to be agreeable to the idea and turned a page in his book, in moments deeply involved once more in the story he'd been reading. Glory watched for a moment, pride alive in her heart for what this boy had accomplished, satisfaction filling her depths because she had had a part in bringing him to this point. And sadness that she had done all it was possible for her to do for him. He needed schooling, more than she could give him, no matter how hard she tried.

And now, with the presence of Cade McAllister in their lives, perhaps she could find the way to do right by the boy.

Chapter Four

"**W**hy don't you take your book to the parlor to read, Buddy. And you can put away your slate and chalk, Essie. I've got to be getting dinner ready. Cade will be hungry, what with working on the fencing all morning."

If the eager look on Cade's face was anything to go by, he was more than ready for dinner when he came through the back door less than an hour later. Glory was alone in the kitchen, mixing dumplings in a bowl to put atop the beef stew she'd readied.

"How'd you get that cooked so quick?" Cade asked, leaning over her shoulder to peer into the kettle simmering on the back of the stove.

"I had beef canned up from a side Mr. Clark bought from the neighbor, Mr. Bradley, last fall. I only had to add a Mason jar of vegetables to it and heat it up good. I'll put dumplings on top in just a minute and cover it tight. We'll be ready to eat in about twenty minutes."

She cast him a dark look, hands on her hips. "At least we'll be ready to eat if you get yourself out of my way so I can get these dumplings on the stew."

He laughed and backed away from the iron range, the sound of his humor a bit rusty as if he hadn't found much to amuse him of late. He watched her from his stance by the table, and when she'd completed her task and then clapped a cover on the bubbling stew where dumplings floated on top, she turned to him.

"You spend a lot of time keeping an eye on me, McAllister."

"Not near as much as I plan to in the future, Miss Glory. And that's something else we have to get straight." His jaw set and a stubborn gleam warned her that the man was putting on his cloak of arrogance again.

"I agree with what you said about Mr. Clark. I feel the same way he did. It looks to me like I'll be here for a good while and I don't think it's a good idea for me to be living here without us being married. The people in town will be talking about you. And that's something we don't want happening. Buddy and Essie don't need any bit of gossip going on about you."

"Can we talk about that later on?" Glory asked quietly. "Maybe tonight?"

Cade nodded a reply, apparently willing to do as she asked. "I want to tell you something I'm thinking about, Glory. I'm going to look at horses at your neighbor's place later on. He's got a fine crop of mares and foals in his fields, and a number of mares about ready to drop their foals. I'd like to make a deal with him."

"There's no money available for new horses," she said firmly.

His grin was quick. "That's where you're wrong, ma'am. I've got more than a bit put aside and if the fella is reasonable, I think I can make a deal with him."

"You're going to invest in my farm?" Her look was skeptical.

"Yes, ma'am. That's exactly what I'm going to do. I can't make a success of this place without putting money into it."

"And will that make it yours? When you've invested in it? Are you planning on the deed being in your name?"

"Not now, Glory. We've got other things to be concerned about. Just know that as long as you and the children live, this place is your home. Nothing I ever do will change that. We'll be partners here, all four of us and any more young'uns who might happen along to join us once we get married. Buddy will someday own this place, just as his father planned for. But in the meantime, you and I have to come to an agreement.

"We need to talk about this marriage thing. Like I said before, I don't want the folks hereabouts talking about you or spreading gossip."

"Why worry about my good name? Won't they gossip about you, too?" she asked, tilting her chin and glaring at him, her heart pumping rapidly from the anger he seemed to inspire in her.

"Women always manage to be the topic of gossip, Glory. Men can get away with most anything, but the woman ends up paying the piper. You know that as well as I do."

"I haven't done anything wrong, Cade. I think the folks in town consider me to be a decent woman."

"You're certainly that, Glory. But you're a good-looking woman, too, and I won't have you being the topic for folks' gossip. We can fix the problem easily with a marriage between us. I've done a lot of traveling around over the past few years, and most of the time I've been looking for a place to settle.

"I wonder if it wasn't the hand of fate that led me here to this town. It was almost like hearing about you from the sheriff and him bringing me out here to meet you was meant to be. I know you came as a surprise to me, for I certainly wasn't looking to find such a perfect spot to settle, with a couple of young'uns and a pretty woman living here. Getting married just seems like a good idea, Glory. For I'll admit I'm attracted to you in a mighty way. I'm hoping you'll agree with me, for it seems like the time is right for us to do this."

"I've often wondered myself how I came to knock at the back door here that day over three years ago," she said. And then she looked up at Cade, her eyes shiny with a glaze of tears.

"I decided that sometimes we don't need to know everything ahead of time, Cade. Sometimes things just work out right for us if we do our best and make our own way in life. It was right for me to marry Mr. Clark and care for his children three years ago. Maybe it's right for me to marry you now and let you take over with caring for the three of us. We sure could use a man's strong arms to do the heavy work here. Some days I get mighty weary, Cade. And lonesome, too, to tell the truth. I don't know about *attraction,* like you said a few minutes ago. But I like you and I think you being here would be good for the children, especially Buddy. But just so you know, I'm not much for fancy love words or flirtin', if you know what I mean."

"You don't have to worry about that sort of thing, Glory. As long as we like each other, we'll have a good beginning. I hope you're at least pondering marriage. I know you've been unsure of it, but I'd like to think you've kinda made a decision today, looking at the future with us a married couple, making a family here. You're a woman needing a man to tend to things and I sure won't mind doing that very thing. Living with you won't be a hardship for me, Glory."

He stepped closer to where she stood and his arm slid around her shoulders, tugging her closer to him. His other hand moved slowly to rest against her waist, and for a moment she felt enclosed, captured by his big body in front of her, the stove behind. She tilted her head back, and without a pause he bent to her, his mouth touching hers carefully, brushing the tender flesh with a kiss of promise. His words were a whisper.

"One thing you need to understand, Glory. When I've said the words in front of a preacher, I won't be sleeping in the bedroom at the back of the house. You can choose where, but you'll be next to me and I'm thinking we'll both fit into your bed."

His breath was fresh, his words spoken softly, as if he would not chance the children hearing him. And then he kissed her again, less of a testing caress, more of a demand for her mouth to welcome his, to return the brush of lips, to accept the promise of intimacy to come.

Glory had never known a man's touch in such a way, for as a young girl, she'd been protected, though she had known young men and even danced with several while her parents looked on. But none had strayed beyond friendship. She'd never been offered the kisses of a man courting a young woman. She trembled beneath his hands— not with fear, for she did not distrust Cade, but with uncertainty. His hands were careful of her, not gripping her tightly, and she knew he would release her if she demurred and stepped away from him.

"Cade?" Even to her own ears her voice sounded wary, uncertain. And from Cade's grin, she suspected he was aware of her flustered state.

"I won't hurt you, Glory. I'll never do anything to cause you pain or give you reason to fear me."

She nodded. "I'm not afraid of you. I just feel… sort of shaky right now. I think you'd better go sit down at the table and let me get supper on."

His grin did not depart from his lips as he obeyed her, pulling out his chair and then watching as she found plates and silverware to set the table. She unwrapped the last of the bread, a loaf she'd baked two days ago that was almost stale. It would be time to set a batch to rise in the morning.

She cut the bread and placed the slices on a plate, then found a fresh jar of jam in the pantry. "Our meal will be a little sparse, I fear. I'll make up for it tomorrow though," she said as she finished putting the food together and carefully lifted the lid of her big kettle on the stove.

The dumplings had risen to the top of the kettle and she touched one with the tip of her index finger, testing it for firmness. "I think these are done. I'll call the children in to eat." And in all her fussing and fluttering around the kitchen, she'd been careful to keep her eyes averted from him, as if she dared not meet his gaze.

Cade felt a wash of desire sweep through him. Not the carnal lust he'd felt in the past for a woman when he'd gone through a long dry spell without a female body to hold close in his bed. This was different, for she appealed to him to the depths that craved a woman of his own.

It was a yearning he'd never experienced, Cade had never thought of any woman in such a way until he'd met Glory, for his job had always come first with him. But it seemed that the way to achieve his goal now was to enter into a marriage. Living here was looking better all the time.

The children came to the table and he watched them closely. Saw the smile Essie shot in Glory's direction, noted the gentle touch of Glory's hand on Buddy's shoulder as he settled into his chair. They were secure in her love and it showed.

The four of them sat around the table, the steaming kettle of stew in the middle, and Cade bowed his head. He hadn't prayed in a long time, only shot small petitions upward as he thought of those he'd loved in his lifetime. His mother and stepfather, still at home in Oklahoma, the friends he'd left behind when he set out to find his own niche in life. But the prayer he offered for their food came easily to him and he spoke the words he'd often heard his stepfather say before meals back home.

Though this was all a part of his mission here, finding the gold would be an easier chore to tackle once he was living in the house. Being settled here was a good feeling, he decided, and he had much to be thankful for, not least of which was the meal before him. One of many meals he would eat here with Glory and the children, who seemed fated to be a large part of his life.

It was not a surprise that the sheriff paid them a visit the next day, for Glory had expected him to be at her door, checking up on Cade, looking in on her and the children. He was a good man and she knew he felt a sense of responsibility for her, after having dropped Cade into her life as he had.

"Have you read the papers Mr. McAllister gave you, Mrs. Clark?" he asked her.

Glory nodded in reply and smiled. She'd been pleased by the facts laid out in the legal documents she'd perused. Cade appeared to be all he'd promised, honest, diligent and possessed of enough ready cash to invest in the farm as he'd promised to do.

"Have you reached any sort of arrangement between you?" the lawman asked, turning to Cade, but asking the question of both the man and woman before him.

"We're still on speaking terms, so I suspect we'll iron things out before long," Cade said with a grin.

"For now, he's sleeping in the barn and working on fencing and such," Glory said.

Cade nodded. "I'm thinking about fencing the pasture. I figure with Buddy's help and a post-hole digger, I can put in enough fencing to keep the animals closed in. We'll see how it goes."

"I'll check back with you, McAllister. Just wanted to make sure that Mrs. Clark had read your credentials and was aware of your plans."

It seemed that the man's life was an open book, Glory decided. The sheriff was prone to trust him, and so, she decided with surprise, was she.

Glory finished her chores in the kitchen and went to the porch, settling on the small rocker there. She'd used this chair when she snapped beans and shelled peas while she rocked back and forth, watching the comings and goings of Mr. Clark.

And now it looked as if Cade would be a fixture on the place, and she could keep track of him while she did her busywork. She wouldn't guarantee anything about a wedding in the next few days, but she was leaning in that direction. And more than willing to let him have his way with the stock and the pasture. As for herself, she had enough to do. Her garden was coming in well, the peas ready to pick, the carrots showing above the ground and her beans blossoming, promising a good crop.

She'd planted three long rows already, for her father had told her years ago that planting beans every two weeks would give them beans for the whole of the summer. And so Glory had done as he'd instructed in those long-ago days of her youth. Every two weeks until mid-July, she planted beans and every two weeks once they were ready to pick, she had a crop to cook or can up in jars.

Her father had taught her well and she'd listened, planting and hoeing, weeding and picking the harvest of vegetables her mother put up in blue Mason jars. Now she canned her own food, thankful for the upbringing she'd had back in Pennsylvania.

She looked up, wrenched from her thoughts as Cade walked to the porch and sat on the steps. "I want to thank you, Cade. I appreciate your working with Buddy and spending time with him in the barn and with the animals."

Cade rose from the steps and walked to stand before her, his hands touching her shoulders. He bent low, turning her face to him. His lips pressed softly against her cheek, then brushed the tender lines of her mouth, a kiss of comfort.

"You've had a tough time of it, Glory. If I can, I'll make things a bit easier for you." His grip on the fragile bones he held within his grasp was light, but the warmth of his palms was welcome and Glory fought back tears as she rose to stand before him.

"I don't mean to be weepy, Cade. I'm usually pretty well in control of myself, but something about having you here, maybe just having a man about the place, seems to give me comfort."

But it was more than comfort that she sought, for she had to admit to herself that Cade made her feel like a woman. A desirable woman. A woman who welcomed the touch of his hand on her cheek as he spoke. "If I can give you comfort of any sort, I'm pleased, Glory," he said softly.

Her voice broke then, and she swallowed hard before she was able to speak. "I had three years here as Harvey's wife, Cade. He slept down the hall, gave me my own room and lived up to his word. He'd said when I met him that he wasn't looking to sleep with me, for he'd had a good marriage with the mother of his children and didn't want another woman in his bed. He was good to me, treated his children well and gave me free rein with his house. I couldn't ask for more."

Cade swallowed, his wondering put to rest. For even though he'd thought from what she'd said early on that her marriage to Harvey Clark had not been one such as he sought with her, she had given him words now that told him without doubt that she'd not slept with the man.

Satisfaction and anticipation filled him as he looked down at her. His hands lifted to her again, palms cradling her face, his gaze captured by the fine wash of color that stained her cheeks. The length of his fingers felt the fragile line of her temples, his fingertips brushing the wispy curls that framed her forehead. She was lovely, her skin finely pored, her lips curving a bit in a smile that trembled. Whether because of the desire he made no attempt to conceal from her, or perhaps her own awakening, she closed her eyes.

"Look at me, Glory." His voice was harsh, and he rued the passion that roughened his words, for he would not have her think him angry.

Her lids fluttered and she opened her eyes fully, brushing aside his hands as she attempted to step away from him. But he would not have it, and his hands once more gripped her shoulders, his touch careful but firm.

It was more than he could resist. Not just the soft lips that parted as if she would speak, or the yielding of her body as she allowed him to take her weight against himself. He bent to her again, and his mouth claimed hers, his indrawn breath holding the womanly scent of her, his heart beating faster as the feel of her breasts against his body brought him to arousal. His kiss was damp, his lips open against hers, and his hands were taut, sliding down her back, pressing her close.

Her hands pressed against his shirt, as if she would gain some bit of room between them. Whether she recognized the thrust of his arousal, or perhaps was frightened at his ardor, she inhaled sharply and turned her head to the side, catching her breath, even as a whimper escaped her lips.

"I've frightened you." His words were heavy with regret, for he'd told her he would not harm her or give her cause for alarm. And unless he missed his guess, she was about as near shedding tears again as a woman could get without the waterworks being turned loose.

"I want to ask you something, Glory. I hope you won't think I'm being crude or trying to embarrass you, but you strike me as a girl who hasn't had much to do with men. Do you know what happens between a man and woman, how they join their bodies together after marriage?"

She trembled against him, yet he must speak, must know the full extent of her knowledge or perhaps ignorance.

"Has no woman explained to you what is involved in the process of giving yourself to the man you've chosen to marry?"

Her eyes filled with tears again as he spoke and she shook her head.

But at least she had answered him, and for that he was thankful, for he'd begun to fear that this was to be a one-sided conversation. "My mama told me one time when I asked her about babies and such that men are usually pretty adept at that sort of thing. She said that all a woman must do was to obey her husband."

Damn. "And didn't she tell you that a man's pleasure is a direct result of the response of his wife?"

Her breath huffed out. "I'd supposed that the room would be dark and things would happen naturally. Mama said that if I married a man who truly loved me, I wouldn't have anything to worry about."

He shook his head and held her before him at arm's length. "I'd say you've got a good bit to learn, Glory. Your education will be more involved than I'd thought." Cade smiled down at her and posed a question. "Have you never dallied with a young man in the moonlight?" He paused as she considered his words and then she flushed becomingly and shook her head.

"I wasn't left alone with any of the young men who came around back home in Pennsylvania. My pa said I was too young for such shenanigans. When I had a gentleman friend come to call, which only happened a couple times, we sat in the parlor and looked at my mama's photograph albums and sorted through picture books about Europe and Greece. It was for sure we weren't allowed to be left alone."

But it seemed Cade was not finished with his subject, and he continued speaking, his tone soft, his words coaxing. "We won't be doing much of what we're speaking about anyway, Glory. Not right away. Certainly not until we're married and even then we'll take our time."

She felt a hot flush cover her cheeks. "Please, Cade. I don't want to talk about this." Her voice broke and he bent to her.

"Glory, I sure wish your mama had explained things to you a little better."

"I was sixteen when she died. And I'm sure, given the chance, we'd have spoken of marriage. But as it turned out, I'm probably about the most ignorant female you've ever met." Her chin tilted upward and her eyes narrowed as she spoke. "I'm not ashamed of not knowing. I'm just embarrassed."

He kissed her cheek then, careful not to infringe, and she looked up at him, anger touching her words.

"I'm young and ignorant, Cade. Are you sure that you want to marry me?" She bent her head and the slender form he held between his hands seemed fragile, as if she was too delicate, perhaps unfit for the life she'd chosen here on the farm. "I fear I won't be very good at this, Cade McAllister, for I'm not willing to do all the things marriage requires of a woman. Not right now, anyway. You ought to find a woman better equipped for marriage than I."

He merely smiled, even as laughter tapped at the door of his dignity and begged for release. But he would not allow it. He was determined to coax her to the point of speaking vows before the minister in town. She might be unaware of what was involved in being his wife, but she was smart enough to recognize that she needed him. Needed a man to protect her and the children she'd taken responsibility for.

"Glory, look at me." His touch was careful on her arms, and he'd captured the length of her body between himself and the wall of the house next to the back door. He'd not put a match to the kerosene lamp over the table and the room was lit only by the soft glow of the black iron range, but he didn't need a bonfire to make out her face.

"Just promise me you'll be thinking about visiting the preacher. We can make it as private as you want, just you and me and the young'uns. The sheriff made sure of my reputation back home and I'm willing to put my money into this place. I'll be good to you and I think you know the children like me. I can't see any reason to put it off."

She looked up at him and her eyes sought his in the dim shadows. "I'll think about it, Cade, but I'm not making any promises yet. And in the meantime, you can sleep in Mr. Clark's bedroom, but I'll have no more of this kissing business. I need a clear mind and I won't have you confusing me with foolishness."

He smiled at her, nodding his agreement as she set the terms of their arrangement. "It'll be just like you want, Glory. I'll give you a week to decide. That should be long enough to make up your mind."

She turned from him and he released her readily. "It's time for Buddy and Essie to be getting ready for bed. I promised to read to them for a bit first." She opened the screen door and went to the kitchen table, reaching up to lift the chimney from the lamp that hung there. Cade scratched a match against the surface of the stove, then touched it to the wick and Glory lowered the chimney into place.

"Buddy? Essie? Are you ready for our reading?"

From the parlor both children answered her and made their way to the kitchen. Buddy carried a book with him and placed it on the table before the chair Glory occupied on a regular basis. Essie scooted her chair around so that she could sit as close to Glory as possible.

"Would you like to listen, Mr. Cade?" she asked politely, swinging her feet as she waited for Glory to take her place beside her.

"Sure thing. I heard a bit last night, when I was sitting on the porch. I've read this book myself. My mama had a copy of it at home and she read it to me before I was old enough to enjoy it for myself."

"Charles Dickens wrote a bunch of books," Buddy said, taking his place across the table from Glory. "I already read two of them, and Glory said I have to write a book report about the one I'm reading now."

"She's done a good job of teaching the pair of you, I'd say," Cade told the boy. "I'll warrant you'll do well in school. I'm going to look for a horse for you to ride back and forth. Mr. Bradley has a dozen or so mares and geldings he's willing to sell. Maybe you and I can go over there tomorrow. If you're gonna ride the horse, I'd say you ought to have some say in which one we get for you."

"Can I do that, Glory?" Buddy looked beseechingly at his stepmother and Cade thought he held his breath as he awaited her answer.

"Sounds like Cade's got things lined up, Buddy. If he wants to get you a horse, he can call the shots, I'd say."

She opened the book, sliding the bookmark from its place and setting it on the oilcloth as she tilted the volume to catch the glow of the lamp overhead. "If we're going to read a whole chapter, we'd better begin," she said, glancing at Cade as he sat down in the available chair.

His grin was aimed at Glory as he settled back to listen. And for the next half hour her audience was held captive by the story of an orphaned boy and the trials inherent in his life without a family of his own.

Glory reached the end of the chapter and slid the bookmark into place, closing the volume and brushing the cover as if she would deny any speck of dust a resting place there. "Time for bed," she said quietly, and both children pushed their chairs back and headed for the stairway in the hall. Buddy picked up a lamp from the table in the hallway and walked ahead of his sister up the stairs.

"Will you be coming up, Glory?" Essie asked, looking back over her shoulder.

"In just a few minutes," Glory answered. "Your clean nightgown is on the bed, Essie. Make sure you change your underwear, Buddy. I put the clothes basket in your room, so be sure you use it."

Cade smiled as she uttered the words she'd no doubt spoken numerous times before. From upstairs, he could hear the sound of two doors opening and Buddy speaking softly to his sister.

"You've done a good job with those children," Cade said quietly. "They love you, Glory. It shows in the way they pay attention to you and mind what you say."

"I made up my mind when I came here that I'd do the best I could to take the place of their mother. I've tried to teach them all the things my own mother taught me when I was comin' up. Mr. Clark gave me a free hand with them and we've always gotten along together. They're smart and willing to work hard to get their schooling."

She rose and went to the doorway, then turned back and met Cade's gaze. "I'm pleased that you've decided to get a horse for Buddy. He's excited about going to school in town and his eyes surely lit up when you said he could go along and help decide on which horse you'd buy for him."

"I'd like to see him on two or three of those geldings. Figure I'll buy him a saddle in town and he can learn how to handle things on his own. He's tall enough to lift a saddle and I'll check into things at the school, see if the boys have a place to keep their tack during the day. I imagine they stake the horses around back of the schoolhouse, but I'll want to see for myself how things are done. I spoke to a fella in town and he said that there's near to a dozen students who ride in from the surrounding farms."

"Buddy knows how to ride pretty well," Glory said. "Mr. Clark let him use the saddle horse, made sure he knew how to handle the animal."

"He'll do well," Cade said confidently. "He's a smart boy and he's old enough to accept responsibility."

Glory nodded her agreement and turned to

climb the stairs. Her steps were light, and she rapped on the doorjamb of Buddy's room, calling his name as she entered. Cade heard her voice, then Buddy's as they spoke together for long minutes before she left his room, closing his door and heading to Essie's room.

She spent a bit longer with Essie, probably helping her with her nightgown, he suspected, and then listening to the girl as she said her prayers. Her voice was but a murmur in his ear, but he smiled, imagining Glory sitting on the bed, her hand on Essie's head as she uttered her petitions aloud. And then Glory left Essie's room, leaving her door open and pausing to call out soft words to the child.

She came back downstairs and into the kitchen. "I'll fry up some sliced ham for breakfast in the morning, I think. Maybe some corn bread instead of biscuits." Glory retrieved the sack of cornmeal from the pantry and bent to lift her mixing bowl from the kitchen dresser, readying things for morning.

She turned then, picking up the book she'd read from and carrying it into the parlor where she put it on the library table in front of the window. Pausing to straighten the pillows on the sofa, she moved a picture, placing it just so as if it must be properly displayed. Cade watched her from the doorway of the parlor, admiring the sway of her skirts, the deft movements of her hands and the easy way she moved about in the home she had established. With little obvious effort, Glory managed to keep things neatened up, creating a place of comfort for her family, a warm atmosphere in which they thrived. She looked up to where Cade stood, as if she had just sensed his presence there.

"I think I'll go up myself and get ready for bed," she said. "It's been a long day."

He leaned forward a bit, his lips touching her forehead in a soft unthreatening kiss. "Good night, Glory. I'll lock up and take care of the lamp in the kitchen. Do you need a light to take with you?"

"No, I've got a candle in my room and I can find it easily in the dark. It looks like it's pretty bright out anyway. No clouds and a full moon. Good night, Cade," she said softly, moving past him and up the stairs, then closing her door behind her.

Chapter Five

She'd done as she said, frying ham and baking corn bread for breakfast. Cade split open his helping of corn bread and buttered it generously.

Settling down to eat, the children talked of plans for the day, Cade and Buddy speaking of the proposed visit to the neighbor once the chores were finished. Essie mentioned that her dolly was in dire need of a new dress, persuading Glory to find a piece of fabric that would be suitable. With the promise of the sewing project Glory had agreed upon, Essie cleared the table quickly and dried the dishes, chattering the whole time.

"First, we're going to wash our hair," Glory said firmly. "The rain barrel is pretty near full and I'll heat some of the water on the stove while we look up the material from the last dress I made for you. I think there's enough left over for the dolly's dress. You can help rinse my hair for me and we'll sit in the sun for a bit and let it dry." Essie was agreeable to the plan and together they carried in water from the barrel, careful to replace the lid so that the rainwater stayed clean.

Cade thought he'd never seen a more beautiful sight. He stood just inside the barn door, his gaze fixed on the two females sitting on the porch drying their hair.

Glory had made use of the rain barrel, water from the roof pouring down to fill it yesterday from an afternoon shower. He'd been in the kitchen, watching as Essie leaned over the washtub and Glory poured the liquid from her quart jar of soap. It quickly formed rich suds and lather in the child's hair.

Glory had declared that she was next and that Essie should pour water over her head on her command. And then she'd looked at Cade, a look that invited him to leave the kitchen. As he'd walked out the door, she was unbuttoning her dress so as not to get it wet, and he was sorely tempted to stay and peek but thought better of it.

He'd seen the nearest neighbor, Earl Bradley by name, in his field yesterday and made arrangements with him regarding the horses he might be willing to sell. It hadn't taken long to sum up their condition and conformation. Three of them were ready to deliver their foals, and it had cost Cade a pretty penny indeed, but worth every red cent, for they were healthy, rounded with the weight of unborn foals, and he had spent an enjoyable hour brushing their sleek coats and learning to know their diverse natures.

Horses were a lot like people, he'd often thought, each with their own quirks and foibles, and these three were placid in their last days of pregnancy. Today he'd return with Buddy for the mount they needed for the boy's transport to school.

Earl had brought the mares by yesterday afternoon and they stood now in the stalls Cade had readied for them. He heard them nicker and whuffle softly behind him as he stood again in the doorway of the barn, watching the two females on the porch.

Essie sat on the second step in the rays of the morning sun, Glory brushing her hair as if it gave them equal pleasure. He knew she would braid it up, keeping it clean and clear of the child's face. But for now, it shone with a radiance that rivaled the sunlight that rained down on the golden locks.

As radiant as the small face that turned to look up at Glory with confidence, those rosy lips parting in a wide smile, even as she spoke of some small thing that pleased her.

Glory's hair was still damp, hanging down her back, her dress protected by a towel around her shoulders. Her tresses curled around her face as they dried, catching the sun and gleaming in a cascade of rich, dark color. Even as he watched, Essie stood and then knelt behind Glory, holding the hairbrush, her small hands on the bone handle, sweeping through the dark length of hair in such a way that Cade knew it was not for the first time the child performed this ritual.

As she bent over Glory's head, her own golden locks blew in the breeze, blending with the darkness that she tamed with her brush. They were like night and day, both darkness and light sitting before him, and he was held immobile by the beauty of the woman he planned to marry.

Even as he watched, a horseman rode up from the town road, his mount in a rolling canter, the silver star on his shirt front glittering. The lawman had come to call, and Cade wondered briefly what had brought him back this way so soon.

Cade stepped from the shadows of the barn,

lifting a hand to the man who rode near. "Hey there, Sheriff. Good to see you."

"McAllister," Joe Lawson's greeting was crisp and to the point. His eyes were sharp, piercing as he measured the man before him, and Cade was happy that Glory had pressed his shirt with the set of sadirons she used. She'd warned that she folded, but didn't iron, so finding it folded just so in his dresser drawer, still showing the marks of the iron, had pleased him. He stood tall before the lawman, feeling that he could speak with this man as he would a friend.

"I've just been looking over my new mares. Want to see them?" It was a friendly gesture, one that would divert attention from the females on the porch, and Joe nodded, lifting himself easily from his saddle. As he led the visitor into the barn, Cade cast one last look over his shoulder to where Glory was hastily plaiting her hair, obviously embarrassed to be seen by the sheriff in such a state. Essie watched patiently as Glory quickly threaded the long strands, as if she knew that her turn would be next.

"They sure are a pair, ain't they," Joe said quietly. "Old Harvey Clark got himself a gem when he took that girl in and gave her a home. Reckon he thought he'd struck gold when she married him."

"I reckon he did," Cade replied, a small smile touching his lips. Once inside the barn, he faced the sheriff and spoke again. "I'm having a hard time, Sheriff. I don't know how I can marry Glory without telling her the truth of my being here. It's not fair to leave her in the dark, but I'm playing both ends against the middle." He waved at a bale of hay and the sheriff settled on it, Cade squatting in front of him.

"I'm thinking I'll probably resign from Pinkerton's once I've completed this assignment and found the gold. I find myself wanting Glory more than I want the career I've had for the past five or six years.

"I've racked my brains trying to think of where a man might hide a stash like that, and so far haven't been able to figure it out. I've searched the barn, but it's not out here. I doubt Clark buried it anywhere—there's too much chance of someone digging it up. He'd more likely have it under his control somewhere in the house. I'm figuring on some building projects that might be a good cover-up for my search, but I've got to lead up to them.

"Right now, I'm just not sure what to tell Glory. I'll have to come up with something right quick. I'm going to push for a wedding within the next week or so. I won't have Glory spoken of without a degree of respect. She's a good woman, and I've just about convinced her that we need to marry up. I'll feel better when she's wearing my ring. So if you'll do me a favor, I'd appreciate it. Will you let the minister in town know that we'll be in on Saturday and I'd like him to speak the words over us, and hear Glory repeat her vows? Will you do that? I'd go myself, but there's a pile of work to be done, and if you can save me the trip, I'd surely appreciate it."

Joe laughed, more of a chuckle actually, Cade decided, as if he was pleased by the turn of events. "I'd be happy to act as your messenger, McAllister, but you have a tough job ahead of you. Are you sure enough of the woman to set the date?"

"As sure as I can be. Glory is smart enough to know that she needs the protection of marriage, and unless some sort of emergency comes up, we'll be in town come Saturday morning. She'll be needing kitchen supplies and I'll have me a few days to make my plans solid."

They stood in the wide aisle of the barn, Joe's hand rising in an automatic gesture to pat the neck of the mare beside him. "This one sure is a beauty, ain't she?" The mare turned her head and nuzzled at his shirt pocket, causing both men to laugh aloud.

"She's used to someone carrying treats for her, I'll warrant," Joe said. "Looks to me like she's about to drop that foal. What do you think?"

"They were all three bred just eleven months ago, and Bradley told me I'd better be ready with a birthing stall right quick."

"Earl Bradley raises good horseflesh, that's for sure," Joe said, admiring the blood bay who stood on three feet beside Cade. As if she would lean against his strength, she edged up to him, and Cade tangled his fingers in her mane, scrubbing his knuckles against her neck.

"Buddy has his eye on this one. I'll get her in shape for him to travel back and forth to school. The bottom line is I got a bargain, is what I did," he told Joe. "When I came to town, I had a nest egg of my own, and with the money from my last job for Pinkerton, I had money enough to invest in this place. I couldn't think of anything more valuable to this farm than new horseflesh. My pa always said horses were a good investment, so long as you fed 'em and kept 'em clean and happy. We always had a pasture full of colts and fillies when I was a boy. This place is exactly what I've always wanted. And Glory is the answer to every dream I've had."

There was a yearning in his voice that seemed to touch a chord in Joe, for he nodded. "I'd say you've got it bad, McAllister. I'm pulling for you." The lawman walked around the black he'd been admiring, past the blood bay to the pinto, who was shorter but stockier. "This one is a good cow pony, I'll bet you," he said admiringly.

"That's what Bradley told me," Cade answered. "We'll see after she drops her foal."

"You gonna breed them back?" Joe asked.

"Soon as they're ready, and if things work out." Cade's hand rested on the pinto. "This is her first time, but the other two have dropped foals for the past two years. They bred well, had pretty little colts last year. Earl showed me what they were leaving behind. I think he hated to see them go, but I made it worth his while."

"Well, I'm going to walk up to the house and pay my respects to Mrs. Clark," Joe said as Cade untied the mares and led them out the back of the barn. In moments, he'd taken the lead ropes from their halters and staked them out in the pasture, where lush grass grew in abundance. Once he'd set a couple dozen posts and strung fencing, he'd be able to turn them loose to graze. Thankfully, the fence line that was in place was secure now after his day-long work tightening the wire against the posts. He'd buy posts and enlarge the grazing area in the next week or so.

He turned back to Joe and lifted a hand. "Thanks for your help, Sheriff. Tell Glory I'll be up to the house in a minute or two."

Joe left the barn and looked at the two females who soaked up the sun's rays, speaking in a low tone to Cade. "She's a pretty little thing, the girl Clark left behind. How a grizzled man like Harvey Clark managed to father such beauty is beyond me," he said. Cade laughed, his agreement apparent.

Joe approached the house. "Mrs. Clark. Are you well? I thought to come out and see how things are going for you and the children." Ever polite, Joe doffed his hat and held it before him.

"I'm well, Sheriff," Glory said politely, her hands full of Essie's golden hair that she was braiding into a long tail. "Mr. McAllister is taking hold with the place. I surely appreciate his help."

"I hear from your hired hand out there that there's to be a wedding come Saturday."

Essie looked up in surprise. "Who's gonna get married, Mr. Sheriff?" Her eyes were wide with wonder as she looked at Glory. "Can we go to the wedding, Glory? I never been to one before."

Glory spoke sharply. "We'll talk it over later, Essie."

From the kitchen a youthful voice spoke a greeting. "Have you seen the new mares, Sheriff? Ain't they a bunch of beauties? My pa always said he wanted horses, but all we ever had was Pa's riding mare and the plow horses. Cade just up and bought those three yesterday, and they're all gonna…" As if he'd thought better of his words, Buddy halted, and the lawman laughed softly.

"Yeah, they sure are, Buddy. Right soon, too."

The boy stepped out onto the porch and stood behind his sister. "We're doing all right out here. You didn't need to check up on us. Cade's taking hold real good."

As if he was the man of the house, Glory thought. And at such a young age, to be put in a position of responsibility. And then the boy spoke again.

"We sure are glad to have Cade here, sir. He's a right good hand at most everything. Got the corral fence all shored up and he's gonna cut hay today. Pa would have liked him."

"You're right, Buddy. Your pa would have thought Cade was a good man." Glory's words were firm, giving support to the boy.

"Glory says I can go to school this year, Sheriff," Buddy announced proudly. "She thinks I'll do just fine."

"He's a good student. Reads well and knows his maths. I've taught him about all I can. It's time for some real schooling," Glory said. "He's a whiz at geography, and he's read all my old history books." She realized she was bragging a bit then, and felt a flush creep up her face.

"You've done well by these children, Mrs. Clark. They're fine young'uns."

Cade appeared, apparently having overheard the last of the conversation, for he spoke quickly, his gaze resting on Buddy. "I think their father deserves a lot of credit for the way these two have dug in and helped Glory the way they do.

Buddy will make a fine horseman and farmer one day, and Essie is already learning skills in the kitchen."

"Can we go to the wedding in town, Cade?" Essie showed no fear in asking, and Cade grinned at her.

"Sure enough you can go, you and Buddy both."

"Is Glory going too?" Essie asked quickly.

Cade's eyes rested on the dark hair, his eyes admiring the sharp blue eyes that met his with anger in their depths, and his words were filled with import. "Glory is going to be the most important part of the wedding, Essie. We'll talk about it at dinnertime."

Essie squirmed on the porch, then slid to the ground. "Can I go find the cat, Glory? She's been hiding in the barn somewhere. I don't know what's wrong with her, but she didn't come when I called her last night."

Cade grinned and rested his hand on the child's golden hair. "I think if you look behind the door in the tack room, you'll find your cat, Essie. She's been busy in there. Walk softly and don't startle her, for she's got a litter of kittens and you won't want to frighten her."

"Oh, can I, Glory? Can I go see?" The child fairly danced as she awaited Glory's words of permission.

"Of course you can. Just do as Cade said. And don't touch the kittens yet. Give them a few days before you handle them."

And then she looked up at the man before her. "I'll see *you* at the dinner table, McAllister." Her tone had turned from honey to vinegar just so quickly, and the sheriff chuckled softly.

"Reckon I'll be on my way, McAllister. I'll tend to that little favor soon as I get to town." He slapped his hat back on his head, then tipped the brim a bit as he nodded at Glory. "I'll be seeing you soon, ma'am. I'm glad things are looking up out here."

Glory nodded, unwilling to speak for the rush of anger that gripped her. She stood abruptly, then turned and stalked across the porch and into the kitchen. The screen door slammed behind her, the spring causing it to almost catch her bottom as she went.

"I reckon you've got your hands full, McAllister." The sheriff reached for his horse's reins and mounted swiftly. With another nod, he was on his way.

"Is Glory mad with you, Cade? She looked kinda put out, didn't she?" Buddy asked his question anxiously, as if he would not take kindly to Glory being upset in any way. Ever protective, the boy tipped his head back and faced Cade.

"I'll take care of Glory, son. She's just a little bit out of sorts, but we'll be fine. Don't you worry. Now, how about you and me using a pair of scythes and getting some hay cut. We can dry it good for a day or two and bring it into the loft." He looked up at the cloudless sky. "Don't look to me like we'll have rain for at least a couple days, long enough for the hay to dry anyway."

"All right, Cade. I don't mind working in the hay field. I used to do it with my pa. Ever since I was a little kid."

And for all that he was a sturdy lad, he was *still* a little kid, Cade thought, his arm encircling the boy's shoulders as they went to the barn.

Dinner was a quiet affair, with Glory serving the food in silence. She sat down after the bowls and platters were arranged to her liking, and nodded at Buddy. He folded his hands and said a short prayer, his noontime duty, it seemed, for he did not hesitate to speak the appropriate words, and then looked up at Glory with a grin. "Sure looks good, ma'am. I like the way you cooked the peas."

"They're fresh from the garden, Buddy. All I did was put some little onions in with them and then creamed them up good, the way my mama used to do."

Cade spoke up then. 'Well, however you did it, I have to agree with Buddy. You're a good cook, Glory." He dug into his potatoes and gravy as if hunger rode him like a thistle clinging to his trousers. "We put in a good few hours out in the hay field, me and Buddy. We've been looking forward to this all morning."

The pork chops were tender, having been baked in the oven, covered with onions and gravy. "Where'd you get the pork?" Cade asked her, lifting a bite of peas.

"Mr. Clark got me a pork barrel to keep the chops and roasts in. It's in the pantry. He showed me how to render out the lard after he butchered the pigs and we filled the barrel. It keeps the pork real good." She cast Cade a speaking glance as if she'd like to bury him with the pork.

"My mother had a pork barrel back home," Cade offered, as if oblivious to her mood. "Pa had a smokehouse and he hung hams and bacon out there, but she kept the fresh pork buried in the lard barrel."

"Mr. Clark did the same," Glory said. "There's a bit left of such things out back in the smokehouse. He kept things up as good as he could, but he was feeling his years of late, and it got almost too much for him."

The children ate rapidly, Essie eager to return to the barn and the four kittens her cat had so miraculously produced overnight. Buddy was anxious to keep an eye on the mares, for Cade had confided in him that their time was very near and they must ready a stall for their use when the time was right.

"May we be excused?" Essie asked politely and Glory nodded her assent. The child walked around the table and stood quietly at her stepmother's side, then lifted on tiptoe to kiss Glory's cheek. "I'll come back in a bit and help with dishes," she whispered as Buddy came around to join her.

The screen door slapped shut behind them and Cade turned to Glory. "I feared that Essie would want to talk about the wedding, and I knew we needed to get things straight first, Glory. I told

Sheriff Lawson that I'd appreciate it if he'd tell the minister in town that we'd be in on Saturday for a wedding."

"Well, you've got a lot of nerve, mister. This is the first I've heard of it." Glory's eyes flared with the anger she'd kept in readiness all during the meal. "I think it might be a good idea to get my approval first, Cade. I never said I'd marry you, did I? I only told you that you could move into the house and have Harvey's bedroom."

"Well, I'll sleep in Harvey's bed till Saturday night, then I'll share yours, ma'am."

"I've told you how I feel about that, Cade. I'd like to smack you a good one—what with you planning my life for me."

When his eyes touched her face, they were dark and filled with determination. "And I've told you how it's gonna be, Glory. Come Saturday, you'll stand up before the preacher and speak your vows to me. I won't have you be the subject of gossip in town. We'll be married and make this whole thing legal. I can't live here any other way."

Glory felt her face burn as if it were on fire. "I don't want you in my bed, Cade McAllister. I've never slept with a man."

He stood and his steps were long and deliberate as he rounded the table. His hands lifted her from her chair and he held her shoulders within his grasp, his head bending to give him better access to her mouth. His lips were firm, his touch not offensive, but Glory shivered in his grasp. As if the heat from a burning coal had touched her mouth, she pulled from his caress.

"Cade?" She spoke his name as a query or perhaps it was a plea, but to no avail.

Cade looked down at the woman he held. His arms ached to enclose that small, slender form against himself, and his patience was almost at an end, for she would not accommodate him as he wanted.

She pressed her hands against his chest and pushed, and her eyes opened wide as she looked up into his. He was immovable, like a tree trunk, and she was captured between him and the table. Should she back up she'd be sitting on her plate, and he wouldn't let her be embarrassed by such a thing happening.

So with a swift tug, he drew her against himself, grasping at the luxury of warmth and soft woman against his long, lean body. She fit well, he thought, her breasts full against his chest, her head just touching his shoulder, her slender hips

held by one hand against the arousal he refused
to hide from her.

And she had no idea what that hard pressure
against her belly was. For Glory did not seem to
recognize the unmistakable signs of his passion
and desire.

She wiggled against him, trying to free herself from his embrace. And yet, his arms around
her felt like a shelter, a sanctuary in which she
was protected from the sticks and stones that
life might pelt her with. Feeling his strength and
knowing he would not use it against her, catching
the scent of man when he neared, yearning for
his touch, even as it made her shiver and quake…
She shook her head, unwilling to face the need
that arose within her when he held her close, as
if she'd found the end of the rainbow and the pot
of gold was hers. Then he spoke, his voice low,
his words chilling her to her depths.

"It's a case of either-or, Glory. Leaving here
wouldn't be my first choice, but it's gonna be
up to you. We'll be married on Saturday. I've
been nice and asked you politely and you shilly-
shallied around, so now I've decided to let you
know just how things are gonna be. I'm moving
my stuff into your bedroom Saturday morning

and when we get home from town, I'll be sleeping in your bed. The children are going to know that we're married and that's the best way to get the message across."

"I know we need you here, Cade, but I'm afraid." She shook her head, meeting his gaze with eyes that shimmered with tears. "I can't do it, Cade. I just can't do what you said." Her words were a plea and he melted, even as her forehead met his chest.

"I'll never force you to—well, I may try to persuade you, but no man can look himself in the mirror when he shaves if he's hurt a woman with his strength. And that's what it would be, Glory, should I take your body against your will."

She lifted her head and met his gaze. "It looks like either I marry you or you'll leave us, and… we need you here, Cade, both the children and me." She tilted her chin higher. "I'll marry you, mainly because I have no choice. I won't refuse your presence in my bedroom or my bed. But know this. I'm fearful of you and I'm not a woman to be fainthearted. I don't know what there is about you that makes me shake deep inside, but whatever it is, I'm frightened of it."

He felt a rush of desire race through his veins

and his voice was rough, as though gravel coated each word. "I know what it is, Glory. But you needn't fear it. Or me. You're a woman, yet a girl. I don't how to explain it to you any better than that. You were never Harvey's *wife*. You were married to him, but he never claimed your body. I don't know why, for any man who lived with you, with legal rights over you, would be insane to let you remain so untouched. I'm not Harvey Clark."

"Well, isn't that the truth!" she muttered.

She made a face and he laughed. "You look like Essie when she's trying to work up her nerve to ask for something," he said easily.

"I feel like Essie around you, only you act differently with her."

"Of course I do. She's a little girl and I hope she'll come to consider me her father one day. I don't feel a bit fatherly about you, sweetheart."

"Sweetheart?" She flushed and he grinned.

"Hasn't anyone ever called you that before?"

"My mother used to, but I don't think that counts."

"It's different when a man says it to a woman, Glory." He set her aside and inhaled sharply. "Now, we're going to change tack here, while I still can. I'll check on the chickens before I go out to the hay field again today. I think your rooster has been working overtime. You've got a broody hen who's determined to sit on a clutch of eggs out there. She won't let Buddy near her, and she tried her best to peck holes in me when I felt beneath her for her eggs."

"I'll let her set," Glory told him, relieved to change the subject. "I've got a barrel cut down and Harvey put a fence around it in a corner of the chicken yard. I'll put her there with her eggs."

"Be careful of her. I don't want to see blood on your hands, sweetheart."

"She knows me. I'm not afraid of her."

"Only of me?" he asked, bending to kiss her again. It was short and sweet, not the sort of caress he yearned to give her, but probably all she would accept for now.

"I'm not afraid of you, Cade. But somehow, I fear what you make me feel. I don't know how else to describe it."

"Just be ready on Saturday morning, Glory. We'll leave early for town. I need to stop at the general store first." He looked her over as if he measured her size and shape. "Do you need a new dress to be married in? We can afford it if you do." He lifted her hand and touched her ringless finger. "And we'll be getting a ring to fit right here, Glory."

"I didn't have a wedding ring when I married Harvey."

He held her hand to his lips, his tongue touching the skin as if he would taste her flesh. "You'll have one from me. After Saturday, you'll be Mrs. Cade McAllister, and I'll be sure you feel like a woman wedded."

Chapter Six

Buddy almost fell asleep over his plate at suppertime. So weary was he from the afternoon in the hay field, he fairly drooped. "I think it's going to be early to bed for you, son," Cade said with a soft chuckle. "I worked you too hard, I fear."

"No, you didn't," Buddy was quick to deny. "And if you're going to work on the birthing stall tonight, I want to help you. Please, Cade. If those mares start having their foals, we need to have a place ready."

Cade cast him a long look. "Why don't I tear down the wall we talked about. I can do it in an hour after supper. Then, in the morning we'll box it in and make a wider gate for the stall. You can put down the straw for the mares to lie on when the time comes, and then we'll just have to wait. Although I don't think it'll be much longer for the pinto. She looks like she's getting ready to deliver, though I don't know all I should about horses having babies."

"You'll be sure to let me help with putting it together, won't you?" Buddy asked, even as he covered a wide yawn with his hand.

Cade laughed softly. "You're going to have an education, young man. You'll learn something you'll never get out of a book."

"Do you think that's a good idea, Cade?" Glory sounded anxious, and he smiled at her.

"He needs to know some things that are important to a young man. And Buddy is definitely that. He'll be just fine, Glory. I feel the need to talk to him about life in general. But I wouldn't do anything to cause him problems. You know that."

She nodded. "Well, we'll keep Essie far away when the time comes. She's too little to understand such things. Matter of fact, I'm not sure I want to participate in this."

"Well, you'll have three chances, and then you'll have to wait till next year."

"You're going to breed them again, right away?" she asked.

"That's why I bought them, sweetheart. This

was an investment for us, and it will pay off in the long run. Wait and see. Land and animals are always a good investment. You've got the land and we bought the animals, so things are all in place."

Buddy touched Glory's hand from his place next to her and she heard his unspoken words.

"I really think it's time for you to be in bed, Buddy. You'll have a big day tomorrow and we'll never get everything fit in as it is. I suspect you'll be in the barn all day with Cade, so you need your sleep."

"All right, Glory. If you say so." He stood and grinned at Cade, his happiness evident. "I'm awful glad you came to live with us, Cade. Things are better with you here." His right hand touched Glory's shoulder and he bent to brush his cheek against hers before he left the kitchen.

"He's a fine boy," Cade said, clearing his throat a bit and then rising from the table.

"Am I a fine girl?" Essie asked, her blue eyes pleading as she met Cade's gaze.

"You're almost the best girl I've ever seen. Except for Glory," he told her, and she basked in his approval.

"It's okay if you like Glory best. I do, too. She's always gonna be here with us, isn't she, Cade?"

He thought she looked a bit worried, probably thinking of her father departing her life so abruptly, and hoping against hope that the woman who had raised her for three years would not disappear one day.

"Glory is your mother now, Essie. She loves you just as if she'd borne you herself. You don't know what that means yet, but someday you will. Just know that Glory and I are going to be with you for a long time. Till you're grown and ready to have a family of your own."

"I'm never gonna leave Glory," the child vowed, stepping to where Glory sat and wrapping her arms around her neck.

Glory pushed her chair back from the table and lifted Essie to her lap, cuddling her close. "You'll always be my little girl, Essie. No matter how old you are or how big you get, you'll always be my little girl. Even when you grow up and have a family of your own, we'll still love each other."

"I think I like that, Glory." The child grinned up at her, her mind seeming to be at peace.

Glory lowered Essie to the floor and clasped her hand loosely. "Now I think it's time to get you into bed, sweetie. Tomorrow is going to be a big day, what with Cade and Buddy working on the new stall and you and I working in the garden. Those weeds just keep on growing, you know."

"I'll help you, Glory." Even as she spoke, the child yawned and headed for her bedroom. "Will you come tuck me in?" she asked.

"Always," Glory replied, sending her on her way.

"You're a good mother, for someone who's never had a child of her own."

She looked up to where Cade stood near the back door. "I've had three years to practice. Harvey gave me all the privileges of a parent when I moved in here. I've always managed to get along with them, and we've had a lot of good times together."

"They love you, Glory. That little fella would do anything in the world you asked of him. You've done well with teaching them and readying him for school. We'll stop and speak with the teacher when we go to town about sending him in September or whenever she starts up classes again. No point in waiting."

"Thank you, Cade. You make it all sound so easy."

"It is easy, sweetheart. That boy is ready to

show his stuff. He'll blow them away with his intelligence."

Glory felt a glow of accomplishment fill her. "Thank you, Cade. You've made me feel that all the hard work was worth it. I've tried hard to do right by the children and keep things up here, and sometimes I felt I wasn't strong enough to do it all."

"I'll bet you Harvey never complained, did he?"

She shook her head. "No, never once. He was kind to me, told me I was a good cook and bought anything I asked for when we went to town."

"I'll warrant you didn't ask for much, Glory. Not for yourself anyway."

Her chin lifted and her eyes flashed. "He bought me material so I could make new kitchen curtains and I picked out a new oilcloth for the table and fabric to make dresses and shirts for Essie and Buddy. And even tea for me, because I don't care much for coffee. Oh, and lilac soap, because I like the way it smells."

Cade grinned. "But no lacy underthings, I'll bet. Or pretty nightgowns, either."

"I didn't need those things. I made my small things from feed sacks. I don't need lace."

"Well, you'll wear lace when you marry me,

sweetheart. In fact, we'll stop first at the general store to check on a dress for you and one for Essie and get your ring then. I suspect they have a good many lacy things in your size in those glass boxes on the shelves."

She opened her mouth to speak, then swallowed the words. It seemed that Cade would have his way in this, and somehow she couldn't find the grit to argue with him. The thought of new underthings against her skin was a temptation. Perhaps even batiste, at least something finer than the feed sacks.

"Nothing to say, sweetheart?" he asked with a grin, and she shook her head.

"Well then, let's plan on leaving here early on Saturday morning. We'll need to plan on an hour at the general store, and the preacher will be looking for us by noon. Then we'll go to the restaurant at the hotel and have a good dinner. So don't plan on cooking. We can piece out a sandwich or something for supper later on. All right?"

She could only nod, for it seemed that Cade had it all worked out and she was not about to rock this particular boat. Although a wedding was not what she had planned so soon, it seemed to her that he had it headed in the right direction, and she decided to ride along. If he was agreeable, if he was willing to be patient with her, she saw no reason to drag her feet. If he was to be her husband, as he'd said, she'd better be thinking along the lines of a real marriage. Perhaps he'd be willing to wait a while before he claimed his rights. *And perhaps pigs might fly.*

Saturday morning came sooner than Glory had thought it would, for she'd looked forward to it anxiously and on the other hand, had feared the changes it would bring about in her life. When she heard Cade and Buddy talking in the kitchen just after dawn, she rolled from her bed and sought out her work dress.

"You're up early," she said to the pair of them as she walked into the kitchen.

"Cade said we gotta get the chores done early and then eat breakfast and do whatever you have for us to do before we can leave for town. So we're about to go out and take care of the cow and chickens and see to the horses. The pinto was looking around the new stall last night, so Cade put her in there for the night."

Glory swung her gaze to where Cade watched

her. "Will we be able to leave them if they're ready to drop their foals this morning?"

"I'm gonna go out to have a look-see right now, sweetheart. Come on, Buddy. No breakfast till the chores are finished. Let's see if we can beat Glory, getting ready to leave for town."

"I'm comin', Cade," the boy answered eagerly, trotting alongside his hero as they stepped from the porch and headed to the barn.

It was but two or three minutes when a call came from the barn door. "Glory, come on out here." It was Buddy's voice, loud and clear, with excitement in every syllable.

She wiped her hands on the dish towel, then slid the pan of biscuits into the oven, for she'd just tossed them together quickly. Now she ran, her feet flying over the dusty ground as she headed for the barn.

Inside it was dim, but Cade had opened the back door and the sunlight shed its glow within that area. "Come on over here, Glory," Cade said quietly. "Take a look."

Glory stepped quietly across the floor to where Cade stood just inside the double stall he had prepared for the animals ready to give birth. The pinto mare stood patiently near him, bending her head as he slid his hand beneath her mane and scratched her there, speaking to her in a low voice.

Beside her was a foal, spraddle-legged and still damp from his journey, for he looked to be barely a few minutes old. "I had to lend a hand to the mama here, but her colt was on his feet like a shot. He's a sturdy little fella, and pretty as a picture."

"He's beautiful," Glory whispered, her eyes damp with tears, although she didn't know why she should feel like crying, for Cade was happy, his dream coming true with the arrival of the first of his new crop of horses.

The tiny colt butted his head against his mother's side, and then, as if he caught a scent that interested him, he bent his head low, reaching beneath her until he found her teats. With a whuffle of delight, he suckled one and choked a bit, milk running from his mouth. He bent his head, stretching his neck as he reached again for the milk she provided and this time was able to hold tight, making Cade laugh aloud.

"You've got the hang of it now, boy." The pinto lowered her own head to turn and keep an eye on her baby, and Buddy slid from the stall to clasp Glory's hand.

"Ain't it grand, Glory? Just look at that little fella. Who would have thought that he could have come out from inside that pinto?"

"That's one of the miracles of life, Buddy. It's the way God designed animals to reproduce. And when the foal grows up he will be able to help a lot of mares have babies of their own. That is, if Cade keeps him as a stallion." She slanted a look at Cade as she spoke.

He laughed aloud. "You're looking way ahead, Glory girl. But if he looks this good when he's a few months old, we may just plan on keeping him for a stud. He's got good markings, and his conformation is right. Hard to say with a foal so young, but I saw his daddy over at Earl Bradley's place, and he looks to be about the same sort of animal. We'll see."

"Will she be all right if we're gone today?" Glory asked, unwilling to do anything that might imperil the new mares and their birthing of foals.

"I think so. I've got the wall pulled down and we'll bring one of the other mares inside before we leave, just in case. The third one doesn't look like she's close enough to worry about yet."

He turned to Buddy then. "If you'll milk the cow, I'll harness up the horse to the wagon for our trip to town, son. And I'll even gather the eggs and feed the chickens."

Buddy's grin was quick. "I can do that." And he was gone to the springhouse, where he collected the extra milk pail and rinsed it at the pump, then brought it back to the barn.

Glory backed from the stall. "I'll take care of the chickens, Cade. I need to check on my old cluck anyway, and feed her. And by that time the biscuits will be done."

Glory hastened to the chicken coop, fed her hens and the rooster, who was feeling pretty spry this morning. The hen she'd put in the corner clucked contentedly on her nest, but deigned to rise long enough to feed when Glory tossed seed within her enclosure.

Essie was in the kitchen when Glory got there, rubbing her eyes and pulling the ribbon from her braid. "Will you have time to do my hair, Glory?"

"Right after breakfast. Now wash up so you can help me, Essie. You'll need to get out plates and silverware. Don't forget a cup for Cade's coffee, and one for me, too. I'll be having the last of the tea."

"You running out of tea, ma'am?" Cade stood on the porch, apparently aware of their conversation. "We'll have to fix that when we go to town."

His hands were still dripping and his head was slick from the water he'd used to smooth it down. "Could I use a towel, ma'am? I thought to dry my hands off out there in the sunshine, but it's not hot enough yet."

Glory smiled at him. "I guess I could spare a towel for you today."

He stood before her, his hands wrapped in the length of cotton toweling she'd given him. He held it in his hands, letting it droop between them.

"I'll take it," she said, but he was too quick for her and his hands lifted, the towel falling over her head, catching her neck and with a steady pull, he drew her closer to him.

"Gotcha," he whispered, his grin melting her defenses. For she leaned just a bit, her breasts barely touching his broad chest, her hands on his shoulders. "Shall I ask for a forfeit, before I let you go?"

"Don't you hurt my Glory!" Essie flew across the kitchen to clutch Glory's waist, peering up at her with anxious eyes.

"Sweet pea, I wouldn't think of hurting your Glory," he said, looking down at Essie with a half smile touching his lips. "In fact, I'd skin anyone who tried to hurt her. Between you and me and Buddy, we'll be taking good care of our Glory. Is that a deal?"

Essie grinned, her worry gone. "Is Glory yours, too? She's been mine and Buddy's for a long time, but we can share her." She glanced to where the door slammed behind Buddy as he entered the kitchen.

"I suspect she belongs to all three of us," Cade said smoothly. "Although, when a man marries a woman like I'm gonna marry Glory today, there's a special bond that forms. It's different than the way Glory loves you and Buddy, but that part will never change. You'll always be Glory's kin, just like she told you the other night. Remember?"

Essie nodded, and when Buddy came up to join the others, he put his arm around Essie's shoulders. "Glory ain't going anywhere just because she's gonna marry up with Cade, Essie. It'll just be better, 'cause Cade will be part of our family, too."

Cade winked at Buddy, and the boy grinned, a wide smile that somehow enclosed the two of them in a relationship. Cade reached one arm for Buddy and drew him close, then nodded at Essie to join the circle. In so doing he was forced to release his hold on Glory, but his lips formed a single word she could not mistake.

Later.

She blushed, but entered into the four-way embrace he had instigated, her arm encircling Essie and bringing her closer. The little girl's smile was wide, her eyes shimmering with tears, and Glory felt her own throat close up as she fought the onset of tears that threatened.

"Don't you girls dare to cry this morning," Cade said. "This is a happy day and we're all going to have a good time. Now, get into your best clothes, young'uns, and you, too, Miss Glory. We're going to a wedding."

Cade had put a box in the back of the wagon for Essie to sit on, lest she soil her dress on the boards of the wagon. She propped herself primly, looking down at her dress, the skirt starched and pressed, her shoes cleaned by Cade till they shone. "I shoulda had a hat," she whispered to Buddy, who sat next to her, and he just laughed and shook his head at her foolishness.

"We'll have to get you one at the store," Cade said, overhearing from the wagon seat. He glanced down at Glory. "You need a hat, too?"

"No. Just a bit of veiling, maybe."

"Whatever you need, Glory. We'll find you a pretty dress. That's why we've started out so early. How about new shoes?"

"These are good enough," she said, though she tucked them back under the seat, for they were worn, not even a good cleaning doing much to hide their wear and tear.

"Not good enough for a bride, Glory," he whispered against her ear, and then laughed as she blushed.

"I've been a bride before," she said, holding her chin high. "Second time around doesn't count."

"You've never been my bride before," he told her. "And believe me, honey, it's gonna count. More than you know."

Her blush was hotter this time, and Essie leaned forward on her box, twisting to peer up at Glory. "You look like you been out in the sun too long, Glory. Are you feeling all right?"

"I'm fine, Essie." Her glare in Cade's direction was met with a chuckle.

The trip went quickly, the horse seeming to

know that a celebration was in order, for she trotted along without pause, harness jingling in time to the quickness of her gait. Before Glory was ready for it, the narrow road widened and they were on the main street through town, with stores and buildings on both sides, the sidewalks full of the Saturday crowd, all of whom seemed to pay special mind to the wagon from the Clark holding, wherein sat the man who'd taken over Harvey Clark's place, the widow beside him.

Behind them were the two children who were essentially orphans, but neither of them looked sad today, for they whispered together and looked around as if anticipating some great event.

The wagon pulled up at the general store and all four occupants climbed down, Cade lifting Glory to the ground and hoisting Essie over the side, where she clasped Glory's hand and murmured soft words audible only to the woman who sheltered her, holding her one hand and gathering her close with her other palm on Essie's shoulder.

Buddy stepped up to the door, opening it wide for the small family to walk inside. Glory waited for Cade's direction. "Come on over to the counter," he said softly, one hand at her waist. And then he smiled at the middle-aged woman who greeted them.

"Well, hello there. It's a pleasure to see you and the children, Mrs. Clark. And you too, Mr. McAllister. What can I do for you today?"

Cade answered for her, for Glory seemed tongue-tied. "First off we have a short list of supplies we'll need," he said, handing the storekeeper's wife the bit of paper with the list Glory had compiled earlier. "Did she remember to put tea on there, Mrs. Nelson?" he asked the lady, who was busily scanning the page.

"Yes, sir, she surely did and I've got a new flavor in I think she'll like." Her smile was wide, as if she considered what profit this shopping expedition might bring to the store this morning.

Cade stepped closer and made his desires known. "First off, our children need to look at the jars of candy and choose some to take home with them. And Glory needs a new dress and a pair of good shoes," he said firmly, his hand at her waist allowing for no denial from her lips. Glory looked up at him with a glare that made him smile.

At his words, Buddy and Essie grinned and

headed for the row of heavy glass jars that held the candy supply, eager to decide on their treat.

Cade turned to the woman behind the counter. "Glory needs some of that froufrou stuff you keep in those glass bins, too. Some underthings or whatever it is women wear beneath their dresses. Oh, and a nightgown." He bent closer to her and whispered against her ear, "You're all done with wearing feed sacks, sweetheart. So don't argue with me or I'll embarrass you right here in front of God and anyone else who might wander in."

Chapter Seven

Glory pressed her lips together and looked at the wall behind the counter. Three shelves were filled with the glass bins he'd mentioned. How he knew what their contents were was a mystery, but if the man was determined to buy things for her, she might as well enjoy the experience of being pampered. It was new to her and she suspected she might just wallow in the joy of it.

"Well, let's see what we have in a dress to suit you, Mrs. Clark." The woman took down two bins and lifted folded garments from within, the first a white batiste fabric with a scattering of lilac-colored flowers over the expanse of skirt and the bodice. A white ruffle formed the collar and the sleeves were puffed and fitted with the same ruffling.

It was more than Glory had ever hoped to own,

for her dresses were plain and serviceable, such as a housewife would wear. She'd made most of them herself, and a store-bought garment was a luxury to her way of thinking.

"Hmm…I think I have another just like it in a smaller size. This one looks to be a little large. Glory's just a mite of a thing, ain't she?" the storekeeper's wife asked Cade with an arch look. She sorted through the box and found the dress she'd decided might fit and laid it before Glory on the counter.

Her breath caught in her throat as Glory held up the garment before her. She need not look further, for the dress she held was perfect. She gazed up at Cade to see his grin aimed in her direction. "Will that one do?" he asked as the storekeeper's wife took the dress and shook out the dainty yards of fabric, holding it up beneath Glory's chin, cocking her head to one side with a smile of approval on her lips.

"Looks like it ought to fit you just fine, Mrs. Clark. Would you like to try it on?"

"Let me take a good look at it," Glory said, gathering the garment before her and holding it against her waist, measuring the width of it. "I think this will do," she said, brushing her hand down the front of the dress. She smiled at Cade then, her cheeks rosy as she folded the dress and placed it on the counter.

"Thank you, Cade," she whispered.

"How about something for Essie?" he asked quietly.

"Perhaps a new pinafore for her to wear over her dress. She can use it on Sundays, too. Her old one is too small and she's been without for a while."

"Well, no longer," Cade told her firmly. "Get whatever she needs, and pick out some froufrou while we're here right in front of the glass boxes."

She nodded, unable to speak for the pure pleasure that rippled through her as four different boxes were deposited before her. The woman behind the counter smiled, pleased at the obvious generosity of the man who made no bones about wanting to spend his money on Glory Clark. Her hands went unerringly to the first bin, this one containing petticoats, one of which she held up for Glory's inspection. It was wide and full, the skirt hemmed with lace, the waist tied with ribbons. Beneath it in the same bin was a stack of chemises, both lacy and sheer, and the first one she held up made Glory blush with the thought of Cade seeing her garbed in such a thing.

He only nodded his approval at Mrs. Nelson, and she placed it atop the petticoat on the counter. "Better give us a couple more of those," Cade said in an undertone, his glance at Glory giving her notice that he would not be swayed from his purpose.

"Stockings?" Glory asked quietly, and was pleased with the woman's choice of three pair, one white, two of them pale brown and more suited to everyday wear.

Cade took her arm then and led her to where stacks of shoe boxes lined another counter, small pictures on the ends divulging the contents to the shoppers who viewed them. He picked up a box with low-cut slippers showing on the label and opened it before Glory's expectant eyes. They were dainty, a far cry from the serviceable and sturdy boots she wore every day. Glory's eyes lit up as she surveyed the shoes in Cade's hands.

"What size do you wear?" he asked, and bent to hear her reply.

"I don't know. Those look about right, I think."

"Well try them on." At his bidding, she sat on a low chair and he half knelt before her, untying the lacings of her boot and slipping it from her foot. His fingers slid the flat shoe into place and tested the fit, pressing on her toes and easing it on and off her heel.

"These are too large," he said briefly, reaching for another box similar to the first. He opened it, revealing the same style of shoes as those he'd discarded, and tried another on her foot. It fit as though it had been made for her, and she felt a jolt of pleasure as she turned her foot this way and that, admiring the fit of the shoe, the slender lines of her own foot within it.

"That one will do, I think. Is it all right, Glory? Does it give you enough room to wiggle your toes?" His smile was warm as he placed her foot on the floor and bid her stand.

She did as he asked and he waved a hand at her, directing her to walk to and fro before him. The shoe was slick on the bottom and she walked with care, lest she slip and lose her balance.

"I think those will do," Cade said to Mrs. Nelson, who watched them with interest. He took Glory's other boot off and replaced it with the mate to the slipper he'd chosen for her.

"She'll wear them, and if you have a place where she can change, I'd like her to try on the dress. If it fits, she'll wear that, too. We'll need a dress and a new hat for Essie while we're at it," Cade said, remembering just in time that he'd promised such a thing to the small girl.

The shopkeeper's wife was obviously pleased with the turn of events, probably envisioning a dandy profit from this bit of business today, for she led Glory to a small room where extra stock for the store lined shelves and sat about in boxes on the floor. "Shall I help you?" she asked the young woman, who seemed dazed by the largesse of the man who accompanied her. Glory shook her head, yearning to see the new dress on her body, her fingers caught up in the lacy underthings Cade had bought to go beneath the fine batiste garment she held.

Mrs. Nelson returned to the front of the shop and smiled widely when Cade motioned to her, obviously pleased by the price he was willing to pay for the gold ring he chose from her supply. He slipped it into his pocket after carefully slid-ing it onto his smallest finger as if checking the size.

"I won't be long," Glory called from the back room, pulling the curtain carefully closed, then unbuttoning her dress, allowing it to fall around her feet. She lifted the new gown and put it over her head, her arms exposed beneath the puffy sleeves, her throat slender above the flowered bodice. A small mirror gave her a bird's-eye view of her face and the upper part of her body, and she looked down with pleasure at the full skirt that fell to the floor around her. In a matter of moments, she'd pulled the new petticoat up beneath the full skirt and tied it firmly, deciding to save the dainty chemise for another day.

The waistline of the dress was just a bit too large, but she reached behind her and tied the ribbon that served as a belt to draw the fabric in a bit, forming it to her own contours. With an easy gesture, she picked up her old dress and folded it, knowing that Cade wanted to see her in the new clothing.

As she stepped from the storeroom, Essie drew in a quick breath and her sigh of approval was obvious. "Oh, Miss Glory, you look so pretty. Like a fairy princess in my storybook."

"You've got that right, young'un," Cade said, his own voice just as awed as that of the child.

Glory walked slowly from the back room of the store, one hand lifting the skirt of the dress lest it touch the floor. "Cade, it makes me feel…"

"Pretty?" Cade asked as he bent to her, his hand touching the shoulder of her gown, his fingers brushing the soft fabric with a gentle touch.

"Yes." She looked up at him and her heart jumped within her breast. "You're a kind man, Cade McAllister. Thank you for being so good to me."

"You deserve every bit of it and more, Glory. Just you being my bride is enough to make me happy, and seeing you all fresh and pretty in a new dress makes me proud. Would you like a new hat, too?"

Glory shook her head. "No thank you. And I don't need the veiling I spoke of either. I'll be fine this way."

He turned back to the counter and his hand lifted, his index finger pointing at another of the glass bins behind the counter. It was taken down and placed before him and he lifted the lid, his eyes warm as he touched the garment folded beneath his hand.

"Will this one fit her?" he asked, and Mrs. Nelson nodded as she lifted it from the box and held it before herself. It was smaller than she, but appeared to be a good fit for the woman he was about to wed. And if he was as smart as he thought he was, it would look like heaven's best when he saw it on Glory's body tonight.

"I now pronounce you husband and wife. Do you have a ring for Mrs. McAllister, sir?" The young minister paused and smiled at Cade as a simple gold circle appeared in his hand and then found its way to Glory's ring finger. Her eyes opened wide as if she were surprised by the ring, and well she might be, Cade thought, for he'd meant it to be a surprise.

And then the final words were spoken. "You may kiss your bride, sir."

Without hesitation, Cade bent to Glory, his lips fitting against hers with precision, leaving behind just a bit of moisture as he ended the brief caress. He'd do better later on, he promised himself. Yet, he could not fault the response he'd felt to his lips just now, for she'd returned the slight pressure he'd exerted, her mouth moving just a bit beneath his. She hadn't denied him his right, that was for sure, and as he reached into his pocket to find a gold piece for the preacher, he considered the money well spent.

He was well and truly married to the girl, a husband in name and soon to be in fact. Once he got her home and the young'uns into bed, he'd set this marriage in motion.

His eyes were lit with a glow Glory hadn't seen before, when he turned to her and offered his arm. She lay her hand atop his sleeve and walked beside him from the small, white church to the grassy expanse of lawn before the building. The children followed them, Essie whispering delightedly to her brother, Buddy unable to hush her words, and in fact adding to her excitement.

"We're gonna eat at the hotel," Glory heard him say to his sister, and she looked back at them, pleased at their happiness. Having Cade in the family had not been difficult for them, for he'd made a place for himself from the first. His care over Essie and his man-to-man friendship with Buddy had endeared him to the pair, and Glory was pleased that they had coped so well with having another man in the household.

The meal at the hotel was up to the children's expectations, although Essie said that Glory could cook better than the lady in the kitchen. With their appetites sated and their excitement at a peak, they piled into the wagon for the ride home.

The four sitting on the board seat were squashed

together, looking for all the world like a true family, and for that Glory was thankful. Essie sat on her lap, chattering happily about the wedding and the new hat Cade had bought for her and Glory's new clothing, even praising Buddy for his handsome appearance in the new shirt he wore. For they'd all used the small back room at the store to change for the ceremony, and even Cade was resplendent in a new white shirt, with a black string tie making him look the part of a gentleman.

They rode up the lane to the farmhouse, Glory plotting her supper preparations, for it was nearing time to think about what she might put together for a meal before dark. "Will canned peaches and toast do for a meal?" she asked Cade.

"I don't think any of us are starved," he said with a grin. "Peaches and toast sound good to me. Maybe some fresh coffee."

"Can we have tea, Glory?" Essie wanted to know.

"Of course. I'll get out the flowered teapot for us and we'll have a party," Glory told her, wanting to make the occasion as cheerful as possible for the children.

Cade went to the bedroom, where he'd earlier moved his belongings, and changed his clothes, preparing to do the chores. Buddy did the same, and quickly reappeared in the kitchen with his overalls on.

Taking the empty milk pail from the pantry, he headed to the barn, Cade fast on his heels. "I'll milk this time, while you take care of the horses," he told Buddy. Make sure they have a measure of grain and see to it there's clean straw in their stalls for tonight. We'll leave them out in the pasture till after supper."

Buddy nodded his agreement and left Cade to the chore of easing the cow's burden of milk. Before long they had left the barn and Cade stopped at the chicken coop, handing Buddy the blue-speckled bowl of corn and chicken feed to scatter over the open yard where the hens gathered.

He checked on the broody hen in the corner, who clucked contentedly at him as he gathered eggs from the empty nests and left the coop. His egg bowl was half full and he carried it to the house, where Essie waited on the porch.

"We're about ready to eat," she said importantly. "Me and Glory fixed the food and I made the tea myself."

Cade covered the child's shoulder with a warm

hand as he went into the kitchen, catching Glory's eye, noting her flushed cheeks as she placed the big bowl of peaches on the table and then poured his cup of coffee.

They sat down to eat and Cade remembered that it was his duty to speak the words of thanks for the meal. He did so with a flourish, mentioning the wedding that had taken place that morning, and his thankfulness for God's blessing on the service.

Glory looked everywhere but at Cade as she served the children and then dished up a bowl of peaches for herself. Cade spread jam with a generous hand on his toast, enjoying the thick slabs Glory cut from a loaf she'd baked just yesterday.

They ate quickly and the children looked out the window at the setting sun, then back at Glory. "Can I read for just a little while before we go to bed?" Buddy asked, looking toward where his current book awaited him on the kitchen dresser. He kept it close by, should a chance come to snatch a few minutes between its pages.

"I think so," Glory said quietly. "I need to take care of my new clothes and clean up the kitchen, so you should have a half hour or so to spare."

His grin was answer enough. Glory brushed

her hand across his head as she left her chair and gathered the bowls, carrying them to the sink. Essie brought a handful of silverware and placed it in the dishpan. A small pan was used to carry warm water from the stove and the few dishes were cleaned up in but minutes.

Glory looked at Cade fleetingly. She didn't see a way of putting it off any longer. She had to get ready for bed, had to take off her clothing and don the new gown he'd bought for her, and then lie down on the bed and await his pleasure.

The things they'd spoken of, the intimacy he'd put into words, were enough to make her tremble, for she had no idea what the man expected of her. She hoped he might let her retain possession of her nightgown; perhaps she'd go on that assumption, and have her own way in this small thing.

She put away the clothing Cade had bought for her, folding and refolding the garments as she placed them in the almost empty drawers of the dresser in the bedroom. It seemed she couldn't dawdle any longer, for she heard Cade speaking with the children in the kitchen, and then Essie called out to her from the bedroom doorway.

"Good night, Glory. I'm going to bed now."

Glory held out her arms and Essie flew to the

shelter she'd come to know so well over the past years. "You're a good girl, Essie, and I love you." It was a whisper against her ear, and Essie leaned back and grinned her happiness.

"It was a good day, wasn't it, Glory. We had fun and the dinner at the hotel was nice. The fried chicken wasn't as good as yours, but the cake was sure delicious."

"It was all a wedding day should be," Glory said softly, brushing her hand over Essie's hair, admiring the way the soft curls framed her dainty features. She dropped a final kiss on the child's cheek and turned her toward the doorway. "I'll see you in the morning."

And at the thought of what would come to pass before the sun rose again in the eastern sky, Glory felt a touch of panic run the length of her spine. Buddy stood just beyond her door and offered a smile.

"I read two chapters, Glory. It sure is a good book."

"Don't forget you'll owe me a book report on it when you finish," she reminded him and he waved a negligent hand in reply, his footsteps taking him down the hallway.

It was quiet in the aftermath of the children's

voices, and when Cade stepped into view, she halted where she was, unable to speak.

"Can I come in, Glory, or did you want to get undressed first?" He watched her, patience being a virtue he planned to exhibit tonight. The girl was frightened, and with good reason. She'd never felt a man's hands on her body, never known a man's touch against her softest parts, and was now faced with a man who outweighed her by a hundred pounds and towered over her by almost a foot.

Well might she be apprehensive.

"It makes no matter to me," she said in a small voice. "I can put on my gown behind the screen in the corner." For, indeed, a corner of her bedroom was shielded from view by a three-paneled screen, meant to set apart the area where she kept her slop jar and dressing table.

"All right." He was agreeable to anything she wanted, he realized. His only stipulation was that they share this bed in which she'd slept alone for three years. He had every intention of sleeping beside her for the rest of his life, of holding her close through long nights and waking with her every morning. Once he'd found that damn hoard, he'd never deceive her again.

And from the looks of the girl, something frightened her half to death. He walked with studied casualness into the room, closing the door behind himself. "I turned out the kitchen lamp and locked the doors," he said, sitting on the chair next to the window and taking off his boots.

"Why don't you get undressed, Glory," he suggested, watching her as she drew her new nightgown from the dresser drawer. It was filmy, sheer, and altogether a delightful bit of froth, with lace in strategic spots. His desire to see her within its folds was urgent.

She nodded and went behind the screen. Soon her dress was hanging over the top and then her petticoat joined it, fluttering its signal that she was halfway into wearing the gown. He waited, watching for her to reappear, and when she did, it was a vision he was not about to forget in a hurry.

She indeed wore the gown. It fell loosely about her slender form, only the firm lines of her bosom shaping it to her body above her waist. It fell from there in a full, almost transparent skirt to the floor. She looked virginal—pure and utterly delicious—and his breath came with difficulty, forcing its way past the constriction in his lungs.

"Come here, Glory," he said, holding out a hand

to her as he waited beside the bed. "I want to kiss you and tell you how pretty you are, sweetheart."

"You want to kiss me?"

"I seem to be thinking about it all the time of late. In fact, I've wanted to kiss you since the first day I saw you. Wanted to hold you close and offer myself as protection against everything that threatened you. I thought how womanly you were, how motherly and kind to two little kids who needed a mother badly."

"All that?" she asked, her eyes wide with surprise.

"All that and more. I sat across the table from you that night and ate the soup you'd cooked. I thought then that you were the most courageous girl I'd ever seen, and if there was any way to have you for my own, I'd move heaven and earth to make it happen."

"And you didn't even have to do all that. I just fell into your hands like a ripe peach from a tree in the orchard."

"You had me worried for a while, Glory. I wanted you to be happy knowing we were to be married, and I wasn't sure I could please you, here..." He waved a hand at the bed beside them. "I want to love you, Glory."

His words were all he had to offer, hoping against hope she would be willing to place herself in his care. This was his chance to show this little bit of woman a degree of patience and tenderness that would perhaps win her heart.

She sat down on the edge of the bed, lifted her feet to slide them beneath the sheet and lay back on the pillow, her hair spreading over the white fabric like a dark cloud, a thing of beauty he'd been anticipating all day. Her eyes were blue as the summer sky tonight, and he realized that they changed color sometimes, turning gray as a storm cloud when he angered her. Blue was better, warmer, he decided, and he circled the bed, unbuttoning his shirt and slipping it from his shoulders to drop it into the laundry basket. His trousers were next and Glory's eyes widened as he lowered them to the floor, sliding off his stockings and dropping them in the basket with his shirt before he folded his trousers and placed them over the back of the chair by the window.

In his cream-colored underwear, he approached the bed, lying down beside her, then lifting himself as an afterthought to blow out the candle she'd carried in here earlier.

He'd have preferred to let it burn, let it illuminate the clean beauty of her features as he loved her, but knew that her modesty would be better served in the dark.

Another time, he told himself. Another night, when he'd wooed her and coaxed her into a more adventurous mood, then he'd leave the candle burn.

As it was, there was enough moonlight to see her, to trace the fine lines of her cheek and temple, to see the lashes flutter against her skin as she looked up at him and then away, too shy to watch him closely. He had no such problem, for he'd waited all day to look at every blessed inch of the girl. If only she'd let him uncover her as he had planned.

His hand went to the buttons of her bodice, undoing them carefully, gently and with a purpose she could not help but understand.

"Must I take off my gown?" she asked as his hand touched the skin beneath the fine cotton. He traced the rise of her breast and she inhaled sharply.

"I'd like you to. I want to see you, Glory. I've waited a long time for this, for my wedding night, for I plan to have only one such night in my life.

We're married now, sweetheart, for the rest of our lives, and I need to see the woman I've married."

"You haven't known me a long time, Cade. Only just less than two weeks."

"It's seemed like an age since you said you'd marry me. You have no idea how long I've wanted to have a wife of my own, a woman who would take care of me and give me her love."

"I'll try, Cade. I know I promised to love, honor and obey you, and I don't think I'll have any trouble with the obeying part, for I want to please you. I suspect I'll grow to love you someday, and honoring my husband is something I've been taught was the right and proper thing to do since I was but a young girl. But—"

He grew a bit impatient, his words overriding her small protest. "Tonight is my night to please you, Glory," he told her, pulling her upright to slide the gown down her arms, allowing the fabric to encircle her as she sat beside him. His hand touched her breast and she flinched from his fingers against her skin.

The memory of the men she'd fled, those on the wagon train who had considered her fair game and had offered marriage, lived deep in her heart, and now the remembrance was alive in her mind.

The night when one of the miners had come to her in the shadows and attempted to embrace her, his hand falling on her breast, his fingers squeezing, his breath hot in her face.

For just a moment, his face was that of Cade's and she stilled beside him, her fear a living thing within her. She pushed at his hand and he placed it instead at her waist. And yet, this was Cade, tonight doing his best to be kind and patient, his dark eyes warm as he smiled down at her. He was a man she could admire, tall and well muscled, strong and handsome, his dark hair falling over his forehead, his cheeks warm with the flush of desire. And the sight pleased her, for he'd said she was the woman he'd waited for, the one he'd chosen to marry. Suddenly, she knew she need not fear him, for even though he was strong, he would not use his strength against her more frail frame. And though he touched her with his long fingers and wide palms, she did not fear him, for he had said he would never harm or hurt her.

And she knew, in her heart of hearts, that she could trust this man she'd married. Knew that he would give her his body in marriage and take hers in turn, and in the taking there would only be joy and pleasure. Her breast warmed from his touch and she looked down to where his big hand once more held her flesh with tender care.

"I won't hurt you, sweetheart. I only want to touch you." When she nodded, he once more fitted his hand beneath the soft curve and held the weight of her breast in his palm, measuring it in silence, looking down at the crumpled bit of flesh that tempted him.

He dropped his head and placed a warm caress there, where the pink crest seemed to reach toward his mouth. His tongue touched it and he heard her breath catch in her throat, as she shivered and trembled at his touch.

With careful hands he eased her back beside him and then his hands were at her waist, folding the gown beneath his fingers till he scooped it from her body and off the bed. She tugged at the sheet, as if she needed the reassurance of a cover to hide herself from his view. But he would not have it, for he took the soft cotton from her fingers and pushed it away, down her body, until her waist, breasts and the soft curves of her hips were exposed to his view.

"Cade, I don't like being naked this way," she protested, her hand covering the vee of her thighs, the other arm lying across her breasts.

"Ah, sweetheart, I won't hurt you." He pulled the sheet up a bit and rued losing sight of the vision he'd covered.

She took his breath, this slender girl with curves that belonged to a woman, for she was rounded nicely, her breasts larger than he'd expected, her waist small, her hips gently flaring and the small mound there at the vee of her thighs fluffy with a covering of dark hair that drew him like a magnet.

She was perfect. And all this beauty belonged to him. It was almost more than his imagination could handle: that Glory was here, within reach, and had given him leave to make love with her.

Chapter Eight

He touched her waist, placed his palm on the curve of her belly beneath the sheet and bent to kiss her again, his lips easing hers open just a bit, tasting the sweetness of her mouth. She returned his kiss, the pressure of his lips seeming to please her, for she sighed and her arms circled his neck.

"It's not you, Cade, that makes me feel so shaky, but the memory of the miners on the wagon train who were determined to get their hands on me. I've felt ever since that I have to protect myself and..."

"It's all right, Glory. You haven't told me that part of your story before, and I didn't know that bad memories lived in your mind. I can only tell you that it isn't just your body that lures me close, although I'd be lying if I said that all your curves and lovely rounded places don't appeal to me in a mighty way. But there's more to you than a body, sweetheart.

"I love the woman you are. I admire the strength and tenderness you show the children, and I want some of that for myself, I guess."

He let his head drop until it pressed against her waist, and her hand lifted to lie on the back of his neck. "I'm truly trying, Cade. I didn't mean to cause you to be angry with me."

"Far from it, sweetheart." And then he paused, lifting himself up and over her again, his lips finding hers and pressing a multitude of kisses there and upon her face, her cheeks and forehead, the soft flesh of her throat. "Will you let me love you, Glory? Will you give your body to me and let me make it mine?" His voice was rough, his tones raw with passion and he hoped once more that she would not fear him, that her answer would be pleasing to him.

Her nod was slight, and he lifted his head, Her eyes were shiny with a hint of tears as she looked up at him. "I want to be a good wife, Cade. I'll do whatever you say."

A man could not desire more than those words, he found, for his heart was touched by the simplicity of her offer. He brushed the dampness from her cheeks, then whispered soft coaxing endearments as he bent lower, his mouth against her breasts, his hands running the length of her body, touching her thighs, her hips, circling her waist and then finally moving her small hand aside, allowing him to explore the warmth she sheltered between her legs. She was soft, damp and willing, and his thankfulness knew no bounds.

It was more than he'd hoped to find, the softness, her flesh yielding to his touch. And Cade felt more a man at that moment than he ever had in his life.

That this fragile, slender reed of a woman would give herself into his care so readily was more than he had thought possible. He'd thought to coax her, perhaps woo her for however long it took to work past her inhibitions. And now, even though she was fearful and fighting off memories of the past, she'd offered him all she had, all she was.

All of her, *his* for the taking.

She moved beneath his hands, lifting to his touch as he ventured farther and discovered the warmth of her womanhood. Her hips rose, seeming to welcome the fingers that explored her soft places. He was careful, seeking out the tight channel he would claim in moments, and he found it to be taut and narrow around his finger. A woman untried, a girl whose innocence drew him.

He rejoiced at her open welcome of his loving. She sighed, her breath coming in quickening puffs against his cheek, then his shoulder, as he found the places that would provide her with pleasure, careful but determined as he explored the body no man had touched before tonight.

And that thought filled him with a joy he'd never known. A thankfulness to the man who had wed her and cared for her, who had left her untouched for this time and this place.

Her body warmed to his touch and Glory welcomed the careful easing of his hand against her softest parts. He slid one long finger within her and she inhaled sharply.

"I didn't hurt you, did I, sweet?" he asked quickly, and she shook her head.

"No, it feels good, but I wasn't expecting you to do that."

He laughed softly. "You're so warm and soft, Glory. I know you're a virgin and I fear I'll cause you some pain, but I'll try not to hurt you, love. Just be patient with me."

But her thoughts were far from fearful, for his movements against her body, the touch of his fingers there where her flesh throbbed warmly against his caresses, brought a pleasure she had not known possible. She sobbed deep within her throat and it was as if she was nearing some great discovery, for her entire body was caught up in the peak of delight he brought her. She found her hips lifting and falling, her flesh meeting his clever hand as he brought her closer to what she sought, and then, as though she had been granted some joy unknown to her before, she felt a shivering, quivering thrill sweep over her and she was caught up in long moments of pleasure.

"Ah, sweetheart." Cade whispered the words in her ear as he swept his hand along the length of her body, spreading her thighs a bit as he turned to settle between her knees. "I'll be careful, love," he swore, lifting her legs and joining their bodies slowly.

As she gasped at the sharp twinge of his taking and would have cried aloud, he kissed her, holding the sound between them, until she almost collapsed in his embrace, her lips touching him where they would, her small cries telling him of her pleasure.

She slid her arms around his neck, pulling him against herself as if she would mold their bodies together, impress her breasts against his chest, her belly against his, her legs entwining with his own. The tears she'd tried to withhold were now being shed against his skin…tears of joy she could not explain.

"Glory, I'm sorry. I didn't want to hurt you, sweetheart, but I knew it would be easier if I did this quickly. It'll never hurt you again, I promise. Only this once."

He lay quietly upon her, feeling the tight grasp her body placed on his manhood, and it was all he could do to remain still, not to thrust into her. But there would be other nights when he could do as he pleased, when his body could take its pleasure without fear of hurting her, and for now he would do what he could to make this easy for her.

He drew back and then penetrated her anew, hearing her small gasp as she accepted him, feeling the clasp of her legs around his, the warmth of her arms as they encircled his neck. He felt the quickening of his flesh that foretold the rush of pleasure that awaited him, and he retreated once more from her, then pressed within, the acute ecstasy branding him. His body trembled against hers and he was awash with the delight she brought him.

She breathed then against his throat, her words soft, almost inaudible, until he lifted from her and looked down at the stunned look of joy on her face.

"Cade...I don't know what to say. It feels so strange, but so right, as if you've made us into one being, one person. Is this what my mother spoke of when she said that a man and his wife would be one flesh?"

"I think she got that out of the Good Book, Glory. Seems like I've seen it in there and heard it spoken in the marriage services when I was a boy. Sounds like a good description to me. It makes sense that we become as one, for from now on we'll be together, you and me."

"I'm glad," she whispered against his ear. "I'm so glad it was you, Cade, that I've never done this with anyone else."

He felt a laugh bubbling up within him and swallowed it. No way would he let her think he laughed at her words. But a wash of pure happiness caught him broadside and he was stunned by the treasure he held in his embrace. He'd known she would be generous with her body, felt sure she would give him all he asked for, but he'd not realized how truly warm and wonderful she was, how fully she was able to set aside her modesty to become his wife. This untried girl who had today turned him into a husband.

Chapter Nine

For the next few weeks, one day seemed to flow into the next, Glory satisfied to work in the house, cleaning, cooking, finding bliss in the joys of marriage. Though Cade was, without a doubt, the head of the home they had formed between them, she knew he considered her to be the warmth that kept things moving along the proper path.

He'd given her no reason to fear his presence here; nor had he treated her as anything other than a woman to be honored and respected. He spoke with her daily of the small happenings on the farm, shared with her every event that transpired in the barn and fields beyond. They sat in the kitchen every morning after breakfast, sharing a cup of coffee while the dishes sat soaking in the sink. And this morning was no exception. He watched as she wiped down the stove and waited for her to take her place across from him, even as the youthful voices of Buddy and Essie rang on the breeze that blew from the yard.

He spoke now, his words seeming to be ones he'd considered for a time before they were said aloud. "Now that all the mares have dropped their foals, I think we need to consider turning the farm into a horse ranch." It sounded more like a done deal than an idea tossed on the table for Glory's consideration, and she turned from the stove to face Cade and discuss his latest project.

"Can't it be both?" she asked, thinking of the tremendous amount of work entailed in raising a herd of horses. Surely just gardening and cutting hay and training the three foals he already had possession of was enough to keep both of them busy. Expanding the farm to that extent would mean investing in more horses and spending money they didn't have. Where Cade had found the cash to purchase the three mares he'd already bought from Earl Bradley was a question Glory had put off asking.

But now seemed like a good time to get things out in the open. "How can we afford a horse ranch, Cade? I have no idea where the money came from when you bought the three mares, but surely you aren't possessed of an endless supply. I had no idea you planned to turn this place upside down and make big changes in the way of life here."

He sat on his chair at the head of the table and motioned Glory closer. "We need to talk about this, sweetheart. Yes, I had some money when I came here, some of it the results of poker playing while I roamed from one place to another. And then I'd saved everything I earned, all but my room and board, when I worked for a while as a sheriff's deputy in Oklahoma for almost a year. I used a bit of it for the mares—"

"A *bit* of it?" she asked, breaking into his explanation. "It took more than a *bit* of cash to buy three pregnant mares and you know it. And now you want to invest further, and won't that give you control over the whole place? The farm Harvey Clark left for his son?"

Cade sent up a silent prayer for patience, a virtue he was short of today. "There's one thing you haven't thought of, Glory. According to the law, when we got married, the farm became mine. Legally, I own the place. And before you fly off into a rage, let me emphasize the fact that when the time comes, this place will be Buddy's. But that isn't going to happen for ten years or so, in my estimation. In the meantime, I'll be building it up into a fine horse ranch, with a pasture full of foals every year and a steady supply of customers who buy them. By the time Buddy takes over here, he'll have a fine living, raising and training horses. It'll still be Buddy's no matter what."

"And when was all this decided?" She sat down as he'd directed, her heart pounding, her lungs seemingly in a vise, for she could barely breathe.

Cade leaned back in his chair. "I've been thinking about it from the first, making plans to enlarge the barn a bit. In fact, fitting out the mare's stalls for birthing and building new ones for the additional animals we've managed to accumulate is just the beginning."

She spoke slowly, deliberately. "This was your plan from the first, wasn't it? That you'd take over the place."

He let his chair thump to the floor and his face fell into angry lines. "I suppose you could say that. My viewpoint is a bit different, but I guess the final line is that I'm not content to cut hay and gather eggs as a full-time job. I'm more interested in doing something that will make money and offer all of us a secure future."

"All of us?" She'd thought things were pretty well on an even keel since the wedding, with Cade in her bed every night and working all day in the barn and the corral, tending his horses and pounding a hammer during the afternoons.

"You're my wife, Glory. And I've taken on the care of Buddy and Essie. I think that speaks for itself."

"I think you're more interested in what you can do to line your pockets than in the three of us, Cade McAllister."

He stood, seeming to loom over her, his palms flat on the table, his eyes flashing an anger she'd never seen exhibited. "And I think you're talking like a blooming idiot, Glory McAllister. In case you've forgotten, you go by the same name I do, and anything I do here will benefit you as much as it does me."

Blooming idiot, indeed. She scooted her chair from the table and rose quickly, crossing the room and running up the stairs to her bedroom door. He was fast on her heels and when she would have shut the door in his face, his big-booted foot held it open.

"Don't ever try to close me out of this room," he said, his words so quiet they only served to frighten her further. He stepped into the bedroom and closed the door. His hands rose to grasp her shoulders, but she backed away, escaping his touch.

And then realized her mistake.

Cade, normally the most peaceable of men, was livid with anger, his face flushed with the fury that drove him, compelling him toward her. He caught up with her in front of her dresser and backed her against it, his big body holding her before him.

"Cade, let me go. I've got things to do out in the garden." She tried the sensible approach, pushing at him with no success, for he did not budge from his stance.

"You started this, Glory. I tried to talk to you about some plans I've been mulling over, and you've made it into a stone wall between us. Now you'll listen to me."

She put her hands over her ears, shaking her head, feeling foolish, but unwilling to obey his edicts.

His palms covered her wrists and he pulled

her hands to his chest, holding them there, even as his body held her right where he wanted her.

She pressed her lips together, unwilling to even speak to him, yet fearful of his mood, his anger and the power he held over her. She stood no chance of escaping him, for if she fought him, he could easily overpower her. In fact, he could have her on the bed in mere seconds, she realized. She was without protection from this man, and the fear of his reprisals against her accusations loomed before her.

He lifted her from her feet then, almost as if he'd read her thoughts, and carried her to the bed, holding her in his lap, his hands firm against her waist and hip. One large hand rose to cup her cheek, and she was held immobile before him.

She would not cry. She would not allow him the knowledge that she was frightened of him, of what his anger might cause to happen. For up until now, Cade had been only gentle and tender with her smaller frame and made concessions for her lesser strength. Yet now he faced her looking like an avenging angel, for when all was said and done, his face held a masculine beauty she could not deny. And even now, if she were to be honest, he had not hurt her nor caused her pain, but only held her across his thighs, perched nicely on his lap.

She had not been fully aware of the depths of the man, she realized. And facing his fury head-on, while two children weeded in her garden and the day was only half begun, was not what she would have chosen to do at this time.

"Cade, you need to let me up. What if the children come in the house? I don't want them to find us in the bedroom in the middle of the morning. I know you're angry with me, but—"

"Hush, Glory. Not another word. You've got me ready to lose my temper in a grand way, and I'm trying to hold it in. And trying to threaten me with two little kids isn't going to gain you any ground."

He met her gaze and his face cleared a bit, the anger giving way to a frustrated look that was new to her. His hands relaxed their hold a bit and he bent to kiss her.

"Don't be kissing me," she said, almost snarling the words. "I don't like you one bit right now, Mr. McAllister."

She turned her head from him but he would not be swayed, grasping her chin and holding her while he pressed his lips to hers. She tried to bite his lip, pushed at him and tried to kick her feet, all to no avail, for he was too strong, his arms a cage about her and she felt at his mercy.

She quieted against his big body, uncertain where his anger might lead. "Please, Cade. Let me up and I'll listen to anything you want to say. Just don't hold me so tightly. It frightens me."

He released her, his arms falling from her as he lifted her to her feet. "I'm sorry, Glory. I was wrong to treat you so. I lost my temper and I'm sorry."

She trembled before him, her fears but naught as she heard his apology, and recognized it as sincere. "Can we just wait until later to talk any more, Cade. I can't think straight right now."

He reached for her, touching her hand gently, rubbing her fingers and then turning it to lift it to his mouth. Pressing a kiss in her palm, he folded her fingers over it. His breathing had slowed a bit, and his voice was softer now, the harsh tones mellowing as he spoke. "Let me help you in the garden today, Glory. I'd like to spend time with you, and if you're going to pick vegetables, I'll help. The chores are done for the morning and we can talk while we work together."

Well, this is something new. Cade picking veg-

etables. She held back a smile and nodded. "All right. There are some stakes to put amid the tomatoes, so I can tie them up, and keep them off the ground. I don't want them to lie on the dirt while they ripen. Makes them get moldy."

"What do you have cooking on the range?" he asked, lifting his head a bit and sniffing the aroma that had wended its way from the kitchen.

"Just a bit of beef I'm fixing for dinner. I thought we'd have pot roast with potatoes and carrots around it. I've got a good crop ready to pull in the garden. They're small yet, but they'll be sweet."

His grin was quick, his hands warm against her waist as he rose from the bed to stand before her. "I sure lucked out when you said you'd marry me, Mrs. McAllister."

This time his use of her legal name sounded more to her liking, and Glory smiled at him.

"Are you done being angry with me?" she asked softly, knowing that her eyes would give her away, what with the tears she was having trouble controlling.

"I'm done being angry. I lost my temper, something I rarely do, Glory. I need to hang on to it better, for I'm ashamed that you saw me having a fit."

"Was that what it was?" she asked.

He reached up and touched the corner of her mouth and higher to brush a tear from her cheek. "Don't cry, sweetheart. I never meant to make you cry."

He caught her off balance and pulled her into his arms. They were warm about her, comforting rather than demanding, for he seemed to have changed tack. "Let's go out to your garden, Glory. You can boss me around all you want and I'll be willing to do whatever you like. At least for an hour or so. Then I've got a few things to tend to in the barn."

His grin did it. She nodded against his chest and then backed away from the warmth of his arms. He followed her from the bedroom, and she made haste to brush her hair back before they reached the kitchen, knowing she was flushed, her hair every which way.

"You look fine," he said from behind her, lifting a hand to tuck a stray tress behind her ear. "More than fine, in fact."

They reached the kitchen and Glory was pleased to hear voices from the garden through the open window. Buddy and Essie were discussing whose turn it was to empty the bucket of weeds, and Cade solved the problem nicely.

Striding out onto the porch, he called their names and when they looked up, motioned at the bucket in question. "I'll take care of it later. Leave it by the end of the row of beans and I'll dump it out back of the barn when I go out. You can both be excused for a while. Glory will do sums with you later, Essie. And perhaps you'd better find a quiet spot to read your book, Buddy. You're about done with it, aren't you?"

Buddy nodded, making haste to leave the gardening to Glory. Essie stood on one foot, her bare toes curling into the dirt, her lifted foot apparently needing attention.

"Cade, will you look and see if I've got a thistle on my toe?" she asked, limping to where he stood. Cade sat her down on the edge of the porch and stood before her, lifting her foot and eyeing the small toes.

"Sure 'nough looks like a thistle to me, little girl. Let me pull it out."

He took hold of the offending bit of weed between his fingernails, noting Essie's wince as he did, and with a swift movement removed it from her flesh. A tiny drop of blood remained and Cade wiped it off, lest she spot it and wail for a bandage. He'd have Glory wash it off and take a look at it later.

"If you're going to the barn, you need to put some shoes on, Essie," he told her. "We can't take a chance on you stepping on anything sharp out there."

Essie put her foot back on the ground and stepped on it fully. "It doesn't hurt anymore, Cade. Thank you." With a grin, she slipped into her shoes, left handy on the porch, and headed off for the barn. Unless he missed his guess, her route would be directly to the tack room where the four kittens were no doubt curled up next to the gray tabby.

Glory came out on the porch then. Cade offered his palm, displaying Essie's thistle for her, and Glory smiled. "She usually wants a bandage if she's hurt herself. Must be she didn't spot any blood."

"There was only a drop, and I figured you'd wash her feet before bedtime and look at the spot. See if it needs anything. But I think it's all right. All taken care of, sweetheart."

"You're good with them, Cade." Glory sat down

where Essie had so recently placed her bottom. "I didn't mean to cause such an uproar. We can talk later about the horse thing, but I want you to know that I won't fight you on it. In fact Buddy will be delighted at the thought of helping with foals and doing whatever you do with young horses. But I'd sure like to know more about where you earned all that money. I'm going to want some answers from you."

Cade grinned at her, his arms itching to hold her against himself, so bright was her smile, so soft her countenance. It would pay, he vowed to himself, to keep her happy. A sense of shame filled him as he remembered his actions in the bedroom, and he thought to make amends.

"Glory, I know I said I was sorry about my temper, but I want you to know that I truly apologize for holding you against your will. And we'll talk later about my money."

"I'm all right," she said, slipping down from the porch and standing before him. "Let's just forget it for now, Cade. I've got tomatoes to stake and beans to pick. The first crop is ready to eat and I thought to have some for supper tonight."

She led him to the garden and he followed at her heels, willing to have the episode so easily put in the past, yet wary lest it come to life again should he mention horses or stalls or building the addition he'd been drawing on a piece of brown paper out in the tack room. It would do well for him to bide his time for a few days and let her cool down.

He staked tomatoes, carried buckets of weeds and then pulled baby carrots from the ground for their dinner. After swiping one specimen across his chest to wipe off the dirt, he bit into it, savoring the sweet flavor as he chewed.

"You're right. They're better when they're small, Glory," he said, bending to pull more of the vegetables from the ground. Snapping off the leafy tops, he deposited them in the weed bucket and held up his double handful to show her.

"Here, put them in my apron, Cade." She moved to where he stood and held her apron open for the carrots, adding them to the beans she'd already picked.

"You want a pan for those?" he asked, willing to go to the kitchen should she need a container for the produce.

"No, I'll carry these to the porch and wash them in a bucket before I take them in the house." Before long, a pile of vegetables sat on the end of the porch—the first of the tomatoes, a good batch of green beans, and the carrots, all blending in a colorful picture of their morning's work.

Cade brought a bucket of water from the pump at the horse trough and sat it on the porch, then watched as Glory washed the food, dumping the water on a small rosebush next to the steps, before she carried the empty pail into the house. Cade toted his third pailful of weeds to the back of the barn, and when he returned, he went into the house.

"Anything else I can do for you before I turn Buddy loose with one of the foals?"

Glory turned from the sink where she was scrubbing carrots and admiring the small tomatoes she'd picked. "No, I'm all set in here."

He looked out to where the lad was sitting beneath a tree, reading his beloved book. "Does the teacher in town have a supply of books she loans you, Glory? He's just a few pages from the end of that one."

"When we go into town, we'll stop and speak with her. But first, Buddy has a book report to do for me. I think he's reading slower so as to put it off a bit."

"Maybe I can help him with it," Cade offered.

"I was pretty good at that sort of thing when I was his age."

Glory's eyes lit, sparkling at him as he turned to look at her. "I'd be so pleased if you helped me with their schooling. It'll give Buddy a head start before he joins the regular classes."

"I'm probably not as good at it as you, Glory, but I'm willing to help if I can."

She turned back to the stove, dumping her pan of carrots into the kettle where the beef simmered. "I'll get the last of the potatoes out of the cellar. We'll be doing without for a couple of weeks till the new ones come in, I'm afraid."

"I'll go down and get them for you. And then leave you to your work while I finish up out back."

He brought the potatoes to her, placing them in the sink and then turned, his arms circling her waist. She was a little bit of a thing—a fact he recognized once again as she stood before him, for she barely came to his shoulders in height— and he lifted her, one arm around her waist and the other beneath her bottom, holding her within reach of his mouth, for he was possessed of a great desire to taste of the woman he'd married.

Behind them the food she was cooking for him

wafted its aroma throughout the room, and in his arms was the beguiling creature who made this house a home. He kissed her, reveling in the soft lips that responded to his touch, the arms that crept around his neck and clung unashamedly to his greater strength. His mouth roamed her face, from temple to throat and back, his murmurs of praise whispered in a steady stream of adulation.

"My mother would love you. My stepfather would think you were the best thing he'd seen since Fido was a pup. I wish they could know you." The yearning he felt in that moment for the family he'd left behind was enormous. Not often given to such a feeling, he recognized that it was Glory's place in his life that had brought back the memories of home and the family he'd left behind.

"You're so lucky to have family, Cade. I have no one, but for you and the children. That's enough, probably more than I'd ever hoped to have, but I miss my folks sometimes, like an aching in my heart that won't go away."

He held her close as she spoke, feeling the pain of her loss, even as he admired the spunk it had taken to make her own way in the world. The day she'd walked away from the wagon train and come to this house had been the turning point of her life. For she'd put aside her past and concentrated on her future, and that was a big job for anyone to tackle.

Let alone a young girl, not even out of her teens. "How old are you, Glory? I'd figured about twenty or so, but I've never asked."

"You hit the nail on the head. I'll be twenty in…" She thought for a moment, and then smiled. "My birthday is next month, Cade. I'd forgotten about it. I came here when I was sixteen. I've always been grateful to Mr. Clark for taking me in and giving me a home."

"Buddy told me it was the best thing that ever happened to them. He remembers well the day you showed up at the door and Harvey told you to come in."

She laughed a bit, remembering. "I was scared to death, for he was a grizzled old fella, hot and sweaty from working in the hay field. But when he put his hand on Essie's head and ruffled her hair, I knew he was a good man, for the children both looked at him like he was something special."

"And he never asked you to sleep in his bed?"

Cade asked, even now seeking an answer to the question that had puzzled him.

"He treated me like another of his children, or his little sister, maybe. He said he'd had a good wife and he wasn't looking for another."

Cade dropped a quick kiss on her lips, unable to resist the lure of the woman he held. "I owe the man a debt I can never repay. Except maybe by doing the right thing for his children."

Glory leaned against him, her head on his shoulder, his long arms holding her close. "I feel safe with you, Cade. That's one of the reasons I married you, knowing you'd take care of us."

His mouth tilted at one corner as she looked up into his face, and she recognized what was coming. Cade was about to spring another of his ideas on her.

"You're not building a new barn, Cade. I don't care what you say, the one we've got is big enough for any number of horses."

His head tipped back and his laughter rose, his eyes dark upon her as he spoke. "You're something else, Glory McAllister. You're always one step ahead of me, aren't you?"

"Not lately, mister. I can't even keep up with you most days."

"Well, this idea I've got is one I think you'll like, Glory. I'd like to fix up my old bedroom, the one where Harvey slept for three years."

"You moving back in?" she asked slyly, intent on the grin he wore.

"Not on your life, honey. But I think it would be a good place for Buddy. He's got that little-bitty room that's not fit for more than a closet. The boy never complains, but I think he should have more space. He's got books and he'll be collecting more as he gets older. On top of that, he needs space to do his schooling. Sitting at the kitchen table is all right, but he should have a quiet spot of his own."

Glory felt surprise trickle through her at his words. "I never thought of that, Cade. But you're right. Maybe he could have shelves for his books and a better place for his clothes. He just hangs them on a couple of nails his father drove into the wall for him. And he's never had a dresser or chest of drawers, just piled his things in boxes."

"Would you mind if I work at it, maybe put in a new window and get it fixed up nice. You could make him some curtains and we'll get him a small chest of some sort."

Cade's eyes were bright, his smile brilliant as

he shared his ideas with Glory and she could only listen and nod as he spoke, for she found his ideas to her liking. Buddy would be thrilled, not only to get a larger bedroom, but for the fact that Cade thought enough of him to want to do this. It was no small task, of that she was well aware.

And yet, it was well within Cade's capabilities, the redoing and tearing out and rebuilding that would take place. And now it seemed he had more than one idea to present, for she saw a gleam in his eyes that could only mean he was not finished with his planning.

"I thought about knocking out the wall between Buddy's little room and the one Essie sleeps in, honey. It would give her a lot more space, and we don't really need that small room for anything, do we?"

"Oh, Cade. She'd be so thrilled. Her things are all squashed up as it is—her doll baby is plopped right in the middle of her underwear and dresses. There's no room to put things."

"That's not a problem for me, Glory. I know how to build pretty well, probably enough to make her a cabinet of some sort to store things in, and I can build a bed frame for her mattress to sit on." And search every nook and cranny in that part of the house.

Glory shivered, a thrill of discovery running through her as she found new things about this man to admire. Cade McAllister was a man among men, as her pa would have said. He stood head and shoulders over anyone she'd met in the past three years, and not just in size, but in his demeanor and behavior.

"Wait till they come in the house and you tell them what you're planning to do for them, Cade. They'll be so happy." She looked up at him and she knew her heart was in her eyes when her gaze met his. "You've let those children know from the very first that you cared about them, and you've treated them as you would your own kinfolk, Cade."

He grinned down at her. "I guess I have, but I just never thought about it that way. They're good young'uns."

"I've just taught them the things my folks thought were important, about keeping clean and doing right, and being good to each other."

He looked over her shoulder at the kettle on the stove. "Don't let that pot roast burn, honey. By the time I get some work done in the barn, we'll be ready to eat, and we've got a job telling those two about our plans."

He looked like a kid himself, she thought as he headed out the door, slapping his hat in place, his strides long and purposeful as he crossed the yard to the barn. There was a swagger about his gait that had appealed to her from the start, and now that she knew the man, she admired it even more. He was handsome, with dark hair and eyes that held knowledge she could only wonder at.

Cade McAllister was a man with ideas aplenty for this house and her farm. And she watched him walk away, even as she wondered just how far his planning would go, what his intentions were for the farm Harvey Clark had left her.

Chapter Ten

"A bigger room of my own? You're gonna knock out a wall?" Buddy was not only surprised but tickled pink, Glory decided, watching the boy as he digested the news Cade gave him.

"I'm going to put another window in it, Buddy, and Glory will make new curtains for you for both windows. We'll build you a desk or table of sorts, where you can do your studying and reading if you like. And I'll find a dresser or make one, maybe a set of shelves for your books and things."

Essie tugged at his shirtsleeve and Cade bent to see her small face. "What is it, Essie?"

"Will I get a shelf, too, Cade?"

"You're going to have a new bedroom, Essie. With the wall of Buddy's old room knocked out, you'll have plenty of space for your doll baby and your clothes and all your belongings."

"I don't have much 'belongings,' Cade. Just the stuff I wear and my dolly."

"Well, maybe we'll have to get you a few new things then. As soon as we sell one of the foals, we'll go shopping for my two young'uns."

"You mean me and Essie, Cade?" Buddy asked quietly, his eyes huge with wonder as he heard Cade's plans revealed.

"You know of any other young'uns around here? Of course I mean you two. I thought when I married Glory, I kinda got the two of you in the bargain. Isn't that how it works?"

"You think me and Buddy are your young'uns, Cade?" Essie stumbled over the words and clutched at Cade's sleeve, as if she would not release him without an answer to her question.

Cade lifted her to his lap and his long arm surrounded Buddy, drawing him near as he spoke to both of them. "I don't have any children of my own, so if Glory doesn't mind, I'd like to pretend that the two of you belong to me. If you don't like the idea, just say so."

"I like it, Cade. I really like it. Me and Buddy will have a pa again, just like before." Essie was eloquent in her desires and Buddy only grinned his acceptance of the state of affairs.

"I can't be your *real* father, but I'll be your stepfather. I had one of those when I was a boy growing up, for my own father died when I was young. When my mama got married again, her new husband was my stepfather and he took care of me."

"Did you call him your pa?" Essie asked solemnly.

"I surely did, for he was a good father to me."

"Well, I think maybe me and Essie should do that, too," Buddy told him. "It sounds more polite than just calling you by your name, don't you think?"

Cade grinned, hugging the two youngsters he held in his embrace. "I think it sounds just dandy."

"All right, Pa," Buddy said quietly, as if he sounded out the single syllable and tested the flavor on his tongue.

Cade looked up to where Glory stood, watching her family. "What do you think, honey? Is it all right with you?"

She fought tears, for she would not spoil their pleasure by crying on such an auspicious occasion. "I think it's wonderful." She could not speak another word without tears falling and she turned to the cupboard, seeking something to lift or move or shift around, lest the children see her tears.

"We gonna eat anytime soon?" Cade asked, his tone playfully cocky.

"In about half an hour. I'm going to make the gravy and put dumplings on top of the beef. Won't be long now." Speaking those words gave her reason to retreat to the pantry where the flour and lard awaited her. She tipped a good measure of each into her crock and went back to the kitchen.

In a matter of minutes, she'd stirred flour and water into the drippings from the roast and made a pan of gravy, adding the vegetables she'd cooked, and prepared the dumplings. In mere minutes they were floating atop the stew and Glory slapped the lid in place.

"Fifteen minutes," she announced. "Remind me of the time, Cade."

"Sure enough," he said, glancing at his pocket watch.

"We need to learn about telling what time it is from looking at the clock," Essie told him, peering at the silver watch he held. "Where did you get that clock?"

Cade grinned widely at her words. "It's not a clock, Essie, but a watch. A pocket watch that my father had all his life, till the day he died. My mama gave it to me after his funeral, and I've carried it ever since."

He looked up at Buddy. "One day, years from now, maybe it could be yours, Buddy, if you want it."

"Really, Cade? You'd really give the watch to me, just like your pa gave it to you?"

"It'll be yours, Buddy. I promise you."

The boy was silent as he absorbed the words Cade had spoken.

"You know what? When I'm old and I have a son, I'll pass it on to him, just like your father did for you. Will that be all right...Pa?"

Glory watched Cade blink rapidly as if there were something in his eye, and his look at her was filled with a tenderness she hadn't seen before. His arm tightened around the boy and he dropped a quick kiss on his head, as if such a gesture was one he was not familiar with.

"You all right?" Buddy asked, peering at Cade's face.

"Got something in my eye and it's all watery." Cade drew his handkerchief from his pocket and blew his nose noisily, and Buddy rested his head on the man's broad shoulder for a moment. Cade sat in his chair, Essie on his lap, Buddy beside him, and Glory wished fervently she could have a picture painted of them, just as they were this very minute.

Cade looked down at the watch he held and then put Essie down on the floor. "You two have five minutes to wash up and get the milk out for supper. Glory's dumplings will be done then and anyone not at the table can't have any."

"I'll be there, Pa," Buddy sang out, hurrying to the sink to wash. Essie made her way to where he stood and he motioned to her to put her hands over the sink. Then with a flourish, he poured a bit of soap on her palms and watched as she followed his lead, washing her hands and then using her fingers to spread the soap on her cheeks, lest they not be clean before she rinsed with clear water.

Buddy grinned at her as he reached with the towel to dab at a smear of soap, then dried her hands for her, before tending to his own. Essie slid onto her chair and watched as Buddy went to the pantry to get the pitcher of milk Glory kept there.

The big kettle of stew sat on the table now, a ladle stuck between the dumplings, ready for Cade to serve their plates. He sat quietly waiting for Glory to be ready, watching as she reached into the oven for her corn bread.

When she sat down in her chair across the table from him, he couldn't resist a wink in her direction, and she flushed nicely at his flirting behavior. "Just tend to business, Mr. McAllister. It's your turn to ask the blessing."

Without delay, he reached for Essie's and Buddy's hands and nodded at Glory to do the same. "My folks always held hands when they prayed, and I thought if we're going to be a real family here, we might want to do the same."

"I like that idea, Pa," Buddy said eagerly, as if using the term was to his liking.

"Me, too," Essie said, her small fingers clamped around Glory's index finger.

Cade spoke familiar phrases and then as he said the final word, he reached for the ladle and looked at Glory.

"Can I help you to some dumplings, ma'am? And maybe some of this tasty roast beef our wonderful cook prepared for our supper?"

"Wonderful cook? That's a new one. Maybe

your cook needs a raise in pay to go along with her title." Glory grinned at him.

"Do you suppose she'd settle for a new wrapper to wear in the mornings when she gets up, in case she doesn't want to get dressed right away?" Cade served the two children as he spoke, and then looked back at Glory.

"A new wrapper? I don't think I've ever seen one."

"They have them at the general store. One of the ladies picked one out the last time I was in there. It kinda wrapped around her and tied with a couple of belt-string things in front. Real pretty, it was, all flowered and bright. I was thinking it would look good on you, Glory. I'll bet they'd have one in your size."

"Can we look when we take in the butter and eggs first of the week? I'd like to see one of those."

"I'd like to see one of those on you." Cade's voice was a low growl, and Glory recognized the tone. She'd heard it several times after the lights were out at night, when he approached the bed where she lay waiting for him.

"Do they have wrappers for little girls, too?" Essie asked politely, her eyes hopeful.

"I don't know, but we can surely find out," Cade told her, and the child fairly bounced in her chair.

"You need a new nightgown worse than you do a wrapper, Essie. Maybe Cade will let us buy enough material for a nightie for you and a bit more for me to make you a wrapper to wear over it."

"Oh, could we, Pa?" Essie's heart was in her eyes as she begged the favor.

"If Glory says so," he said, clearing his throat and making a fuss over the pan of stew before him. He took another dumpling onto his plate, for the first one had done a disappearing act in mere minutes. "What do you think, Glory?"

"I think I can figure out how to make one for her if I can get a good look at the ones they have at the general store."

"You'll get yours store-bought, Glory. You can use it for a sort of pattern for Essie. It'll be easier if you have it here to look at, I'd think."

The beef roast was fast disappearing by the time supper was over, and Glory served the corn bread. The children liked it with butter and syrup on it, and Cade was agreeable to trying it for his dessert, too.

Glory had made it numerous times for just such a reason, and Cade made his opinion known quickly.

"This is good stuff, Glory. Never heard of syrup on it before. We only ate it like bread with a meal when I was growin' up. I'll bet my father would like it this way."

"We like it, too," Buddy said, "and our first pa said it was better than pie."

"Your first pa? You can call him your real father if you want, Buddy. It won't make me feel a bit bad being the second father for you and your sister."

"You'll be our real father, too. We'll have you here longer than our first father, but we won't ever forget him, Pa. He'll always be kinda with us."

"As long as you remember your father, and keep him alive in your mind, he'll be with you, Buddy," Cade said quietly. "He was a good father and taught you a lot of good things, like how to behave and how to treat your sister and Glory. Things that are important."

"Yeah, I learned how to milk a cow from him and all about cutting hay and bringing it in for the animals. He wasn't much for gardening stuff, said that was women's work, but Glory didn't mind doing it, so it was all right."

"So long as she doesn't lift things that are too heavy for her," Cade said.

"You mean like the wash basket you carry out for her?" Essie asked.

"Like the wash basket, and the bushels of fruit from the trees when it ripens. Glory can help pick the peaches and apples, but she's not going to tote the baskets full of fruit."

"She did before, when our pa was busy in the field or in the barn."

"Maybe so, but not anymore. I'm here now and you and I are going to be in charge of taking care of our womenfolk. That means both Glory and Essie."

Cade leaned closer to Buddy and his voice lowered as he spoke to the boy. "Females are special people, Buddy. They were made to take care of their children and their husbands and to have babies sometimes. They weren't meant to do men's work. That's gonna be our job, son."

Glory rose from the table, her eyes blurry as she picked up the plates and silverware and carried them to the sink. She put them into the dishpan and added soap, then watched as Cade toted a kettle of water from the reservoir for her.

"Thanks, Mr. McAllister." She looked up at him and thought anew how strong and handsome this man was. He had the right words for the children, knew the way to teach them without sounding as if he was giving a lesson on life to them.

And now she saw the gleam in his eyes that sent a message she especially held dear. Cade was ready to put the children to bed and then take his wife to bed. His mouth was near and she lifted on tiptoe to touch her lips to his.

"Kinda sassy there, lady," he said in a whisper, returning her caress with a brush of his lips over her cheek and then her mouth, where he lingered a bit.

"Are you complaining?" she asked, leaning close to speak into his ear.

Her words were quick, and his eyes sparkled as he answered. "Are you kidding? Me? Complain? Not on your life, sweetheart. Not on your life."

Chapter Eleven

The sound of hammering was with her constantly, it seemed. For Cade was as good as his word, tearing down a wall to enlarge the back bedroom, and this morning, he'd determined to replace the window in Buddy's new room. To that end, they'd all piled into the wagon for a trip to town, where the window could be purchased at the lumberyard.

The mood was joyous, the children chattering and Cade was his usual cocky self. And so the trip to town went quickly. The general store was the first stop, where they delivered Glory's eggs and butter to the storekeeper. The credit she received would cover her grocery list and then some. As she did her shopping, Cade had taken the children with him to the lumberyard. They would purchase the window, along with various items needed for the work he was doing, such as wood for shelves.

But Glory's thoughts now were on her food supplies, and she listed her needs aloud to Mr. Nelson. "Coffee, baking powder, sugar, a pail of lard..." She hesitated, trying to read a scribbled note. "Oh, yes, I'd like to see one of your wrappers for ladies."

The glass bin from the wall was lowered to the counter and the storekeeper's wife approached, lifting a garment from within and holding it up for Glory's inspection. "This is the latest thing from back East. A nice wraparound garment made especially for wear in the house. Very popular with the ladies," she said, holding up the garment she'd described.

Glory undid the fastenings, first the four buttons and then the belt that wrapped around a lady's waist and tied at the front, holding the garment in place. She laid it out on the counter, inspecting the seams and the way it was constructed, then admired the brightly flowered fabric.

The woman folded the garment neatly and placed it in the proper bin, then looked back at

Glory. "Pretty woman like you should be wearing bright colors."

"He likes me in whatever I wear, it seems," Glory announced quietly.

The woman grinned widely and bent close. "I'll just bet he does, honey. He's a looker, all right. A fine figure of a man. Just the right fella for you. Even if it did take a tragedy to bring you together."

"Well, we're doing well. The children have adjusted to having Cade as their stepfather. And the farm is thriving."

The bell on the door rang, announcing another customer and Glory hastened to finish her shopping, lest she deter the proprietor from new business. But it was Cade who appeared at her side, Essie and Buddy fast on his heels.

"We got a window, Glory. Pa bought it for my new room." Buddy's words were confident as he looked up at the man beside him. "We're gonna work on it later today."

"And I'm gonna have shelves and a dresser for my clothes," Essie added quickly, tugging on Glory's skirt to gain her attention.

"Won't that be grand?" Glory cast a quick look

at the woman behind the counter, as if to put proof to her earlier words about Cade's prowess.

"Anything else for you today, ma'am?" Properly impressed by the four in front of her, Mrs. Nelson was pleased to help Glory out with her needs.

"Maybe a couple of dill pickles from the barrel. I didn't put up any pickles yet this year and my dills from last year are all gone. And a ring of pickled bologna, please. Maybe brown sugar if you have any. Mr. McAllister likes it on his oatmeal in the mornings."

Cade nudged Glory and bent to whisper in her ear, "Did you check out the wrapper we spoke of?"

"Oh, yes. I need a few yards of fabric, ma'am. Six yards should be more than enough. Maybe that blue-checked one on top of the pile."

The lady hurried to the bolts of yard goods that sat atop a counter at the other end of the store, lifting one to show Glory. "Is this the one you want?"

"No, she'll take the one to your right, with red-and-yellow flowers on it." Cade's voice stilled Glory's quick protest. "I like my wife in pretty colors. She'll look like a princess in that one."

Glory flushed, embarrassed by Cade's words,

yet pleased by his choice of fabric. It was pretty, she thought, with the flowers and green leaves against a creamy background. A gift she would cherish because Cade had chosen it. She lifted onto her tiptoes and whispered her thanks in his ear. A wide grin appeared on his face and he bent to her, his lips against her ear as he responded.

"You can thank me properly tonight, ma'am. I'll be looking forward to it."

She cast a look at Buddy and Essie, who were both oblivious to the byplay of the adults, and her next words were for them.

"Why don't you two pick out some candy today."

"Can we, Glory?" And then they looked at Cade for his approval, which was immediate, accompanied by a smile that offered his permission. They scampered to the counter where candy was kept in round glass containers. They found licorice whips and pretzel knots, then consulted between themselves over a multitude of hard-candy shapes.

"How much should we get, Pa?" Buddy asked Cade, looking up for guidance in his purchases.

"How about five cents for each of you?" Cade answered, to which Essie could only gasp at such largesse.

Their purchases filled two small bags and the children literally danced to the door, Buddy more staid, due to his advanced age, Essie oblivious to the smiles that came her way, so pleased was she with her prize.

The foodstuffs Glory purchased were put into boxes and carried to the wagon by Cade and Mr. Nelson. Then Cade lifted Glory to her seat and checked to see that the children were settled behind him before he lifted the reins and directed his team to take them home.

Buddy sat in the back of the wagon, ever vigilant of the ruts and bumps in the road, tending to the stack of lumber for the shelves and the much-admired window with six glass panes and raw-wood frame. They'd also bought a gallon bucket of paint, a bag of nails and a new saw, which were placed beside the lumber, wood for shelving and a cabinet of sorts that would hold Buddy's clothing.

The boy was excited, his words filled with anticipation. "I never had a room with two windows, Pa. It'll be great to be able to look out over the backyard and see the side where the lane is, too. Will there be room for a shelf between the two windows, do you think?"

Cade looked at Glory, sharing the joy of the boy behind them. "I figure you can have a shelf there with your new dresser or whatever beneath it, and another shelf next to your bed. Enough room for your books and maybe we'll put your desk there, too."

"Oh, boy." His exclamation was almost silent, but audible to the two who sat together on the wagon seat. Glory reached for Cade's arm, and tugged it close to her.

"Me, too, Pa? Will I have a desk like Buddy's? Or a dresser, maybe?" Essie was bound and determined to gain her share of Cade's attention, and she was not to be disappointed.

"Essie, we'll get Buddy's room fixed up first and then work on yours. And yes, you'll have lots of room for your clothes and your baby doll, just like we told you the other night."

"Is Glory gonna get a new room, too?" Essie asked, obviously concerned that Glory would not share in the fun.

"No, she's stuck in her old room with me. But she's going to have a new closet built for her clothes." *And I'll have reason to get behind the walls in our room. Maybe Harvey Clark kept his cache that close at hand.*

"She's already got her screen in the corner."

"Well, now she's gonna get a space that's more private." Cade grinned at Glory as he spoke.

The afternoon went quickly, Cade deciding to tear out the wall between the two rooms and then ready the space for the window right after dinner He cautioned the children to give him an hour to accomplish his task, without interruption, for tearing out the wall was a messy job and he didn't want Buddy hurt by flying chips of plaster or Essie stumbling over the wood he would uncover as he worked. And perhaps find some trace of the gold he sought within the wall.

And so as he began his chosen task, he decided on the proper distance from each corner of the room, centering the space for the window before he began. His hammer struck the plastered wall repeatedly before he made a breakthrough and saw the first of the wall hit the floor.

With a pry bar and sturdy arms, he managed to empty the space before him. Then, as he looked down between the studs that held up the wall, he caught sight of fabric or perhaps leather. Curious, he pulled a bag out and read the words printed on the heavy cloth.

"St. Louis Bank of Missouri." Plain and clear, it lay in his hands and bid him read it again. He did, several times, his heart beating rapidly. For in his possession was the gold Harvey Clark had hidden inside this wall. The plaster over the space was fresher than the rest of the room, and Cade realized that Clark had indeed been the criminal and been justly punished.

If he'd thought it untrue that Harvey Clark had stolen gold and hidden it somewhere, he now had the proof in his hands that the man had been a thief and his death had been the result of his own folly.

He held the bag before him, studying it closely before he opened it, allowing the gold coins within to pour out into his palm. Riches beyond his own experience filled his hands and he was stunned by the revelation. What to do? Should he tell Glory? Report this to the sheriff? Probably, to get this job finished and done with. But then again... His heart slowed as he considered the effect such a thing would have on his family.

The children were barely over the tragedy of their father's death. To bring this up would label the man in their eyes as a thief, would make them the brunt of renewed scorn by the townsfolk.

Indeed, even Glory would be tarred by the brush of circumstance, for she had been the man's wife and thus might be considered an accomplice.

Cade returned the bag to its place in the wall and looked down within the studs to where the gold had been, undisturbed for over ten years already. And to where it would lay for however long it took to make the decision to turn it over to the sheriff. He found new boards, cut them to fit and replaced the wall beneath the new window, hiding away the gold from his family.

With a can of paint, the room would look like new, the wall repaired nicely, the curtains of the window he'd just installed blowing in the wind. Buddy's new room would be complete.

The wall he'd begun to tear down was next on his agenda and he finished his cutting and pounding by late afternoon. The raw look of the opening would be finished off with the fresh wood he'd purchased, painted over with the bucket of white paint.

He heard Glory call his name and noted the sun from the window facing west. It was fast moving toward the horizon, and he'd best hurry to be sure the window was secure, with no spaces left open lest it rain.

"I'll be there in a few minutes," he called back to Glory and then fitted one more board at the top of the window, sealing off an area that needed to be secured. No daylight showed through any other part of the wall, and he was satisfied that it was finished for tonight. Tomorrow would be time enough to paint a first coat on the wall and window frame.

Then he'd finish off the raw wood on the opening he'd cut, and let Buddy come in and help with the painting while he measured shelves and put them in place.

Glory was ready to sit down at the table when he came downstairs. Two shiny faces greeted him with grins a mile wide as he sat between them.

"I saw my new window from out back, Pa," Buddy said happily. "It sure looks nice, especially with the sun shining on the glass. Can I help you tomorrow?"

"I'm counting on it, son. There's wood to paint and shelves to build and a place on the floor to fix where the wall was. We'll have our work cut out for us."

He turned to Glory then, questioning her about her afternoon. "Did you get everything put up from your shopping trip, sweetheart? I wondered if you'd paid any mind to the wrappers they had at the store, and then I figured you had when you bought the material we saw."

"Everything got put away, Cade, and yes, I saw a wrapper and looked it over real good. I think it will be easy enough to make. I'll have to figure out if it's a circle of fabric and how to cut my material to do that. But I think I can do it. I counted all the seams and saw how the skirt was put together."

"You're sure smart, Glory." Essie was clearly impressed by the discussion, for she hadn't ever shown an interest in the work invested in the clothing Glory made for her. Many a night, after the children were abed and the house was quiet, Glory had sat by lamplight, sewing buttonholes and seams and hems, so that both children would be dressed well.

"She surely is smart," Cade agreed. "I just wish you'd gotten yourself the store-bought wrapper like I wanted you to."

"I can make one just like it," Glory said firmly.

He reached to spear a plump chicken thigh and Glory sighed. "This is the last of the young roosters from this spring," she said. "We won't have more until my old clucks hatch their eggs.

It doesn't take long before the chicks are grown enough to provide food for the table, though."

"What will you do with the old hens, Glory?" he asked, curious about her knowledge of such things. "How do you know when the younger hens will start laying?"

"We just cull them out every year, Cade. The older hens I put in canning jars and use the meat throughout the winter. I can make stew or dumplings or soup or whatever from them. The pullets start laying right early, and their eggs are small to start with, but it doesn't take long till they're producing eggs every day."

"Is this a job you're going to do soon?" he asked.

"You'll be involved in the job, Cade. I'll let you know to keep a whole day free to help with killing the old hens and plucking feathers. I'll keep the soft feathers for pillows, and throw out the rest."

"That all sounds like women's work to me," he said smoothly, his smile superior.

"Sounds to me like a man had best help with it if he wants chicken soup this winter."

"Well, you have a point there, Mrs. McAllister," he said finally, yielding the argument to her. And yet it had been bantering at its best, he decided, for neither of them had held the upper hand, only shared their opinions.

The sun had set before they finished their meal, and Cade lit the kerosene lamp over the table. Buddy rose and went to the parlor, his book in hand, a tablet tucked under his arm and a pencil behind his ear.

"I think we have a book report taking place," Glory said to Cade in an undertone, and he was quick to take the hint. He followed Buddy, and Glory could hear their voices as they spoke of books and the stories they'd both read in the past. Cade almost treated Buddy as an equal in this discussion, for they shared a love for books, and Cade was more than willing to help Buddy with the task he faced tonight.

Glory sat Essie down at the table and gave her the lesson she'd prepared earlier, then did her dishes as Essie bent over the sheet of paper full of numbers before her. Her tongue was caught in the corner of her mouth and she mumbled beneath her breath as she laboriously wrote down the answers.

"I think I got them all, Glory. Do you want to check and see if they're right?"

Glory dried her hands, coming to the table to sit beside the child. "Let's see now. This one is right and this one, Essie. In fact, out of all of them, only this last one is not quite right. You forgot to carry a number here."

And since this was a new phase in Essie's education—the carrying of numbers in addition—she wasn't surprised that the child had missed it.

"We'll do some more tomorrow. You've caught on so well, I can hardly believe it. I think you must be more advanced than the children in school who are your age. And arithmetic is important in life. All these things you're learning are useful when you cook or sew or whatever, later on."

"Ma'am?" Cade stood before them, his hands in his pockets, and Glory looked up to see his grin.

"Got that book report finished?" she asked.

"Buddy's working on it now. We'll read it over together when he's done. In the meantime, I wanted to tell Essie that arithmetic is used in lots of ways. When I measured the wall for Buddy's new window, I used a yardstick your pa had in the barn. It measures the inches and feet for me so I could put the window in the right place."

"Will you show it to me when you work on my

room?" Essie asked, wide-eyed at Cade's words. "Did my pa know how to use one, too?"

Cade assured the child of her father's prowess in such things. "I'm sure he did, for this one is not new, but looks to me like he made good use of it in the past. In fact, I'll warrant that Glory has a tape measure she uses when she sews."

"A tape measure? Can I see it?"

Glory laughed. "It's nothing special, Essie. Just a long piece of linen with the inches marked on it. When I put it around your waist, I know how big to make your dresses and petticoats."

The child seemed a bit subdued. "I didn't know that, Glory. I'll be sure to be better about my arithmetic from now on. I want to grow up to be like you and have my own tape measure and stuff. Maybe I can learn how to sew things for my doll baby."

"Maybe you can. We'll figure something out. Perhaps a nightie for her to begin with. That should be easy for you to make."

Essie was obviously thrilled at the news, for she danced into the parlor, and Glory did not have the heart to halt her progress, knowing how pleased the child was.

She needn't have worried about Essie disturbing Buddy in his work though, for they came back together to the kitchen in mere minutes, Buddy holding the tablet with two pages covered in his neat writing. He offered it to Cade for his approval and it was given back with only one word changed. Buddy made the suggested revision quickly and then offered it to Glory for her perusal.

She read it quickly, impressed by Buddy's vocabulary and his passion for the book he'd read. His enthusiasm shone from the pages—his pencil had flown over the lines, painting a picture of the French and their revolution, and the effect it had on the people of those days in history.

"This is fine, Buddy. Better than I'd thought you could accomplish on your first try. Did Cade help you or is it all your own work?"

"He explained the things I needed to tell about in the report, how to describe the people in the book and how important they were to the story. But I did all the writing by myself, and added the things I thought were important. Do you really think it's good, Glory? Good enough to take to the schoolteacher in town?"

"Oh, my, yes," she said, grasping the boy close

to her for a hug. "I'm so proud of you, Buddy. You've done so well."

"When can we see the teacher?" It was clearly a question that had preyed on his mind, for he looked so hopeful Glory could not bear to disappoint him.

"We should have done it before this," Glory said.

"I think the next time we go to town, we'll look her up for certain and let her know you'll be coming to school at the end of summer. Maybe she has another book she'd like you to read before then. We can take back the one you've finished and get another for you."

"I hate to give it back, Glory. I know we have to, but I'd really like to keep it for my own."

"We'll see about getting you your own copy one day," Cade said, speaking words Glory had hoped to hear.

Buddy's eyes were lit with anticipation of new books and Essie was enthralled by the idea of yardsticks and tape measures being used on a daily basis. She made it her business to bring Glory's sewing basket to the table and search within for the tape measure she'd seen before but never realized what it was used for.

Now she unrolled it and measured the table across the middle, bidding Cade to hold the end for her so she could better get an accurate answer. Next she held it around her waist and then had to have Glory read the numbers for she could not see them herself.

She went to the kitchen window and inspected it anew, as if she'd never seen it before, measuring the panes, one after the other. "Do you know these are all the same size?" she asked.

"That's how they make them, Essie. They have to fit inside the frame and be the same size so they can be lined up properly." Cade walked to where the child stood and showed her how the panes were held in place by the narrow strips of wood.

It was a lesson in arithmetic Glory would not have known to show the child and she watched in appreciation as Essie asked questions and Cade supplied the answers, Buddy standing by to listen.

And then it was bedtime, for darkness had enveloped the earth and Cade closed up the house for the night. He slid the bolt on the back door and checked the front, a task he had taken on the first day of their marriage and continued on a daily basis. She'd noticed that he always checked the latches on the windows on the ground floor, but seemed not to be concerned about the ones in their bedroom, for those windows were opened to the fresh air most nights.

"You take good care of us, Cade," she told him later as they were readying for bed. She watched him as he pulled back the quilt to fold it at the foot of the bed, then drew down the sheet and fluffed her pillow before he tended to his own undressing.

"That's my job, sweetheart. It's what I promised to do in our wedding ceremony. When I married you, I took on the responsibility of those children, too."

"I'm so pleased that you've taken hold and made this place what it is today," Glory said.

"And what is it, exactly, Glory? This farm you hold so dear, is it different than you'd planned for it to be?"

"Better, Cade. With the horses out in the pasture and the children's bedrooms being enlarged. Even the chickens are laying better than they ever have before. You've gotten in the spring hay and the loft is half full already. My garden is thriving, thanks to your help, and the children and I are happy. What more could I ask?"

"Nothing for yourself, Glory? Isn't there anything else you'd like to have?"

"I'd like to feel a little better, Cade. Of late, I'm sleepy a lot and I'm not usually given to taking naps, but some days I feel like I just have to lie down for a few minutes. And in the mornings the smell of your coffee makes me feel kinda like upchucking. I don't know what's come over me, but I just feel strange, not like myself. But that's not something you can fix, so don't worry about it. It'll work itself out."

He viewed her as she stepped from behind her screen, the gown he'd bought for her falling gracefully about her. The sight made him thankful that the girl belonged to him, for there was within him a mighty yearning for her, a need for her youthful body beneath his, for her arms to encircle him with the passion she held in abeyance for just such a time as this.

"Come here, Glory." He held out his arms and she crossed the floor, her look puzzled, for her normal pattern was to lie down on the bed and await his presence beside her. Now he held her close in the middle of the room, and her arms went around his waist, holding him against herself, feeling the rise of his manhood against her belly and between her thighs. Her eyes were closed and her cheeks were flushed with a faint rosy hue, and he felt at that moment that he was the richest man in the world. For in his arms he held a woman who was warm and willing and would cuddle beside him for this night and countless nights to come.

What more could a man ask of life?

But his sensible mind answered quickly. All the more reason to get the gold to the sheriff and let Pinkerton's know he was done with this job. Then he could settle down and take up his new life with Glory.

His thoughts prodded him to see the sheriff right soon.

He lifted Glory and carried her easily to his bed, lowering her to the middle and joining her there, his clothing already scattered across the floor, for he'd known enough to ready himself for her while she'd been behind the screen.

Now he bent over her, welcoming her arms as they clasped his neck. He lowered his head a bit, his lips touching the mouth that opened to his kiss, then spent long minutes pleasuring his wife, readying her for his presence within her tender body.

"I could spend the next week right here, Glory. Just holding you and loving you and feeling your soft breasts against me and your sweet scent rising to tempt me."

Glory muffled her laughter, and then discounted his hopes as futile. "I fear you can't do that, Cade, or your work will never get done. You have exactly six hours or so to spend here and then it will be time to get up and get busy."

"But just think what I can do in those six hours, sweetheart," he said, his voice dark as black velvet to her ears.

"Shall we think about it or do it, Cade?" she asked, her eyes on his, her body moving beneath him. Her legs opened for him and he was there, where she'd planned for him to be.

"Ah, Glory. You're such a wonder. I don't know what I ever did without you. I'm so thankful you're mine."

And then with a stealth born of long practice where Glory was concerned, Cade pulled her gown from beneath her and then over her head and dropped it on the floor.

"You're sneaky, Mr. McAllister," she pronounced as she clasped him even closer.

"Yeah, I know. But I wanted us on even ground. You may not have noticed that I came to bed without any clothes on at all."

"Oh, I noticed. From the time I came out of the corner behind the screen, I noticed. Couldn't help but see that you have a problem here."

"Where?" he asked, posing his query even as his problem twitched between her legs.

She laughed aloud now as she responded to his teasing. "As if you didn't know. That thing that keeps trying to get my attention."

"And is it working? Are you paying mind to my problem, maybe with an eye to taking care of it, sweetheart?"

Her body beneath his was most accommodating, for she wiggled to the proper place and then lifted her hips, solving his dilemma neatly.

"How's that, McAllister?" she asked, breathless as he took advantage of her willingness.

"About the most perfect thing that's happened to me for the past two days."

Chapter Twelve

The house fairly sang with enthusiasm as Cade cut wood and put it together to form the things he had promised to Buddy and Essie. The boy was with him a good share of the day, for Cade had given him a paintbrush, covering the floor first with a tarp he'd found in the barn. Buddy industriously painted the woodwork around the hole Cade had made in the wall, excited to see how large the room would be when finished. His desk was taking form this week, and the boy was already planning for his things to be placed there.

Cade told him he'd see about making a drawer for the table he'd created, and told Buddy he'd not done such a thing before, but he thought it was something he could tackle and accomplish.

Cade produced the drawer. It wasn't deep, but wide, fitting beneath the middle of the desk.

Made to hold pencils and paper and erasers and other such things that Buddy might use for his schoolwork, it was exactly what he'd needed.

Glory went up to the room to inspect it and praised Buddy to the skies for the painting he'd done and for cleaning up Cade's mess as needed. The new window looked as if it had always been there, so well had Cade fitted it into place. Even the boards he'd put in place beneath it were painted, as were the surrounding walls.

Buddy's room was almost ready to move into and he could hardly wait, begging for the chance to sleep there, even without his bed in place.

"I could sleep on the floor tonight," he said, his words a plea.

"We'll move your stuff in later on this afternoon, and you'll be able to sleep in your bed tonight." Cade spoke the words firmly, wanting Buddy to be settled by nightfall.

"Oh, boy. I'll start getting things ready to move, Pa." And he was off, gone to his old bedroom on flying feet.

"You've made him so happy, Cade." Glory stood behind him as he smoothed a piece of wood with sandpaper. "I don't know how you managed to know so much about building, but I'm sure glad you're using your knowledge for us."

"Who else should I work for, Glory? You're my family and I love all three of you."

She was stunned, looking up into his face as he rose to stand before her. "You love us? Me and the children?"

His smile was warm, his arms strong around her as he bent to kiss her with a tenderness that almost made her cry, so sweet was his manner. "Of course I love you, Glory. I haven't said the words to you, and I shouldn't have assumed you knew without my telling you, but my love is yours. I knew when I first saw you that you could steal my heart, and doggoned if you haven't."

Her arms crept around his neck and she leaned her head against his chest, hearing his heart beat beneath her ear. He said she'd stolen his heart, and the thought of that filled her with a joy she could barely contain.

"I've never told a man I loved him before now, Cade. I'll probably never say those words to an-other man, but you're the most important per-son in my world. I feel for you as I've never felt for any other person in my life. I love the children like they were my own, but for you there's a different sort of love. It fills me and overwhelms me sometimes. When you hold me close, when you kiss me, when you make yourself part of me…it all seems to blend in together in a marvelous sort of way that makes me want to be close to you, to touch you and have you hold me."

"Sure sounds like love to me," Cade drawled slowly, his grin wide, his eyes sparkling. He looked down at her as he lowered his head, his mouth touching hers in a kiss that seemed a promise of forever. Their bodies were close, drawn by the power that made them man and wife, their flesh crying out for the act that would join them together as one.

"We can't do this here," Glory said quietly, knowing what his thoughts were, even as she was tempted to obey her own desire.

"No. But we can wait till tonight, sweetheart. After it's dark and the children are sleeping, we can remember where we were right now. It's like reading a book and marking the page so you won't forget where you are. We'll remember once the light goes out tonight. In fact, maybe I'll just leave it on, so I can tell what I'm doing."

"Cade McAllister, you seem to do your best work in the dark, if I know anything about it," she retorted, and then collapsed against him as his fingertips found a ticklish spot just beneath her armpit, where her ribs began.

"No fair, no fair," she protested, trying to escape his hold.

"I'll let you tickle me tonight," he promised, drawing her close, forsaking the fun of tickling her for the joy of kissing her.

"You aren't ticklish," she said, pouting.

"No, but it would be fun, having you look for places where I might be," he told her.

"Is that all you think about?" Her voice was prim now, as if the impropriety of the situation had just struck her.

"Most of the time," he admitted. And then his grin appeared again. His dimple even showed, a rare occurrence, for he seldom smiled so widely. "Don't you know that husbands are addicted to the marriage bed? And with good reason, love. It's the most beautiful part of being married, the taking of a wife into your arms and coaxing her to accept you into her body."

"You didn't have to do much coaxing, Cade. I fear I was an easy target for you."

"You have no idea how I worried about the process of loving you the first time, Glory. I feared I would hurt you and scare you off. And then I didn't know if I would be able to give you pleasure in our bed."

Her eyebrows lifted and she tipped her head back, the better to look up into his eyes. "You didn't hurt me, Cade. Only a little, and I expected that. As for the pleasure part, I don't know if I could stand much more than you offer."

His face took on a look of happiness she had not seen before. "I didn't know that, Glory. That you enjoy so much the loving part of our marriage. Oh, I knew you were pleased with things, but not that you truly wanted to make love to me without any coaxing."

Her tongue traveled the length of her upper lip as if she thought long and hard about her words. "I kinda like the coaxing part, Cade. Please, don't quit that part of it."

He laughed aloud, and she put her fingers on his mouth to hush the sound. "Don't let the children hear you."

"Who cares. They'll just know that their pa loves their mama. And there's nothing wrong with that, sweetheart."

Essie nagged at the supper table, pleased that Buddy's room was almost finished, but worried that her room was not even begun.

"Can we start tomorrow, Pa? Can we work on my room, please?"

And Cade, even though he was tired from the chores and the added work upstairs, managed a smile when he answered the child. "We'll see, Essie. I need to work on a set of stalls in the barn, and I may have to put your room on hold for a couple of days."

"More stalls?" Glory asked on her way from the table to the cupboard where she stored her pies. She'd baked a custard pie, one Buddy liked especially well.

She brought him a large piece, placing it before him.

"Oh, boy, Glory! That sure looks good. You even whipped up some cream for it and everything."

"I sure did, Buddy. You're almost my favorite fella, you know."

Glory looked over at Cade, enjoying his obvious pleasure in the dessert she'd given him. "This seems like a good time to bring it up, Cade, while you're happy with the pie and the lady who baked it. I'd like to go to town in the next day or so if we can. I want to buy some material for curtains for the children's rooms. And they need to pick out the colors they want. And we have to look up the schoolteacher and get things settled. We've been to town twice since you mentioned seeing her and it's past time to do it."

"You're right, Glory. How about the day after tomorrow? You'll have another batch of butter done by then for the general store, and maybe three or four dozen more eggs."

"All right. That'll do, I think. In the meantime I'll do the baking and see about cutting out a dress for Essie from the material we bought."

"I thought that was for you, sweetheart," he said quietly.

"Oh, not the flowered piece, but another of pink-and-white gingham. I got it a while back and saved it for summer for her."

"A new dress for me?" Essie jumped down from her chair, having listened intently to the conversation.

"Yes, a new dress for you, Essie." Glory held the small body tightly against herself, her heart filled with love for the child.

"You didn't drink your coffee, Glory. Would you like tea, instead?" Cade asked, his gaze fixed on her face.

"It didn't agree with me for some reason. No, I'll have tea later when my food has settled a bit."

But the food didn't settle well at all, and Glory found herself leaning over the slop pail in their bedroom a half hour later, losing the supper she'd consumed.

She carried it out to dump it in the outhouse and washed it out near the horse trough, aggravated at herself for ailing again. It was getting to be a regular thing and she wondered at it, although she had a suspicion as to what her problem might be.

Sleeping with Cade had resulted in a baby, of that she was almost certain. She'd realized just today that her monthly had not arrived as scheduled, and then began counting back, finally concluding that she hadn't had that flow of blood for well over two months. As close as she could figure, she was almost three months along, and it was no wonder she'd tossed up her meals several times of late.

The idea of a baby had always fascinated Glory, for she was curious about the changes in a woman's body leading up to childbirth. The women in town almost went into hiding when they carried a child, it seemed, for in the over three years she'd lived here, she'd rarely seen a woman swollen with child. And that seemed strange to her. It seemed that there was almost a shame attached to the condition.

But not for me, Glory thought staunchly. No matter how enlarged her body grew, she would not be ashamed of it, or fearful of letting folks know of her pregnancy. Pregnancy. It was a word she'd thought of, but not in connection with herself.

And now she faced the fact that she was heading in that direction, and found that she could think of no one to speak about it with, for she hadn't made friends with the women in town. Her closest friend was Cade, and she wasn't sure how much good he'd be under the circumstances.

Essie was in the parlor and Glory joined her there, watching from the doorway as Essie played quietly with her doll baby. "Should we make some clothes for that baby?" Glory asked, remembering an earlier conversation about the subject.

"I'd sure like to, but I know you've been busy, Glory."

"Not too busy for that. How about if we make her a dress out of the scraps of your pink-and-white-checked fabric? When I finish with yours, I'll do one for her, and you can be dressed alike," Glory said, taking a seat on the sofa.

"Would you really?" As though she could not conceive of such a wonderful thing, Essie approached Glory and climbed up to sit beside her, her doll in her arms.

"I'd think we could get a remnant of flannel from the store and make her a small quilt if you want to, Essie. I think I can remember how to do that. My mama used to sew for my babies when I was a little girl."

"Was your mama good to you, like you are to me and Buddy? Did she teach you stuff, like your arithmetic and reading? And what's a *remnant*, Glory?"

"To begin with, a remnant is a piece of fabric left over on the bolt, once the storekeeper has sold most of it to the women in town. Usually it's just a bit of a piece, less than a yard, and they put a lower price on it so that someone will pick it up and decide they'll save money by buying it. As to the rest of your questions, I went to school when I was a little girl, and when I was old enough I went to college for two years. That's how I learned how to teach children a bit."

"I don't think I need to go to school in town, Glory. Not while I've got you to teach me."

"Well, in a couple of years, I'd like you to go, Essie. The teacher there can do much better than I, and you'll learn so much from her. You'll be coming home and telling me all the wonderful things she's talked about in class. Wait and see, when the time comes you'll like going to school."

"I like it right here with you." Essie scooted closer to Glory's side, leaning her head against her stepmother and yawning widely.

"I think we'd better talk about bedtime, sweet. You've had a big day and we've got things to do tomorrow so we can go to town the day after. Maybe you can help with the churning a little. I'll bet you're strong enough to hold the handle and lift the dasher in the churn."

"Can I really? I'd like to try that. And I can wipe off the eggs for you, Glory, and pack them for town."

"You're a big help to me," Glory said, lifting the child into her arms and carrying her through the house.

As they reached the kitchen, Cade and Buddy came in the back door and Cade's glance caught Glory with her arms full.

"I'm not sure you should be toting her around, Glory. She's getting pretty heavy for you to lift."

"Not any heavier than she was four months ago, Cade, and I carried her then."

"That's true, but things have changed a little since then." His brow furrowed and he shrugged, turning away. "We'll talk about it later, sweetheart."

She lowered Essie to the floor and went up the stairs with her, entering the child's bedroom and noticing how small it truly was. It was time enough they did something about it.

Essie's gown was under her pillow and Glory helped her get undressed, pulling the garment over her head. "There you go. All ready for bed."

"I need to say my prayers, Glory."

"I know, love. You kneel here beside me and I'll sit on the bed and listen to you."

Essie knelt quickly to whisper her prayer, one Glory had taught her three years ago. She finished up with a long list of people and even animals to be blessed, including the four kittens that were almost big enough to be called cats now.

"We need to see about finding a home for a couple of those cats, Essie. Why don't you pick out the two you'd like to keep and we'll let the other two go. There's lots of farms hereabouts that probably need a barn cat, and we'll check around and find homes for them."

"Do we hafta?" The plea was to be expected, for Essie had become attached to the small animals, carrying them about in her apron or in the skirt of her dress.

"Well, it would be a good idea, for the tabby cat will probably have another litter before too long and then we'll have more than we need. I'll ask at the general store and we'll find homes for them. Some other little girl might like to have a kitten, too."

"I didn't think of that. It would be nice of me to give one to someone who doesn't have any kittens, wouldn't it? After all, I have four of my own." Sounding beneficent, Essie yawned again and closed her eyes. "I can give two away, Glory. It's a nice thing to do, isn't it?"

And with that the child fell asleep, the sleep

of the innocent and pure of heart. Glory bent to kiss Essie's forehead, murmuring a few words of praise for being such a good girl, and then she rose, ready to walk down the hall and seek out her own bed, because she was tired.

From Essie's doorway, Cade watched her. She looked tired and well she might, for he suspected that she had reason to be weary, for her body to require more rest than of yore. His Glory was going to have a child, he'd bet a five-dollar gold piece on it should he find a taker. But that seemed unlikely, he thought with a smile as she rose and turned to face him.

Her smile was immediate and for that he was thankful, for he doubted that any man of his acquaintance had ever had such a responsive wife as he. Glory was fresh and lovely and all things enjoyable. Her smile was but a forecast of things to come, for she was prone to welcome him nightly for a long session of loving, never offering excuses or claiming weariness.

He held out his hand and she grasped it willingly. "Where's Buddy?"

"He's already gone to his new bedroom. It's not all sorted out yet, but he's managed to get things pretty much the way he wants them. I gave him a lamp to read by, since I doubt he's ready to sleep yet. He's too excited about seeing the teacher and giving her his book report and finding out about school next month."

"Did you lock up the house? And blow out the lamp in the kitchen?"

"All of that and more, Glory. I'm ready for bed and I think you are, too."

"Does it show?" She winced, rubbing her forehead with her fingertips.

"Do you have a headache?" he asked quietly.

She shook her head. "No, just a nagging set of muscles in my neck. Makes my head tired. A long session with my pillow will help, I think."

"I'll do better than that. I'll rub your back and neck and get rid of the aches."

They went into their bedroom and shut the door, effectively shutting out the world, for unless one of the children was ill or in need, their bedroom was off limits and no one would enter unless invited.

Cade watched as Glory began undressing, hanging her dress on a hook then going behind the screen to don her nightgown. He waited patiently for her, shedding his clothing while he watched the screen move a bit with her shifting about behind it. He heard the water pour into the basin, heard the sound of her pleasure as she washed with the warm cloth. He knew what she looked like back there because he'd watched her on several occasions and enjoyed the sight of Glory getting ready for bed.

Now he lay on his pillow, naked beneath the sheet, and watched as the screen was pushed to one side a bit and Glory came into the bedroom proper. The light from the lamp beside the bed lit the room well, and Glory was resplendent in her gown, a picture of womanhood, seemingly made for his pleasure.

He held out his arms and she came to him, settling beside him on the wide bed, her head on his shoulder, his arms around her and his body warm against her flesh.

"Do we really need this gown?" he asked, and it seemed that Glory was willing, for she simply sat upright and tugged off the gown and then tossed it to the floor.

"Now you get to blow out the lamp," she said firmly, as if an even exchange had been made.

"All right, but you know I'd like to see you by lamplight some night."

"Some other night. Just not now, Cade. We have some talking to do and I think I'd do it better in the dark."

"Whatever you say, love." He leaned up and lifted the glass lampshade, blowing out the flame and settling the globe back in place. She rested her head once more on his shoulder and settled in there as if she was content with her position in life.

"What are we talking about, Glory?" He knew, as surely as his mama was a lady, that his Glory was going to tell him news he had already guessed on his own.

"I don't know how you'll take to this, Cade, but I have to tell you, for it wouldn't be right to keep it to myself."

"Are you worried about something?"

"Not worried exactly, Cade. Just wondering how to tell you what's happening."

He couldn't bear it, couldn't stand for Glory to be upset. For if her being pregnant was a source of distress for her, it was better to have it out in the open now. He touched her chin, tilting her head back, the better to view her face in the shadows of the room. The moon was high, shining through the window, and it cast its glow on the bed and its inhabitants.

"Tell me right now, sweetheart. Whatever it is, we'll take care of it together."

A tear dropped from her cheek and touched his shoulder.

"Glory, you're crying. I won't have it. Just spit it out and I'll fix whatever's wrong, sweetheart."

"Cade, I think I'm… No, that's not right. I *know* I'm pregnant. There's no think about it. I realized today that it's true. I've not had my monthly for over two months and unless I'm sick with a terrible disease, I think I'm going to have your child. And I don't know how you're going to feel about it. After all, we already have two children in the house and you've put out your money for horses and fixing thing up, and I'm not sure we can afford to have a baby. It will involve outing flannel to make diapers and little gowns and things. And I'll probably have to have a couple of dresses to fit me for the next six months or so, and—"

"That's enough, Glory. You just listen to me, sweetheart. Having a child is the most wonderful thing that can happen to a man and his wife. Don't you know that? If you are truly having my child, I'll be the happiest of men. It's an end result of our love for each other, sweetheart, and having a new baby in the house will be plum wonderful. I couldn't be happier."

Now she was crying in earnest, her tears dropping like rain upon his shoulder and chest. "Oh, Cade, I can't tell you how much it means to have you say that. My mama said that babies were a gift from God."

"Your mama was dead right, sweetheart, and any man worth his salt is proud when his wife is with child. It's proof that their love is strong enough to form a child within her body, and give sustenance to that child for nine months. I'll be so proud of you, Glory. Don't you worry about anything, for I'll take care of you and help you all I can."

"You're so good to me, Cade, and I don't deserve it. I gave you a hard time about getting married, and made you sleep in the barn—"

"Not for long you didn't," he reminded her. "If I remember right, I slept in the barn for a night or two and then I moved into the room down the hall. And it didn't take long before I was in here with you. And you had the right to hold me off, Glory, for it was a tough choice for you to make, marrying so soon. I know I put a lot of pressure on you, but time has proved me right."

"I'm glad it was you who warmed my bed for the first time."

"And the last time, sweet. For the last time. Should we live another sixty years or so, I'll still be warming your bed and loving you with my last breath."

"That's a mighty powerful promise, Cade. You might get tired of me someday."

"Ah, Glory, my love, I'll never tire of your sweet lips and the warmth of your body. You fill my arms and my heart. And now you've given me news of a child to add to our household. I couldn't be happier."

"And to think I was fearful of telling you. I threw up my supper tonight and I didn't want you to know, lest you guessed what was wrong with me."

"I've sorta guessed anyway, what with you being so sleepy all the time and not wanting coffee and turning green when you smelled certain foods."

He looked down at her and his smile gave him away. "I think I knew the other night when you told me how funny you were feeling, Glory. I guessed then, for I knew you hadn't had your monthly in a long time.

"Glory, my love, I'm full of thankfulness tonight. My wife is going to give me a child and I'm tickled pink."

Chapter Thirteen

Essie was full of her own importance in the morning, working at the churn while Glory fixed breakfast. From the yard Cade's and Buddy's voices sounded out, and Glory looked up to see them washing in the horse trough. They walked to the house and she opened the door for them.

"Breakfast is all ready. Essie's been working the churn while we waited for you to come in."

Cade took the hint and walked to where the girl was industriously lifting the dasher and then dropping it into the churn. "I'm makin' butter, Pa," she said with a grin.

"So I see."

Glory carried jam from the pantry and checked the butter dish to be sure there was enough on the table. "Well, this helper had better come and eat her breakfast. We'll finish the butter after a while."

Cade ate two helpings of the potatoes, telling Glory he'd never had them fixed with onions before. "These taste real good with the ham. Are you running low on ham and bacon yet? It'll be time to butcher soon, and we'll fill the smokehouse again. I don't want you cut short on breakfast food."

"There's still a whole one out there and I've got over half a ham in the pantry. Bacon's kinda in short supply, but we'll stretch it out. I've used the last of the pork sausage, so we'll need to make some as soon as you butcher."

"I don't want you working too hard on that sort of thing, Glory. We may have to get you some help for a week or so when the time comes."

"I'll be fine, Cade. I'm strong and healthy." The look she shot in his direction was a clear warning that he wasn't to spill the beans about her condition.

"Can I work with the foals this morning?" Buddy wanted to know as he finished eating and made ready to go outdoors.

"A good idea, son. They all have halters on, so bring a lead rope with you out to the pasture and work them one at a time. About ten minutes each should do it for this morning. Take them twice around the pasture. Then brush them down good and talk to them all the time. It doesn't matter what you say, for the tone of your voice is what's important. Keep your voice kinda soft and low. It makes them learn to trust you, for they'll begin to recognize your voice and look forward to hearing you the next time you work with them. They won't be spooky around you. That's important."

"How do you know so much about taking care of them, Pa? Did you do this kind of thing when you were young?"

"I sure did. My stepfather taught me all he knew about horses, and we had a barn full of them. He trained them and sold them to all the ranchers around the county. Most of the farmers and ranchers raised beef and had to buy their horses from someone else. So we made a good business of it."

"Is that what you want to do, Pa?" Buddy asked, intent on hearing all he could about the process of training the foals and working with them.

"It's part of what we'll do on this farm."

Glory spoke up then. "Harvey Clark always said it was important to have good crops, raise enough hay to feed your animals and concentrate on selling corn and taking wheat to the mill."

Cade turned to Glory. "All of that is important stuff, honey. But a good horse is worth as much as an acre of hay. Maybe even more if you wait till it's three years old and ready to ride. The hay is important for we'd be up the creek without a paddle if we didn't have enough to last through the winter. But the real money is in animals, the horses and young steers we can raise."

Glory looked up at him, her attention caught by his talk of young steers, her eyes glittering. "And where are we going to get these young steers you're planning on raising?"

"I'm gonna buy heifers, already bred, from Earl Bradley. I spoke with him the other day about it when we were in town and he stopped by the lumberyard while I was there. He said he has more cows than he knows what to do with and I told him I'd be pleased to take three or four heifers off his hands. If they were bred first, we'd have a nice crop of calves, come next spring. We settled on a price and he agreed to guarantee their breeding."

"And when are we getting these animals?" Glory asked, wondering where the young cows would be housed.

"Right soon. Earl said he'd bring them by in a

few days. I suspect he wants to be sure they've been visited by his bull before he brings them."

"Why does his bull want to visit with the cows, Pa? Does he want to say goodbye to them?" Essie was sober as a judge as she asked her questions, and Cade wore a puzzled look as he looked at Glory for help. In fact, as she watched him, his face began to look downright ruddy, and he tipped his chair back a bit, as if he pondered an answer that might be suitable for a small girl.

Glory took him off the hook. "The bull is going to be the father of the babies of all the lady cows. He has to visit with them and make sure they're ready to leave home and come live with us."

"Oh. All right. I'm glad he likes the lady cows. Will he come and visit his babies when the lady cows…" She looked at Glory expectantly. "How will the lady cows know when to give us their babies? Are they like the horses Pa bought? Will they just lay down and then a baby cow will be there?"

"I think we'll talk about it after a while, sweet. It's a little more complicated than that, I fear." She looked at Buddy, who was hiding his smile behind his hand and trading winks with Cade. "And you two had better get out there and get a place ready for our new heifers to be turned loose to graze."

"They can graze with the horses. Cows and horses seem to do well together, Glory. I'll have to separate them when it's time, in the spring, for the cows don't need to be in the barn for the actual births, but the horses do. Cows seem to do all right out in the open. They're different than horses."

Glory only nodded, realizing that Cade's explanations were for Buddy's benefit, for the boy seemed to drink in everything Cade had to say about the animals. And on top of that, she was hoping that Essie would turn loose the idea of calves and cows and the bull. She feared the explanation might be too much for her to cope with right now.

She turned to Cade, still wondering about putting all the animals in the same pasture. "I won't argue about any of that, for I'm sure you know more than I do about the matter. But won't there be too many animals for the amount of grass growing out there?"

Cade nodded, drinking the last of his coffee. "That's another thing we'll be thinking about, because we'll need a bit more fencing before too long. I'm going to order it when we go to town tomorrow. I'd rather be ready ahead of time, and fencing takes a lot of work. Buddy and I will be spending a good bit of time putting in posts and stringing wire. It'll take three strands to keep the animals contained.

"Cattle are dumb animals. If you turn them loose on open range, they don't know enough to stay near the barn, but just keep on moving. We're not set up for rounding up cattle spring and fall, so we'll have to keep ours fenced for now."

"Can we afford it, Cade?" She had to ask, for the question was burning in her mind.

"I'll start out small, Glory. Enough posts and wire for an acre or so. We can add on later, but that'll be enough for the next year. When we have to enlarge, we'll just add on. In the meantime, I think I have a buyer for the little filly. The fella wants her trained to follow and he's interested in putting a harness on her in a year or so. He's talking about putting her in front of a pony cart for his children. She'll need to be two years old before she's ready for that, but he can work with her once he takes her home."

"Is she worth enough yet to make it worthwhile

selling her now? Will we make more if we keep her another couple of years?"

"Yeah, we'd do better if she were three and ready to ride, but we'll keep the other two and next year we'll have three more foals to work with. Earl said to bring the three mares by and he'd see to breeding them later on this month, when they're ready."

"How do they get ready?" Essie wanted to know.

"Well, sweetheart, they decide when they want to visit with the father again. If they decide he's a nice fella, they'll be friendly with him and he'll give them foals for next year."

Essie looked puzzled, but Glory reminded her that the churn was awaiting her attention, and she put the issue of horses and foals aside in favor of working on the butter.

When Essie's small arms grew weary, Glory took over the task and before long they had six rounds of butter on the table, arrayed on a strip of a newfangled sort of stuff called waxed paper. The general store had gotten in a few rolls of it, and Glory purchased three yards for just such a use.

When the butter had sat for a while, she would wrap it up in the waxed paper for the trip to the general store tomorrow. The eggs would be wrapped in newspaper and layered in a box to travel. Essie liked to help with the eggs and Glory had given her several lessons in the importance of not cracking the fragile shells. The child seemed to have caught on well, and took great pride in her chore.

They worked together in the kitchen all morning, stopping only to begin dinner, for the menfolk would be in shortly after noon for their meal. Cade liked a full meal at noontime, as did most of the farmers, since they worked hard during the morning hours and needed the sustenance of a good midday meal.

She brought out a Mason jar of chicken, canned up last fall, when she'd culled out her old laying hens and butchered them. A kettle of chicken and dumplings would set well with Cade, she decided. Essie was sent to the garden to pull a dozen carrots, Glory instructing her to find the ones with the biggest shoulders showing aboveground.

"That's one for each finger and two extra. Is that right, Glory?" The child stood at the door, double-checking Glory's orders, and received a nod of approval.

"That's exactly right, sweetheart. There are

twelve in a dozen and you have ten fingers and thumbs. So ten and two extra make twelve. You've done well with your arithmetic, haven't you? And while you're out there, see if there are any peas on the vines. I don't think the strings are too tall for you to check between the leaves."

Essie beamed at the pride aimed in her direction and danced out the door and off the porch to perform the task.

Glory found a medium-size metal bowl, a blue-speckled one like the coffeepot she used every day. She had three such bowls, which she used often in the garden during harvesttime.

She carried it out to the porch and called to Essie to come and get it, for it was a good size to put the carrots and peas into. The air was clear, the sky without clouds this morning, and she inhaled deeply of the fresh breeze, her eyes on the corn she'd planted just beyond the tomato plants. It was ready to tassel out, and they'd have sweet corn for supper by the end of the month. She'd planted five rows, enough to keep them in fresh corn and have some left over to can up for winter.

She knew that Harvey had also planted several acres with field corn just before he'd been arrested and taken to town, and there would be enough in that crop to fill the corn crib in the fall.

She thought of him, could almost see him working in his fields, and rued the day he'd been taken from their lives. The children had adjusted well to being without him, for Cade had filled the place of a father, and allowed them to get used to his being here gradually. She thought of Harvey's death, of the crime he'd been accused of, and wondered anew if he'd had any knowledge of such a sum of gold.

Surely he'd have spoken of it to her, or she would have somehow come across a trace of it in the house or barn. Unless he'd been guilty of the crime and perhaps buried it on the property. She knew it was still spoken of in town; she had borne the looks of those who wondered at her own innocence in the matter.

But after all, if Harvey had been a bank robber, he'd surely paid a high price for his crime. Somehow, she couldn't believe that he would have been the one chosen to hold the gold, to hide it or be responsible for it. He'd been an ordinary man, a man of moderate intelligence, but not what she would have considered the type to mastermind such a robbery. Harvey had not been what Glory would call a leader of men.

As opposed to Cade McAllister, who could do most anything he set his mind to, Glory thought, looking up as his tall figure caught her eye. He was in the pasture, surrounded by his foals and the three mares, and as she watched, he circled the three of them, his casual manner belying his close attention to them, checking for readiness, his mind on the breeding to come.

Cade's attention was caught by the sound of horses coming from the road. He looked up, attuned to the visitors he had been expecting. Earl Bradley and one of his hired hands appeared, four cows ambling between their horses, heading for their barn, if he wasn't mistaken. He lifted a hand in greeting.

"Hey, there, Earl. Didn't expect you till tomorrow, but today will work as well. We'll just put these young ladies in the pasture with the horses for now." He opened the gate and the men readily guided the cows into their new grazing area.

"Buddy and I will be putting up some new fencing in the next week or so," he told Earl.

"They'll do well right here for a while," the

farmer said, dismounting to close the pasture gate. He leaned on it and Cade joined him.

"Those are good-looking heifers. I'm glad you were willing to part with them."

"I've got more than I need, and if they all breed true, I'll have enough to take to the stockyards next year. There's those that really like young beef, and I've got a goodly amount of young steers."

"I'm hoping to get a good bull," Cade told him.

"Well, mine is available till you get one of your own. In fact, you might get a young one in the spring, and if he looks like his daddy, he'd be worth setting aside when it comes time to cut them and do your branding. Have you got a brand yet for your place?"

Cade shook his head. "Hadn't thought of it, to tell the truth. I'll want something that includes Buddy. I won't use just my initials or name. This is his place, after all. When he's old enough, I'll turn it over to him."

"You're putting a lot of work into it, McAllister, to just turn it over to a boy later on. Not only work, but hard cold cash, too."

"We'll run it together for a lot of years, I figure. But if the boy turns out to be as good a rancher as I think he will, he'll have the know-how to run a big spread."

"The piece that butts up against your property is available, probably could be bought for taxes in a couple years. The fella that had it walked away and left it empty. There's even a cabin on it, not much to look at, but pretty sturdy. Looks to be watertight and well built."

"I took a look at it one day when Buddy and I were out riding the property line, checking on fences and deciding about what land to fence for pasture. It seems a dirty shame to me for it to sit empty over there. If I buy the land down the road a ways, I'd probably need to hire someone to live over there."

"You got any men in mind to hire on here?" Earl asked him.

"No, not yet. I'm not earning enough to hire help, but another year or two should make a difference. We'll have hay to sell this fall and the corn crop looks good. I thought about raising wheat next year on some acreage out back."

Earl nodded, his approval of Cade's plans apparent. "I'll put the word out that you might have extra hay. There's always fellas needing feed for their stock. Harvey Clark made sure he had plenty of hay to cut. Usually three cuttings a year."

"Yeah, we'll cut for the third time in September. I'll not have Buddy here to help with it though, for he'll be going to school in town this year."

"You could keep him home till the hay's in," Earl suggested, as if schooling wasn't nearly as important as a crop of hay.

"I know a lot of the young boys help out at home till October or so, but I think it's important for Buddy to be regular in his schooling, this first year especially."

"Problem is that the boys turn into young men and then they get to thinking they should go to the big city and make a lot of money, and some of them leave for greener pastures."

Cade smiled as he considered the boy he'd taken as his son. "I don't think Buddy will turn out that way. He's a born farmer. You ought to see him with the foals. He's got a real knack for training."

"These young'uns are lucky to have you here lookin' after them, McAllister. It could have turned out different for the missus and these children."

"I'm the lucky one," Cade told him, his grin

wide as he thought of the woman he'd married and the children who had become his own. "Glory's a good wife, knows her stuff, with cooking and sewing and putting food away for the winter months."

"Folks hereabouts are happy that she ain't alone, that's for sure," Earl said. He turned then and mounted his horse, his farmhand having gone to the horse trough to water his mount. "We'll be gettin' back home. Good luck with the fencing."

Cade held up a hand, halting his departure. "I'll stop at the bank and drop by your place tomorrow to pay you for the heifers."

"Not anything to worry about. I'm in no hurry." Earl Bradley turned his gelding and rode toward the man who waited for him, then lifted a hand to Glory, who was watching from the porch. She waved at them, then headed to the pasture.

Cade leaned on the gate and waited for her to join him. "I thought heifers would be smaller," she said as she approached, looking at the three who grazed just a few feet from where Cade stood.

"No, they get their full growth pretty young. By the time they're ready to have their calves late next spring, they'll be full-grown cows." He covered Glory's hand with his own, holding it in a firm grip. "You'll beat them to it, Glory, for it takes cows eleven months to have a calf, and we'll have our child before our pasture fills up next year."

"I suspect you'd like a boy, wouldn't you, Cade?" She turned to look up at him, her eyes sparkling, because she obviously was thinking of the baby she carried.

She was too much to resist and he bent to kiss her, brushing his lips across hers as he looked down into her eyes. "I'll take whatever we're given, Glory. Every man probably wants a son, but I already have Buddy and he'll not take second place when we have a boy born to us. He'll always be our firstborn, no matter how many children you and I manage to bring into the world. I think a little girl, with dark hair and blue eyes, would be just about perfect. I'd like a little Glory running around here, and Essie would no doubt love to have a baby sister."

A tear trickled from Glory's eye and left a damp trail on her cheek. "You really don't care, do you, Cade? It's all right if we have a girl? I'd thought you'd be set on a son, and perhaps you will be the second time around if this one is a girl."

"You won't mind doing this again?" he asked, thinking of her queasy stomach and the early-morning and late-night retching he'd heard several times.

"You have no idea how happy I am to be giving you a child. My mama said it was what a woman was made for, that it was the high point of her life to bear children."

"Your mama was a wise lady, wasn't she?"

Glory nodded, looking a bit lost at this very moment.

"You need another woman to talk to, don't you, sweetheart?" He hadn't thought of it before, because Glory seemed so capable, so well equipped to cope with her everyday life. But this was a different thing altogether. A young woman bearing her first child was sure to be in need of another female to speak with. He wondered if she'd considered any of the ladies in town for just such a friend. And then thought of an even closer woman who might be just the ticket for Glory.

"Have you ever met Earl Bradley's wife?" he asked.

She nodded. "I've seen her in town a few times, and when she had extra apples, she asked Mr. Bradley to bring me a couple of bushels one time a year or so ago. She seems very nice. They have four children, all of them school age."

"Maybe we could ride over and you could pay her a visit one day," Cade said, and then enlarged on the idea. "I have to stop by there tomorrow on the way home from town to pay him for the heifers. It would be a good chance for you to spend a few minutes with her, maybe, and see if you might become closer neighbors than what you've been before."

"I always thought Etta Bradley was a nice lady. Maybe I could take her some strawberry jam or ask her about her garden."

Glory sounded eager to fall in with his idea, and Cade felt a sense of accomplishment that he'd neatly solved the problem of her being so much on her own. He put his arms around her, drawing her close, and bent to nuzzle her throat a bit, the faint scent of her soap drawing him there.

"You sure smell good, honey. You're always so clean and pretty. I'm proud of you, did you know that?"

"Me? You're proud of *me?* And here I was just thinking a little while ago how smart you are and how you know so much and have such a knack for doing things."

"We're lucky to have each other, Glory." He held her close, thinking ahead to the times in the coming months when he'd lay his hands on Glory's belly and feel the baby move.

"I'd like to let my folks know about us, Glory. I want my father to know that I'm to have a child with you. Maybe we can even ask them to visit, if you like."

She leaned her head back, looking up at him. "Would your mama like me, do you think?"

"She'd think you were top-notch, Glory. I'll sit down and write a letter tonight after supper and tell them all about you and the children and the farm. They'll be pleased, for I haven't written to them in months."

Essie had apparently decided that nagging would get her bedroom in order, for she sat at the supper table and spoke of the lack of space for her dolly's bed, and her solitary window looking out upon the lane beside the house while Buddy had a wealth of windows in his room. When she spoke of shelves, Cade took the bait.

"What are you trying to tell me, sweet? Are you feeling left out of the general scheme of things?"

She looked puzzled. "I don't know what that

means, Pa, but I sure do need some more room to put my stuff."

"I got the message, Essie. Give me a few days to work on the pasture and I'll get back to pounding nails and tearing out the wall for your room."

Glory touched the child's hand. "Sometimes we have to be patient, Essie, because men have plans made days and weeks in advance, and Cade is no different than any other farmer. His livestock has to come first, for that's where he makes the money that we live on. He has to take care of his new heifers and the foals and provide for them. I fear you'll have to wait your turn. And in the meantime, we'll pick out material for your new curtains tomorrow and work on them, along with Buddy's. Maybe we can make you a new set of pillowcases to match your curtains. Would you like that?"

"And a piece of flannel for a quilt for my baby?" Essie asked, reminding Glory of her promise.

"Yes, a bit of flannel for your dolly's new quilt. We'll piece together some squares of fabric I've put aside from other things I've made and we'll put a pretty top on the quilt for her. You can help me tie it with yarn."

Essie beamed, her mind obviously working at

top speed. "And then when my room is finished, I'll be all ready to fix it up real pretty, won't I?"

"But first, we need to clear off the table and do up the dishes, Essie. I'll get the dishwater ready and you can bring the plates and silverware to the sink for me. And while we're doing that, Buddy, I want you to finish your reading in the history book the teacher in town lent to us. I'd like to be able to return it to her tomorrow. You only have one more chapter to go, right? It's about the war between the United States and Great Britain. You'll find it interesting, Buddy."

He looked sheepish as he met Glory's gaze. "I've already read it, Glory, a couple days ago when I ran out of stuff to read. I didn't know all that stuff about our country having to fight for freedom. I guess I didn't appreciate the guys who were running the country, and all they did to make the government strong."

Cade's brow rose as Buddy spoke. "I didn't know you were interested in history, Buddy. I always thought that Benjamin Franklin was one of the smartest men that ever lived. And Thomas Jefferson was a good president. I have a book about his life somewhere in my things. I'd forgotten about it, but I'll get it out for you."

"Not tonight," Glory said, reminding him of his prior commitment for the hour after supper. "I'll find the writing paper and see if we don't have some envelopes in the desk. Mr. Clark used to keep a supply of them in his top drawer."

"Who you gonna write to, Pa?" Buddy asked.

"I'm going to send my folks a letter when we go to town in the morning. They don't know about my new family, and I need to catch them up to date on the happenings around here. They need to know they have two new grandchildren."

Essie's eyes grew large as she heard his words. "Is that me and Buddy, Pa? Are you talking about us being grandchildren?"

"You're sure enough their grandchildren, Essie. The both of you. They'll be so pleased to know that I have a son and daughter now."

"I guess I hadn't thought about it that way, Pa," Buddy said wonderingly. "We're really your children, aren't we? Almost as good as blood kin?"

"Better, maybe. For we chose each other, and when you have blood kin, you just have to take them whether it's your first choice or not. In our case, we made a family, just the four of us, and shaped it to suit us. Glory and I are your folks, just as much as your real mother and father were."

"And come next spring..." Glory hesitated, looking to Cade for guidance, and he took her hand and stood behind her, his arm around her waist.

"Come next spring, there'll be five of us, Buddy. Listen up, Essie, for this is important. Glory is gonna have a baby, too. We'll have more than new foals and calves in the spring. We're gonna have a real baby of our own before then. You'll have a new brother or sister and there'll be one more McAllister living here with our family. What do you think of that?"

"Really? We'll have a real baby? A sister or maybe a brother?" Essie was bursting with smiles and giggles. Buddy looked solemn, eyeing Glory wisely.

"We'll have to take good care of Glory, won't we, Pa? Make sure she doesn't work too hard and stuff like that."

"How do you know about that sort of thing, Buddy?" Cade asked, truly puzzled that the boy would be so perceptive.

"When my mama was gonna have Essie, my pa and me took good care of her. She was right sickly and she didn't live long after Essie was born, but it wasn't 'cause we didn't tend to her real good. She was just too sickly to make it." He halted and his gaze was intent on the woman who'd been his mother for the past three years or so.

"Glory ain't gonna be sickly, is she? If we take good care of her, she'll be all right, won't she? I sure wouldn't want anything to happen to Glory."

"She'll be fine, Buddy. I can almost guarantee it, for Glory is healthy and strong and she'll be just fine. Women have all the special equipment it takes to have babies and take care of them afterward. Between the three of us, we'll look out for her and come next spring, we'll have a new baby for all four of us to love.

"Our whole family will be blessed, for this is the most wonderful gift in the world. A new baby here in our home."

Chapter Fourteen

They were ready for the trip to town bright and early, breakfast out of the way and the chores finished before the sun had reached the treetops in the east pasture. Essie wiggled, standing on one foot then the other as Glory braided her hair.

"I've got the list you made, Glory. Did we remember everything?"

Glory smiled, recalling the fuss made over the listing of each item Essie could dredge up from memory. They'd included the bit of flannel, fabric for curtains and the promised pillowcases, along with the list of foodstuffs that were in short supply in the kitchen.

"Don't forget you wanted to see about new Mason jars for canning, too, Glory," the child reminded her.

"I'll write it down, Essie. And lids and rubber rings, too."

"And maybe a piece of stuff to make my dolly a dress." Essie forgot nothing, Glory had found, especially those items relating to her doll and the bedroom she was intent on furnishing.

The wagon was before the back door and Cade and Buddy awaited their womenfolk, Cade jumping to the ground to lift his wife onto the high seat. She straightened her skirts and looked over her shoulder at the two behind her. Essie could barely sit still, she was so excited thinking of the list she held in her pocket.

The wagon rolled down the road that wound through the countryside, past the first few houses and then the church, the bank and the establishments that made up the business area of Green River. The storekeeper, Jeremiah Nelson, was sweeping the sidewalk in front of his establishment, a bucket of water near the door awaiting his attention. It was Friday, the day for his stint of window washing, because Saturday was the busiest day of the week for a general store and he liked to have his place clean and ready for his customers.

"I see the schoolteacher inside the store, Cade.

Do you think this is a good time to speak with her about Buddy?"

"Can't think of a better time. I'll have him with me, so go ahead and see what she says."

Cade dropped Glory and Essie off at the general store, taking Buddy with him to make a stop over at the bank. "I'll be back with you right soon," he said.

Essie held her list ready as she and Glory entered the store, peering down at it to read the items Glory had written down. "Can I help you, young lady?" Mrs. Nelson asked kindly, exchanging an understanding look with Glory.

"Yes, ma'am, Mrs. Nelson. Me and Glory got a whole list of stuff we need today." She looked up at Glory and offered her the paper she held. "I'll go look at the material while you talk to the lady, Glory. Is that all right?"

"I'd like to speak with the schoolteacher for just a minute," Glory told Mrs. Nelson. "Then I'll be right back."

Mrs. Nelson nodded, and Glory approached Sally Thomas, the woman who taught all grades at the local schoolhouse.

"Good morning, ma'am. I need to speak with you about my stepson, Buddy."

"I've seen Buddy in town," the woman said with a smile. "He's the young man you've borrowed books for, isn't he? Will I be having him in school this year?"

"I surely hope so. I've worked with him at home for three years and I think he's pretty well up to his age level. And he's read everything you've lent us, too.

"Buddy has learned about all I can teach him, Miss Thomas. He's a right good reader and his maths are excellent, and he's working on history right now. I think he's more than ready for real learning."

"I'd enjoy having him. School starts in two weeks, you know."

Glory nodded. She was aware that classes began early so that the older boys could be excused for harvest later on. "I've had Buddy write a book report on *A Tale of Two Cities* for you. I'll send it with him, if that's all right. I'd say he's at sixth-grade level in most everything. He's had a little trouble with long division, but he's a whiz at reading. I'm sure he'll be willing to take any tests you want to offer him."

"There's a younger child too, am I right?"

"Yes. Essie is just learning to read, and has

been working on arithmetic for me. But I think we'll keep her home another year. Perhaps next year I'll feel better about sending her along with Buddy."

"I'll be happy to have him, and Essie, too, when you think she's ready," Miss Thomas said.

"Will there be a problem with Buddy riding a horse to town? It's too far for him to walk and my husband said that Buddy's a good rider, so he wouldn't be fearful of sending him off on a mare."

"Several of the older boys ride to school. There's a fine place for them to stake their horses during school."

"I'm so glad we had time to speak. I'll talk to Buddy when we go home and be sure he's ready for you. I'll send the books I've borrowed from you back with him when he shows up for the first day of school, too."

"I have a lot of books in my own library and the children are always free to borrow them," Miss Thomas said. "I'll look forward to meeting Buddy."

Glory was pleased at the progress made today and fairly itched to speak with Cade and Buddy on the way home, because she knew the boy would be delighted to make preparations for schooling.

She made her way back to the shopkeeper's wife, glancing over to where Essie stood before the bolts of yard goods that lay on the counter across the store. The child lifted one hand, gingerly touching a pretty, flowered bit of percale. She looked back at Glory for approval and then moved on to where several small remnants lay at the end of the counter.

A bit of flannel caught the child's eye and she picked it up, shaking it open to see how long it might be. Not quite a yard, Glory saw from her vantage point. And best of all, it wasn't the usual white offered for baby things and winter nightgowns. It was pink, a shade that would enhance Essie's doll. Another bit of remnant caught the child's attention and she reached for it, this one yellow, perhaps a little larger than the first.

With care, Essie refolded the piece she'd already examined and then added the second bit, bringing them to where Glory waited and watched. "Will these be all right, Glory? We could get the pink and make the dress. Or maybe we could get the yellow for the quilt."

"You in the market for outing flannel, Mrs. McAllister?" Jenny Nelson asked archly, her gaze twitching to Glory's flat stomach.

"No, not for myself, but for Essie's doll baby. I promised her I'd make a quilt and perhaps a kimono." She turned to Essie and nodded her approval of the two pieces of fabric.

"I thought just one of them, Glory. We don't need to get them both." And yet her hand brushed the nap of the flannel as she spoke, and her eyes fixed on both the pink and yellow material.

"We can get them both, Essie. Cade won't mind if you have them."

"He's a right generous man, ain't he?" Mrs. Nelson said. She peered down at the list she held and reached to the shelf behind her for a sack of coffee. "How many pounds, Mrs. McAllister?"

"I think five will be fine. And I'll need twenty-five pounds of flour. I'm almost out."

"Don't forget the curtains, Glory." Essie tugged at her sleeve, looking up beseechingly.

"I won't, sweet. We'll go look right now."

"You're doing a heap of sewing these days," Mrs. Nelson said. "Going to make any new clothes for the two of you?"

"Not this week. Just curtain material for the children's rooms."

"And new pillowcases for me, too," Essie said proudly.

They sorted through the gingham fabric, both checks and plaids available in the stack. Essie voted for pink-and-white checks for her room and Glory settled on a darker color for Buddy, wavering for a moment between the green and blue gingham, finally selecting ten yards of the blue.

Essie watched wide-eyed as Mrs. Nelson measured it off. "I won't need but half that much, for I only have one window, and Buddy has two," she offered brightly.

Glory chose thread for her sewing projects, adding a card of small white buttons to the stack, along with the flannel Essie had chosen.

By the time Cade joined them in the store, they had quite a selection to carry home with them. Essie held up a remnant Glory had chosen for her, large enough to make new drawers and a petticoat for her Sunday dress. Her old ones were well worn, and almost too small, and Glory could not resist the fine batiste remnant she'd spotted.

"You girls about done in here?" Cade asked,

watching as Mrs. Nelson began adding up the prices of Glory's purchases.

"I can pay for most of this from my egg-and-butter money," Glory told him in an undertone, but he only gave her a sharp look and shook his head.

"Put it on my page in your book, Mrs. Nelson. I'll pay you at the end of the month."

"That'll be just fine, sir," the woman said. "Your wife got some real bargains today, what with the remnants she and the little girl picked out."

"My daughter is learning fast, isn't she?" Cade asked, one hand reaching to touch Essie's golden hair.

"She's sure enough lucky to have such a generous Pa, I'd say." She wrapped the package of fabric and sewing notions in brown paper, tied it with a length of string and put it aside. Then she packed the food into an empty box from the storeroom.

"I'd say I was the lucky one, Mrs. Nelson," Cade said quietly, his smile backing up the words he spoke. With one arm around Glory's waist, the other filled with the box of groceries, he nodded at the door. Essie picked up the bundle from the counter, saying her goodbyes with a grin.

Buddy sat in the wagon, jumping up to lend a hand as Cade brought the box to the tailgate. "Is that it, Glory?" he called out.

"Oh, my, I forgot the Mason jar and rings and lids I need for canning," she said, turning to go back into the store.

"I'll get them for you. How many do you need?"

"I think I can get by with a dozen quart jars and a dozen pints, and enough rubber rings and lids to cover them. If we can't afford that many, I'll make do, Cade."

"Are there any more left in the cellar?" he asked.

"Enough for the tomatoes when they ripen. But the beans will be ready right soon, and I need the pints for the last of the peas and the carrots. Oh, and I forgot to look at a piece of ribbon for Essie's hair. Maybe pink to match her new dress."

Cade grinned at Essie. "You need a ribbon, girl?"

"I can get along without a ribbon, sir. Glory is gonna make me a new dress and new curtains and stuff for my dolly, so I don't really need a hair ribbon."

"We'll see about that," he said, entering the store again, the bell ringing as the door opened.

Glory sat atop the wagon and watched as a group of menfolk passed by the store, one of them looking to where an old man snoozed, sitting on a bench outside the big window.

"Say, fella. Do you know where the Clark place is located?" one of the men asked in an undertone.

Glory's ears picked up the name he mentioned and she turned to look at Buddy, motioning for him to be quiet, lest he offer his knowledge to the man who asked after their place.

He nodded, as if he understood that he'd best listen and not speak up.

The old man who sat on the bench only nodded and pointed to the west, in the direction of the farm, and then leaned back on the bench, his eyes closing once more.

Glory was silent, her eyes averted as the men walked down the sidewalk, turning in to the newspaper office.

When Cade came from the store, Glory lifted a hand, indicating he should come closer so she could speak to him. After depositing his big box of supplies on the back of the wagon, he walked over to stand beside her.

"What's wrong, sweetheart? What happened?"

Glory leaned close to him and spoke quietly. "There were three men here in front of the store just a minute ago, wanting to know where the Clark farm was. I didn't recognize them, but I didn't like their looks, Cade. They frightened me. The gentleman on the bench didn't give them very good directions, just pointed to the west. They went into the newspaper office." She scooted over to make room for him on the wagon bench.

Cade nodded and lifted himself to sit beside her, then picked up the reins and snapped them in the air over the draft horses' backs. The big animals turned the wagon around and it moved down the road, heading toward the east.

Buddy leaned over the seat, speaking softly into Cade's ear. "Are you going the wrong direction on purpose, Pa?"

Cade nodded. "No sense in leading the fellas to our front door, I figure," he said, looking back at the boy. "We'll just go a roundabout way."

"Who do you suppose they were?" Glory asked, fear rising in her throat as if it would choke her.

"I don't know, but I don't like the idea of strangers asking after Harvey. We'd best keep our eyes sharp and let the sheriff know what you heard."

Cade pulled the team over in front of the jailhouse and stepped down. "I'll be right back, Glory. Don't worry. It'll be all right."

He went into the building, finding the lawman behind his desk. "Say there, McAllister. How are things going out on the farm? I've been meaning to stop by and speak with you. Maybe next week one day."

"Maybe you'd better hear what I have to say first, sir," Cade told him, quickly relating the details of what Glory had overheard.

"I'll step outside and keep a lookout for them. They may even stop here and ask for directions. Don't worry about it, McAllister, I won't send them your way."

Cade nodded briefly. "I'd appreciate your help. I don't cotton to strangers coming around asking questions. There's been a new development out at the farm and Glory and the children don't need any trouble."

He went back out to the wagon and drove along an alleyway out of town. The route he took added three miles to their trip, but he was unwilling to lead anyone to the farm, lest the men follow them. As they passed all the fenced-in property along the way, he looked behind the wagon frequently to be sure no one followed them.

When they reached the lane leading to Earl Bradley's farm, Cade turned in, driving his team to the back of the house. Earl came from the barn to greet him, even as his wife came out onto the porch.

"You remember Etta, don't you, Mrs. McAllister?" Earl asked. His wife stepped down from the porch and approached the wagon.

"Would you like to come in for a cup of coffee or maybe tea?" she asked nicely.

Glory stepped down, her hands going to Cade's shoulders as he moved closer to the wagon to help her. "I'll be in the barn for a few minutes," he said quietly against her ear.

Glory followed Etta Bradley into the house, looking around her at the kitchen. It was neat, clean and well organized, just what she would have expected. Etta Bradley had a good reputation with the ladies in town.

"I'm glad you stopped by today. I've been meaning to have Earl take me with him when he went to see your husband, but it hasn't worked out. I wondered how you and the children are doing. I know it had to be a jolt to the young'uns having their pa taken the way he was."

Glory sat down at the table, accepting the cup and saucer Etta handed her. "Tea will be fine, ma'am. Coffee hasn't been agreeing with me of late."

Etta shot her a quick look. "Any special reason for that?"

Glory knew she blushed, but there was no help for it, and she dived in headfirst. "Well, to begin with, I think I'm having a baby. In fact, I'm certain that's what the problem is. I've been losing at least one meal a day, and I'm getting right sick and tired of it. In fact, that about describes me lately. Sick and tired."

Etta laughed. "That sounds mighty familiar to me. Each time I got in the family way, I spent about six months moping around, yawning and retching. It seems to be a common symptom for most women."

"Well, I didn't plan on it. I thought I was healthy and able to handle most anything," Glory said.

"You probably are. But having a baby is a condition like no other. It ain't like measles or mumps, but some days it's about as bad. You feel like bawlin' some mornings, and other days you wonder how you ever got into such a mess. Just wait till you start growin' out of all your dresses and you feel like a tub of lard." She laughed as if she was describing her own woes as a pregnant woman.

"That sounds familiar to me. Things are starting to get tight already and I'm only about three months along, I figure."

"That sounds about right. What does your new husband have to say about it?" Etta asked, settling into her chair, the teapot before her.

"He's tickled to death, and the children are delighted."

Etta laughed, pouring tea into both their cups. "Well, that leaves you, Glory. How do you feel about it?"

"Most days I'm as pleased as Cade, except when I get so sleepy in the middle of the day. I haven't felt like scrubbin' out the wash or cleaning out the chicken coop in two weeks. Of course, you just go ahead and do what you have to, but it's no fun."

"Well, cleaning the chicken coop is a job I wouldn't do on a bet. I figure I got four kids for a reason or two, and one of them is the chicken coop. If they don't clean it, then Earl gets the job. Cooking and cleaning and that sort of thing is enough for any woman to do."

"I like your way of thinking," Glory said with a grin.

"Stick around, honey. I've been in this business for a long time, and I've figured out the best way to beat the system. Men have it pretty good. They work in the fields and the barn and then come in and sit down at the table and get waited on. Women have to figure the best way to get all the help they can. So we have kids and start training them young. My oldest girl is twelve and doggone if she can't fix a meal pret' near as good as me."

"I shouldn't complain, and I guess I really don't mean to," Glory said, sipping her tea.

"Go ahead and complain all you want, honey. I've got a broad shoulder, and I know all about marriage and menfolk."

"Well, I made a good choice when I married Cade McAllister. He's been good to me and the children, and he works hard to keep things up and make a good living for all of us."

"Yeah, and he got a good deal out of it too, Glory. He got a farm and a wife and a ready-made family. Can't ask for better than that."

"Well, the farm is still Buddy's. His pa wanted it that way. Cade is just looking after things till Buddy is old enough to do for himself."

Etta's gaze narrowed and she bent across the table to speak softly to Glory. "Don't you know that when you married the man, he got title to everything you own? Anything he does is for his benefit as much as yours and the children's."

"I don't think of it that way," she said. "Cade's put money out for stock, the mares he bought and the heifers he got from your husband, but it's still my farm. At least I thought it was."

"You better check that out. I think things changed once you married him."

Essie and Buddy came to the back door, and Buddy knocked, speaking to Glory. "Glory, Pa says he's ready whenever you are."

She swallowed the rest of her tea and smiled at Etta. "Stop by sometime. I'd like to talk to you more about having a baby. This is all new to me, and I'm likely to need some advice before I get done."

"I surely will, Glory. You take care of yourself, and don't be fussing about what I said. I know you have a good husband. Earl thinks he's a good man, and he's pretty good at sizing up menfolk."

With a hand from Cade, Glory lifted herself up to the wagon seat. Then Cade turned the team about, heading for the town road. "I made it right with Earl for the heifers. Told him I might be interested in another couple of them if I sell the colt like I'm planning."

"You know best," Glory said. "Far be it from me to take care of buying and selling livestock. I just gather eggs and churn butter."

"And do a right good job of it, too, ma'am," Cade said with a grin.

When they reached the lane leading to the farmhouse, he looked up at the sign he'd recently hung over the entrance. McAllister Family, it read in bold lettering, and Buddy shared a moment of pleasure with Cade as he paid special mind to the name on the sign.

"My pa never called the place anything but the Clark farm," he said quietly, looking back to where the sign swung from two posts.

"Well, it's under different management these days, son. Our whole family is involved in the place, not just me and you. And I wouldn't be a bit surprised if we don't have more than two or three sons in the family before we're done. Glory and I plan on having a big family, so you and Essie will have lots of relations."

He turned his head to where Essie sat behind him, delving into his pocket and pulling forth three lengths of ribbon he'd tucked inside. "You like any of these colors, Essie?" he asked, holding them out for her inspection.

"Oh, Pa! They're all pretty, ain't they? I think the pink one would be nice with the new dress Glory is gonna make me, and the blue one would go with my other Sunday dress, wouldn't it? But the purple one is just beautiful, Pa."

"Well, I'd say it's a good thing you don't have to choose then, Essie. They're all for you, so when we get in the house you can put them up in your room and then wear a bow on your braid every day. Each morning, you'll have to choose the color to go with your clothes for the day."

The child reached her small hand over Cade's shoulder and he placed the ribbons across her palm, his sidelong glance at Glory one of joy, for the child's response to his gift was enough to make a grown man cry. Essie bent forward and kissed Cade on his cheek, and then squealed aloud.

"Oh, Pa, you've got whiskery cheeks."

Glory laughed at her, and tugged the child forward to sit on her lap.

"Here, let me put one of your ribbons on your braid, Essie. You might as well enjoy them today."

"Which one, Glory? My dress is kinda faded out, but it used to be blue."

Glory made a production of holding the three ribbons next to Essie's skirt, finally choosing the purple one to use. "This one will make your dress look a bit purple, I think. And the next time we buy some fabric for you, we'll get a print with purple flowers in it. Will that work?"

"Oh, yes." The child was ecstatic, wiggling on Glory's lap, trying to see the bow Glory formed for her. She reached for her braid, which was long enough to lay across her chest, and carefully brushed the chosen ribbon with her small fingers as she admired it up close.

"I feel so special, Pa. Thank you again." Essie curled up on Glory's lap, her index finger again making contact with the bit of cloth that had so delighted her.

Cade leaned closer to Glory as he pulled the wagon up to the back porch. "Sure doesn't take much to make her happy, does it?"

"She's never had anyone pay much mind to

her before, only me. Essie doesn't ask for much in life."

"Kinda like her mama, ain't she?" He lifted Essie to the ground and then held up his arms for Glory, grasping her waist and lowering her to stand in his embrace. His kiss was brief, but offered promise, his mouth touching her cheek and temple with a caress she leaned into.

"You're a good father, Cade," Glory whispered against his ear. "The children love you. Now, hand me one of those boxes and I'll carry it in."

He grinned at her and turned her toward the porch. "You don't need to do any totin' boxes, sweetheart. Buddy and I will carry stuff in and Essie can handle the bundle of fabric."

"I need to talk to Buddy, too. I spoke with Sally Thomas, the schoolteacher in town, and she's real pleased that Buddy will be coming to school in a couple weeks. I asked her about him riding a horse and she said several of the older boys ride in every day. There's a place to stake the horses during school."

"We'll have to decide for sure which horse he'll ride, Glory. I think he likes the black mare the best. But he can make a choice for himself. He's a good rider."

"Well, maybe you should speak with him, Cade. He'd likely rather hear all that from you."

She hastened ahead of him then, watching as Buddy lifted his share of the load from the wagon, handing Essie the bundle of fabric to carry.

Glory opened the back door and held it for her menfolk, waving at the table as the preferred spot to place her purchases. Essie carefully undid the package she carried and rolled the string up to save in the pantry. The brown paper was smoothed out and folded over to be used for various things. Schoolwork could be done and lists made on any scrap of paper available, and such a large piece was a treasure.

"I'll use that piece for drawing out the plans for your room, Essie," Cade told her, halting her progress to the pantry.

Essie grinned happily, and placed the paper on the kitchen dresser for Cade's use later on. "Don't forget my shelves, Pa. I'd like to have two of them, one for my clothes and one for my schoolwork and stuff."

"This box the Mason jars are in would do well for your dolly, Essie. We could cut it down and make her a bed out of it, and then when we finish her quilt, we'll put together some of the chicken feathers I've put aside and make a pillow for her, too," Glory told her. She bent down to remove the jars from the carton in question and set them carefully on the pantry shelf, upside down, lest bugs get inside.

Essie ran up the stairs to her bedroom and returned just moments later with her doll. She knelt on the floor where Glory had put the box and laid her dolly inside. "She fits real good, Glory. Come look and see."

And Glory did, bending to inspect the space the doll inhabited. "This will work out just fine, Essie. Carry it to your room, and we'll work on it later."

Once they'd finished putting away their purchases, Glory had thought to make Essie's pink-and-white dress right away, but the child protested loudly. "You promised we'd make a quilt. I want to do that first," Essie cried, her short little arms trying in vain to reach around Glory's middle. "You promised, Glory. You promised, remember?"

"Yes, I remember." It was all she could do not to laugh aloud, for the child was grimly determined to have her own way in this, and Glory would not deny her the right to choose her own priorities. "We'll make the quilt first, Essie. But you need to help me find the right pieces for the top of it. We'll go through my fabric scraps and see what we can find. I'll show you my special place for keeping things in my room."

"Can we go up now, Glory?" Essie asked.

"I don't know why not," Glory said.

Cade was out back and Glory made a mental note to ask him about the men in town—for she was fearful of them finding the place, even though it was called by a new name. For the sign no longer designated it The Clark Farm, but instead read McAllister Family, a phrase that warmed her heart.

Chapter Fifteen

Together they went to Glory's bedroom. It was a room Essie was very seldom allowed in, so she had decided that this was an occasion worth celebrating. "Is this your special trunk, Glory? Do you have your very own things in it?"

Essie knelt beside a trunk Harvey Clark had bought her soon after her appearance at his back door. He'd brought it home from the general store, presented it to her and announced that she must keep her belongings inside it.

"A cardboard box would do as well," Glory had said, amazed at the gift.

Never had Glory possessed anything so fine, and now as she handed Essie the key and directed her to open it, she told her the story of the day the child's father had brought it home from town and given it to her.

"My pa, my *real* pa, gave you this?" Essie was stunned by the revelation and Glory explained further.

"He wanted me to have a place for my own things, and even gave me a key for it, so that what I kept inside would be for my eyes alone, unless I chose to share the contents with someone else."

"Am I *someone else*?" Essie asked softly.

"You're my very own girl, Essie. And I want you to see the things I've kept in a special place," Glory told her, watching as the small fingers worked to fit the key into the brass lock. It turned with a *snick,* and Essie lifted the lid with care, allowing the hinges to take its weight, even as she knelt before the wooden chest to survey its contents.

Glory knelt beside her, gathering up various pieces of fabric, left over from things she had sewn in the past three years. "I thought we could use these pieces to patch together a quilt top for your bed and one for your dolly, too, Essie."

"Oh, yes, Glory. That would be grand." The child wiggled in excitement, barely able to be still as she picked up piece after piece of the fabric bits that Glory had set aside. At the bottom of the trunk lay a dress, faded and worn, patched and mended by careful hands, until there was little left but the seams to hold the worn stuff together.

"What is this piece, Glory?" Essie held it up, puzzled by its condition, for Glory had used less worn items for rags when she scrubbed the floor or dusted the furniture.

"That's the dress I was wearing the day I came to your back door, Essie. It was the only thing I had to my name when I left the wagon train and walked across the prairie, looking for a place to stay. I had it on the first time you saw me."

"I don't remember for sure." Her eyes searched out the worn garment, then held it up against Glory's apron. "Did you wear it a lot after you came here?"

"It was all I had, until your pa went to the store and bought me some material to make a dress from. I'd mended it and sewn up the seams and tried to keep it in one piece, but it almost fell apart one day when I washed it."

"And you kept it anyway? You didn't want to use it for a rag?"

Glory shook her head. "No, I wanted it to remind me of how little I had when I came here, and how much your pa did for me. I was poor as a church mouse, and someday I'll tell you what that means, sweet. And your pa gave me a home and a family and let me live with you and Buddy. And one day, when you're older, this trunk your pa gave me will be yours. Maybe he was thinking of that when he gave it to me."

"I'm glad he got it for you, Glory." She leaned against the woman who'd been her mother for three years and her arms fit better this time as she hugged her tightly.

"So am I." From behind them, a strong, deep voice echoed the sentiments expressed by the child as Cade stepped into the bedroom. "What are you two doing in here, anyway? Telling secrets?" He grinned at Essie and shot Glory a look filled with tenderness.

"Glory's gonna make me a quilt for my bed when you get my bedroom fixed up, Pa. And she said we can make one for my dolly, too. See all the pretty scraps of fabric she has in her trunk? She's been saving them for a special occasion."

"She never let me look in her trunk," Cade said mournfully, making Essie break out in uninhibited laughter.

"You can look if you want to, Pa. Glory won't care, will you?"

"There's not much in here, just bits and pieces

of things I set aside until I needed them," Glory said, rising from where she'd knelt beside Essie.

"No nest egg? No hidey-hole hard cold cash?" Cade asked, teasing her as he bent to kiss her lightly.

"I should be so rich," Glory said, leaning to close the lid once more. "My butter-and-egg money is in the kitchen, on the kitchen dresser in the old sugar bowl. Everyone in the family knows where I keep my riches."

"And what riches do you have, Glory?" Cade asked soberly.

"I have Essie and Buddy and you, Cade McAllister. That's all any woman could ask for." She looked down at Essie's lap, full now with the assortment of fabric pieces. "And I have the makings for a quilt for Essie's bed and one for her dolly's new bed."

"So I see," Cade said, bending to inspect the stack of material Essie had found. "Don't I recognize this bit of stuff?" He held up a blue flowered scrap.

"That's like my dress I had on yesterday, Pa." Essie squealed with delight that Cade should recognize it. "Only, my dress is old now and all faded out, but that was what it looked like when Glory first made it."

"And when will we see this quilt take shape?" he asked Essie.

"Maybe tomorrow we'll start it, if Glory says so."

"All right. And now, if you'll take your bits and pieces to your room, Essie, I need to talk to Glory for a minute or two."

Essie rose and left the room clutching her find tightly. They heard her door opening and closing behind her down the hallway.

Cade held Glory close. "We need to talk about something," he said softly. "I don't want to frighten the children, but you need to be very careful when I'm not in the house with you. If those men show up here, we'll need to be ready for them, Glory. I brought my shotgun into the house and put it in the pantry, along with a box of shells on the top shelf. I have a rifle in the barn, and my pistols are in the tack room.

"And now for the big question. Can you fire a gun? Have you ever shot a long gun?"

"Yes, on the wagon train, everyone had to learn how to load a gun, aim and fire and know enough to protect themselves. The wagon master took all the women out one day and gave us instructions. I was pretty good at it, too."

"Well, I hope you never have to prove that, sweetheart, for I don't want to ever see you be forced to lift a gun against another human being. But if you have to, I want to know that you can. Those men may be looking for gold."

"I don't think Harvey had any gold, Cade. I told you, I've never seen hide nor hair of it, and I looked."

He hesitated, wondering if he should tell her of his discovery in the wall of Buddy's room, and decided she deserved to know what he had found there.

"He had the gold, all right, love. But he managed to hide it away and didn't tell you about it. I found it in the wall when I was tearing up things for Buddy's room. I put it back and nailed the boards over it again, for I wasn't sure what to do about it, when we should tell the sheriff about it. I'm afraid that if the townsfolk know the gold has been here all along they might decide you knew about it. And I don't want anyone talking about you or making judgments about your character."

"I think we need to let the law know that the gold is here, Cade. It's not ours to keep and Mr.

Clark was wrong to hide it and leave me holding the bag, so to speak."

He grinned. "I'd say you're right there, sweetheart. But on the other hand, perhaps now isn't the right time to spill the beans on the old fella."

Glory shivered. "I still remember how adamant he was that he not be blamed for the robbery. And perhaps he wasn't the leader behind the whole thing, for I don't think Mr. Clark was all that brainy. I think if he was involved, he must have followed the man in charge, who led him in the wrong direction. And he ended up losing his life because he was the fall guy."

"I think you're probably right, Glory. And for now, I'm going to leave the gold where it is. We'll give it back a bit further down the line, when we can do so without involving you or the children in the whole mess. Although I don't think you're going to come out lily-white no matter how we figure it out.

"The problem is, should it be known that you were aware of the gold, you could be accused of collaborating with Harvey, and be blamed for the gold being in your home. The Pinkerton Agency is certain of the gold being here—in fact, they hired me to search for it. There's no way, I'd allow you to be so unfairly involved in Harvey Clark's problems. Better that the gold be forever hidden than that you be in the midst of such a mess. We'll talk more about that later on," he said, for Glory looked fit to blow.

"The bottom line is, I want you to be able to keep yourself and Essie safe, here in the house, in case visitors arrive unexpectedly. I'll keep Buddy with me as much as I can. You just keep a good eye on Essie."

Cade felt regret that he had been required to make an armed camp of his home, but he knew it was better that they be prepared than to be taken unaware by strangers.

Cade and Buddy left the house daily, working with the horses, tending to the cattle and readying the barn for the additional stalls to be built before winter. For a week, life went on in an orderly fashion. Glory and Essie patched pieces of fabric together on the parlor floor, making a colorful quilt top for Essie's bed, and another, much smaller one for her doll.

Each morning, Glory went to the pantry, checking on the shotgun before she began the day, unable to hide a shiver of dismay as she thought of ever shooting the weapon at a man, but determined that Essie should not be harmed because of her own fears.

It was a week after they'd seen the men in town that Cade went to the hay field, along with Buddy and Earl Bradley's eldest boy, Robert, a lad of fifteen, who had been hired to help out with the gathering of the hay into the barn. Cade told Glory they would be in just after noontime for dinner and she kissed him at the door, apprehensive for some reason, but unwilling to let him know of her unease.

"I'm going to put the mares and foals into the barn this morning, Glory. We'll be in and out of the pasture and I don't want them running loose out there. If they should take it into their heads to run off I'll be half the day rounding them up."

She watched him as he drove the mares and their foals into the corral, then into their stalls inside the barn for the day. It was hot out, an ideal time to pick the last of the tomatoes. So with Essie by her side, she took the gun from the pantry, loaded both barrels and put extra shells into her apron pocket before heading for her garden. The tomatoes were dead ripe and she'd carried one bucketful into the house and was well on her way to filling it again when she heard horses approaching, heard the whinny of a mare from the pasture and looked up from her work.

Her gun lay just a foot or so from where she knelt and Glory reached for it, grasping it tightly. Kneeling between the tomato plants, heavy with ripe fruit, she heard the mare from the pasture whinny again.

From behind her, another horse answered the greeting, and Glory turned to see two riders coming up the lane, effectively cutting her off from the house.

She called to Essie and whispered to her quickly, "Go get Cade. Tell him that there are two men here. Run fast, Essie."

The child did as Glory instructed her, running for the barn, through the wide front door and out the back. Glory watched uneasily, for Essie did not reappear in the pasture, and she heard nothing from the child. Not her voice calling out to Cade or any sort of outcry.

And then a large shadow filled the barn door, a man, holding Essie before him, his hand over her mouth, the child kicking and squirming in his clasp.

She reached for her shotgun and held it to her

shoulder and then recognized the futility of such a move, for if she were to fire, she would no doubt find a target in Essie. And not for the world would Glory take a chance on hitting the child.

Even as she watched, the man turned back into the barn and, carrying Essie with him, ran into the corral. From the lane near the house, the other two men dismounted and headed for Glory. One of them aimed a pistol at her.

"Drop that gun, lady, or you're dead where you stand." There wasn't a doubt in her mind that the man would follow up on his threat, but Glory took one chance, lifting the barrel of her shotgun and firing both shells into the air. It vibrated against her shoulder and she held it before her as the men sped to where she stood.

If only Cade heard the weapon, and realized it was a call for help. And of course he would, Glory knew, for they had planned for just such an event perhaps taking place.

"If you need me, fire the gun, both barrels, and I'll come 'arunning," he'd said just this morning before he left her for the work awaiting him in the hay field.

And so she had, and what if he ran right into trouble? What if the man in the barn saw him coming and shot him? Glory cried aloud, holding her weapon before her, even as the two men reached her and tore it from her grasp.

From behind the barn, the third man rode past them, heading for the town road, Essie perched on the saddle before him, the child crying loudly, calling to Glory for help.

"Don't worry about the young'un, lady. She'll be fine so long as you cooperate with us and tell us what we need to know."

They dragged Glory into the house, her feet making deep trails in the garden, for she was not willing to be of any help to them. "I don't know what you want with me," she cried aloud.

"All we want is the gold old man Clark brought home with him," one of the men said, his arm tight around Glory's neck. She choked and gagged as he tightened his hold on her, and she began to retch violently. He released her a bit, and she bent to vomit on the ground near the porch, aggravating him beyond his endurance, for he cuffed her on the side of the head and lifted her from her feet to carry her into the house.

Cade's scythe swept through the ripened hay. Buddy was to one side of him with a smaller version of the tool, and Earl's boy, Robert, with his father's scythe, worked just a few feet away. When the sound of the shotgun split the air with a double report, Cade stood erect, looking toward the house, the roof barely visible beyond the barn and corral.

He dropped his scythe and set off at a dead run, heading for the barn, only to halt when a horse left the corral, ridden by a man in dark clothing, with Essie held before him on the saddle. Even as he ran through the back of the barn, he saw Glory dragged to the house, then carried into the kitchen by two men.

"Damn, and I left her alone. I should have stayed in the house with her." He ran full tilt through the barn, stopping only to pick up his pistols and strap his holster on in the tack room. Buddy was fast on his heels, and he turned to the boy.

"Use the black mare, Buddy. Ride bareback and get the sheriff. There's no time to waste, for those two fellas have Glory in the house and Essie's been kidnapped." Without a word, Buddy slid a bridle into place on the black mare and left by the back door of the barn, riding across the hay field to the woods and beyond, taking a shortcut to the road leading to town.

From the kitchen window, a gun barrel emerged and a shot was fired toward the barn, pinning Cade and Robert where they stood behind the barn door.

Glory found herself on the kitchen floor, one of the men shooting from the window, the other one intent on questioning her.

"No sense in worrying about that fella out back, lady. He ain't gonna help you any. You might as well tell us where the gold is while you're still able to talk. If I have to start pounding it out of you, you'll be sorry you didn't spill the beans while you had a chance."

Glory looked up at dark, hate-filled eyes, a mouth that spewed obscenities and hands that were fisted. She could only shake her head and whimper, pleading with the man to let her go.

He laughed loudly, his hand unclenching long enough to reach for her, his wide palm slapping her roundly, almost knocking her insensible as he brutally hit her across the face and on the side of the head.

"You'd better tell us what we want to know,"

he said from between clenched teeth. "I've killed before and I'll do it again. And if I have to, I'll tear this house apart, one piece at a time, till we find that gold. We know it's here. Harvey took it with him when he left St. Louis, and me and the boys got stuck in jail. We was supposed to hang for the robbery, but there was a jailbreak a month ago and we got loose.

"Harvey told us he was headin' this way, and that he'd stash the gold for us until we were ready for it. We heard he's been hanged for his trouble and now we're here to collect."

Glory shook her head, stunned by the sharp blows dealt her, half conscious as she hung in his grasp. He dragged her to the stairway, hauling her behind him as he climbed the stairs.

"Keep that fella out there busy," he called back to his crony, and Glory could only think of Cade in the barn, knowing that he was worrying about Essie and herself at the mercy of two madmen.

"Your fella ain't gonna help you, lady. He only married you for the gold and he ain't about to risk his neck for you, no way in hell."

The man dragged her down the hallway, into the first bedroom, the one she shared with Cade, and looked around the room, as if the gold might be in plain sight. "Where is it, lady? Might as well tell me before I take it out of your hide."

He headed for her wooden trunk and looked at the brass fixings on the front, then took aim and fired at the lock. He lifted the cover as she wept, there on the floor, knowing that her possessions were exposed to his view.

"Nothin' much in here, unless you got it buried under all this junk." He bent and turned the trunk onto its side, the fabric and items from Glory's three years here in this house falling to the floor. He kicked the trunk against the wall and turned back to where she lay.

"Is it in the dresser?" Without pause, he pulled the drawers out, tossing them to the floor, Cade's clothing and her own heaped in a jumble as he emptied them without care for the contents. He bent and peered behind the space where the drawers had been, finding but emptiness there.

"How about the bed?" he muttered, tearing the quilt away, then bending to look beneath the frame. He went to the corner where her commode stood, her pitcher and bowl atop it, her slop jar beneath. He tore the screen aside and the pitcher and bowl hit the floor, bits and pieces of china flying hither and yon. Glory watched him in silence, unwilling to say or do anything to bring his attention to rest on her again.

He dragged her with him as he left the room, threw open the other bedroom doors and looked within the rooms, his anger growing as there seemed to be nothing of any value to be found.

"We'll go back downstairs. Maybe in the parlor," he said beneath his breath, grasping Glory's arm and dragging her with him. She stumbled and fell to her knees in the hallway and was jerked harshly to her feet and then down the stairs. Then they entered the kitchen once more. "You stay right here, lady. If she moves, shoot her, Ralph," he told the man, who was still shooting sporadically from the window.

With a wave of his hand, and a look back at Glory on the floor, he ran from the kitchen, down the hall and into the parlor. She could hear the furniture being tossed hither and yon, the sound of glass breaking as he apparently broke into the library case and tore the books from the shelves.

Returning to the kitchen, he approached her again, and Glory feigned weakness, holding her hands to her head and collapsing full length onto the floor, falling on top of her shotgun, one of the men having dropped it there, uncaring, for it held no shells now.

From the open back door, she saw the barn door open wider and the two mares and three foals run from the barn. Both of the men in the kitchen were looking out the window now.

Glory lifted herself up a bit, found the two shells she'd put into her pocket earlier, moaned to cover the faint sound as she quietly opened the gun, slid the shells into place, then lay back on the floor. One of the men turned to look at her and she watched from beneath her eyelids as he scanned her body on the floor, then turned back to the window, his attention taken by the open barn door.

She watched as the mares and foals headed to the watering trough and bent their heads to drink from the cool water. Then she caught sight of Cade's denim-clad legs, his body low to the ground as he hid amidst the four-legged animals, half out of sight behind the trough.

A shout rang out from the lane beyond the house and one of the men ran to the parlor, apparently intent on firing at the newcomer. Cade rose from his prone position and the man at the window sighted his long gun on him.

Glory moved quietly, lifting the shotgun and firing once at the man's back. The pellets hit him in a widespread pattern, felling him with a single shot. Cade stood then, shouting one word.

"Glory!"

"I'm here, Cade," she answered, her voice strong, even though she shook with terror as the crook lay bleeding profusely just a few feet from her.

With a shiver of dread, she realized she had killed him, and yet no remorse touched her, for he had been intent on firing at Cade, and not for anything on God's green earth would she have acted differently.

From the front of the house, she heard a shot fired and then the second man ran along the side of the house, apparently intent on reaching his horse. Behind him rode the sheriff, his handgun blazing as he closed in on the man fleeing toward the horses.

Cade came from behind the trough, lifted his pistol and let loose with two shots. Cade's aim was true. For as the man reached the horses, he fell to the ground, his leg bleeding. But he was still holding his gun. He rolled to his stomach and returned Cade's fire, then was the target of the sheriff's handgun as the lawman rounded the house. Finally, the robber slumped forward and his gun fell from his hand.

Cade ran for the back door, bursting into the kitchen where Glory sat in bewilderment on the floor. "Honey, are you all right?" He squatted beside her, lifting her a bit, his sharp eyes seeming to inspect every inch of her with one sweeping glance.

"I'm fine, but Essie is gone, Cade. And I shot a man."

"I know, sweetheart. Go on upstairs. I sent Buddy to town to fetch the sheriff. Take your gun with you and stay in Buddy's room. You can see both the back and side of the house from there. I'm going after Essie."

She nodded. Rising quickly and taking the shotgun with her she ran for the stairway, eager to do as Cade told her.

She entered Buddy's new bedroom and shut the door, pushing a heavy box against it, then went to the window, lifting the sash and leaning her shotgun against the sill. She heard Cade's voice, then that of the sheriff and Robert Bradley, and then watched as they rode down the lane to the town road, following the path taken by Essie's kidnapper.

Glory slouched by the window, trembling as she imagined what Essie must be going through, her heart feeling heavy in her chest at the thought of the child's terror. And then, as if she had somehow conjured up the image, she caught sight of a rider coming across the pasture from the woods, headed for the barn.

He called out as he rode, apparently warning his cohorts that he was nearing the house. But no voices answered him and he rode into the barn and slid from his horse.

Glory called from the window. "Drop your gun, mister. I've got you covered."

"Fat chance, lady. I've got the girl and if you aim at me, you'll hit her."

He grabbed at Essie, but she slid from the other side of the horse and ran from him, apparently intent on reaching the safety of the house. He lifted his gun and took aim at the window where Glory knelt, firing his shotgun twice.

The shots hit the window, shattering the glass, and several of the pellets found a target in Glory, penetrating her shoulder and arm. She fell to the floor as he fired again and this time his aim was lower, blasting a hole through the wall beneath the window. The wood splintered and cracked and from the wall, Glory watched in amazement as gold coins poured forth in a stream.

The leather bags were split by the shots fired and released their contents from the hiding place beneath the window. She heard Essie cry out her name and then as she crawled to the other window, she saw the child running to the house. The gunman opened the barrel of his gun and loaded it quickly, intent on the child who fled from him.

Glory heard the sound of the gun and lifted herself up. Her left arm was bleeding and useless, but her right hand still held the shotgun. She propped it on the windowsill and took aim at the man, aware that she had only one chance, for she'd used the first shell in the kitchen, and her pocket was empty.

She knew she presented a clear target, and watched as the man lifted his gun to his shoulder. With a prayer on her lips, she pulled the trigger and shot her remaining shell, then fell to the floor, the shotgun dropping from her hand.

Essie called out from the kitchen. "I'm coming up, Glory," and Glory heard her pounding footsteps on the stairs. The door was barricaded, but she crawled to that side of the room and lifted herself, grabbing the box and then shoving it from before the door.

Essie pushed the door open and her face reflected the terror of her ordeal. "I'm here, Glory. I ran from the bad man and then he musta got shot, 'cause he's lyin' on the ground out back. And there's another fella in the kitchen, all bloody, just lying there on the floor."

She knelt beside Glory and her cries faded as Glory sank into oblivion. Darkness seemed to surround her and she could only cry out Essie's name before she lost consciousness.

Cade and the sheriff rode until they could no longer find a trace of tracks made by the man who'd fled with Essie. Buddy was on the black mare beside Cade, and even Robert was with them, eager to help. "I think we'd better head back and see if there's any sign of the fella in the woods beyond your pasture, Cade," the sheriff said.

"I agree. And I want to make sure Glory is all right. If that man shows up, she's all alone in the house."

They turned in the middle of the road and headed back to the farm. Buddy clung to his mount, his hands tangled in the mare's mane, for without a saddle, he was clinging to the animal, his legs not able to hold him erect.

"Go ahead, Cade. I'll catch up," he called out. "Be sure Glory is all right."

The horses increased their speed as Cade dug his heels in and the sheriff followed suit, Robert staying to ride beside Buddy. Cade was fearful of having to tell Glory they hadn't found the child because he knew she would be beyond horror at the thought of Essie alone with a man intent on revenge.

Once they arrived back at the farm they left their horses near the porch and rushed to the house. When Cade opened the door, Essie ran into his arms.

"Pa, Glory's shot. She's bleeding something awful. Come quick, Pa."

Chapter Sixteen

Barely able to understand the child for the sobs racking her small body, Cade took the stairs two at a time, heading for the bedroom where he'd told Glory to hide.

She lay on the floor, blood flowing freely from her shoulder and arm. He tore off his shirt as he entered the room, folding it over to form a pad and holding it to her shoulder when he reached her.

He turned her on the floor, finding no exit hole for the wounds, and recognized that she had shotgun pellets in her flesh.

"Joe, send Buddy for the doctor. Have him ride my horse. He'll do better with a saddle. Tell him to hurry."

From the stairway, he heard the sheriff call for Buddy, and then the sound of Joe Lawson heading downstairs to give Buddy his instructions.

The sound of a horse galloping from the house told of Buddy's departure, and Cade turned back to Glory. The pressure of his shirt on her shoulder had been enough to stop the rapid flow of blood. He continued to hold it firmly in place with one hand until the sheriff came back upstairs.

"Hold this, Joe. I need to find something of Buddy's to tie around her shoulders. Got to keep that pad in place till the doctor can take a look at her."

The sheriff did as Cade had bid him, even as his gaze widened at the sight of the gold coins that had spilled out on the floor. Cade rifled through the boxes containing Buddy's clothing until he found a shirt that would serve his purpose. He tore strips from it, tied them together and held Glory erect in his arms so that Joe could bind her tightly.

"Looks like you've found the old man's gold, Cade," Joe said quietly, and Cade nodded.

"I discovered it there a couple days ago. Our friend out in the yard apparently shot through the window and then hit the siding below it. Ripped right through and tore open the wall. I hid it from Glory and the children until I could tell you about it."

He bent to Glory's side, intent on stopping the flow of blood that stained the dress she wore. He tore the sleeve from the shoulder seam and exposed the wounded flesh underneath. The shot in her upper arm had ripped through her skin, leaving a long gash. Cade fashioned a smaller pad from Buddy's clothing to press against the wound.

She was regaining consciousness and groaned aloud as he worked. Her eyelids fluttered as she tried to peer up at him. She even attempted to whisper in a faint voice.

Cade shushed her quietly, bending to kiss her forehead. "It's all right, honey. You'll be fine. Buddy went for the doctor and I'm going to carry you into our room while we wait. Don't wiggle around any, Glory. The bleeding's pretty well slowed down and I'm going to pick you up now."

He lifted her in his arms and Joe held the door wide, then went to the bedroom at the head of the stairs where Cade's nod had directed him. He opened the door and Cade carried Glory inside, laying her with care on their bed. Essie quietly followed them into the room.

"They must have taken this place apart," Cade

said, looking at the clothing strewn over the floor and the screen lying in the corner.

"Looking for the gold, I'd bet," Joe said. "For all the good it did them, with all three of them dead. Old Harvey Clark must have hidden it in the wall and not told anyone about it. I doubt that Glory had any idea it was there. She seemed to be in the dark about it."

"You're right there," Cade said firmly. Leaving Glory for a few seconds, he snatched up towels from the corner where her commode stood. Then, raising her a bit, he placed two towels beneath her shoulder, for the blood was seeping into the quilt and he knew Glory would have a fit when she saw the mess he'd made.

"Cade?" She lifted her right hand, trying to touch her left arm, then winced as she moved. "It hurts real bad, Cade."

"It'll be all right, Glory. You've got a couple pellets in your shoulder, and one sliced your arm open, but we got the bleeding pretty well stopped and I'm gonna wash the wound up a little so I can see how bad it is."

"I'll get some warm water from the kitchen," Joe said, heading for the door as he heard Cade's words. His footsteps clattered down the stairs, and then in minutes he was back, carrying Glory's largest kettle, almost filled with warm water from the reservoir.

"Get me another towel or two," Cade told him, reaching into his pocket for the knife he carried there. With swift movements, he slit the fabric of her dress, cutting the bodice open, fully revealing the damage done. The pad fell aside and blood oozed sullenly from the wound on her shoulder.

Cade heard Glory's groan of pain as he wet a towel and laid it on the bleeding area. With gentle movements, he bathed her skin, then put a clean pad against the wound. Her dress was soaked and he cut it from her, lifting her just a bit to allow Joe to pull it from beneath her upper body.

"Cover me, Cade." Her voice was weak, but her eyes met his as she raised her hand to cover her bared breast.

"Another towel, Joe," he said quietly, placing it over her shoulder and breast, whispering to her as he leaned close. "You're all covered up, Glory. Don't move, sweetheart."

"I shot two men, Cade. I think I killed them both," she whispered.

Joe Lawson heard her words and stepped closer to the bed. "Don't you worry about those men,

Mrs. McAllister. If anybody ever deserved to die it was the fella that took the little girl. You were just protecting your family, and sometimes shooting a gun is a part of that. Just don't fret about it, you hear?"

Glory nodded, closing her eyes, tears running from beneath her lashes.

Cade bent over her. "Don't cry, sweetheart. It makes my heart ache to see you hurting this way."

"Water, please," Glory whispered, and Joe was quick to make another trip down the stairs to pump a glass full from the sink, returning in less than a minute to hand it to Cade.

"Just pick up your head a little, Glory. Don't try to sit up." He slid his arm beneath her neck, lifted her a few inches and held the glass to her lips. She sipped at it, swallowed a bit and shook her head.

"That's enough for now." Her eyes closed again. Cade felt her go limp against his arm and recognized that she was unconscious.

"Keep an eye out for the doctor, Joe. I'll stay here with her." The sheriff nodded and went downstairs.

Essie remained in the corner of the bedroom,

her eyes intent on Glory. "Will she be all right, Pa?" she asked, her voice trembling. She was sitting on the floor, her knees pulled up to her chest, her arms squeezed tightly around them as if she wanted to be as small as possible, so that no one would send her away from her chosen spot.

"She'll be all right in a few days, Essie. The doctor will tend to her. He'll have to look at the place where the bad man shot her and fix it up a bit, but Glory will be back in the garden and the kitchen by the end of the week. And you can be a big help to her, with the churning and such."

"I'll help her, Pa. I always do."

Glory awakened again, her voice sounding raspy to Cade's ears. "Don't let Essie be frightened, Cade. Send her out when the doctor gets here. In case I make a fuss, I don't want her to know about it."

"I'll be here with you, sweetheart. I'll hold your hand and give you a good slug of whiskey to help with the pain."

From outdoors they heard the sound of voices and then Buddy made his way up the stairs. "Can I come in, Pa?" he asked from the doorway.

"Sure you can, son. You made good time getting to town and back, didn't you? Come say hello to Glory and then you and Essie had best go out to the barn and make sure the kittens have a good big saucer of milk for their dinner." He shot Buddy a man-to-man look and was rewarded by a nod of acknowledgment.

"I understand, Pa," he said in an undertone. "I'll take care of Essie and keep her away from the bedroom for a while."

"Thank you, Buddy." Glory's voice seemed stronger, Cade thought, even though her fingers against his hand were pale and limp.

Buddy approached the bed and looked down at Glory. "I'm sure sorry you got hurt, Glory. But I'm awful glad you're a good shot. I expect Essie owes her life to you, you know. If that man had fired at her—" His voice broke and he turned away, heading for his little sister.

"Come on, Essie. Let's you and me go for a walk. We'll take out a cupful of milk for the kittens and check them over. And then we need to take care of the eggs and feeding the chickens. Glory needs some extra help today, and you and me have to pitch in."

"All right, Buddy." Essie rose from her spot in the corner and Buddy took her hand, leading her past the bed and then to the doorway into the hall. They passed the doctor as he came up the stairway, and he spoke to them briefly before he came into the room where Glory lay.

"What's been going on here, Mrs. McAllister? Seems like you're the heroine of the day, if your boy has the story straight."

Cade looked up, attempting a smile, but found it difficult. "She's got a gash on her arm from a shotgun pellet and I think there's one in her shoulder somewhere. Maybe two of them," he said quietly.

"Well, we'll take a look and see how things stand. You got any good whiskey, McAllister?" he asked briskly.

"Yeah, there's some in the kitchen downstairs."

"Your wife is gonna be in pain, if I know anything about it. We'll have to go in after those pellets. Can't let them fester under the skin. Maybe they'll be close to the surface and in that case, it won't be too bad, getting them out. Why don't you get the whiskey and we'll see if it helps."

Cade released Glory's hand and she looked up at him pleadingly. "Don't be long, Cade. Hurry back?"

He bent to kiss her, his lips tender against hers, and assured her of his quick return.

"You got yourself a fine husband, Mrs. McAllister," the doctor said, opening his bag and removing several items. "I told the sheriff to send some good hot water up with your husband. I'll need to wash my hands and I'll need a small dish to put alcohol in to make sure my instruments are clean. We don't want any infection."

Cade came back up the stairs in mere moments, a whiskey bottle in one hand, a bucket of hot water in the other, one of Glory's small bowls inside the bucket.

"You can see if Glory's basin survived the fella who tore this room up, Doc," he said. "Otherwise, I'll go back down and fetch a pan for you to wash in."

The corner of the room held the overturned screen and various items from Glory's commode. The pitcher was shattered, but luckily the basin had survived with but a small chip on the rim.

The doctor poured hot water into it and scrubbed with a liquid soap he'd brought with him and then let his hands air dry, coming back to the bedside.

Cade brought a straight chair for him to sit on and then took his place on the other side of the bed beside Glory. He reached for her hand

and held it between both of his, lending her his strength. The bottle of whiskey was beside the doctor and he poured a few ounces into the drinking glass that sat on Glory's bedside table.

"I want you to drink this, ma'am. Not all at once, but in tiny sips. It'll help with the sore spot on your shoulder, for I can almost guarantee you it's gonna hurt like the dickens when I start looking for those pellets."

Cade put the second pillow beneath Glory's head and lifted her a bit, holding the glass to her mouth. She sipped, choked and inhaled, trying not to make a fuss. With a nod of her head, she signified her readiness and he tilted it again, allowing a small bit to enter her mouth. The doctor waited quietly, arranging his instruments in the bowl Cade had brought from the kitchen, pouring alcohol from a bottle over them, and then watched as Glory did her best to swallow the whiskey he'd prescribed.

"I think we're ready now, Doc," Cade said, holding Glory's gaze with his own, leaning over her as if to somehow protect her from the pain he knew she must endure. If she cried aloud, he didn't know what he'd do, for watching her in pain was almost more than he could handle. And if the doctor was planning on cutting into her shoulder with that sharp instrument he held in his hand, it was sure to involve pain.

Cade bent low, covering Glory with his body, his head against hers on the pillow, his arm holding her fast, lest she move and harm herself inadvertently. She turned her face to his, opened her lips against his cheek and whispered something he could not decipher.

"What, sweetheart? What do you need?"

She whispered again, and he felt his heart melt within him, for the words she spoke were guaranteed to make him weep. "I love you, Cade. I love you. You're so good to me." She sobbed with the final word she spoke, for the doctor cut into her shoulder with a quick turn of the knife.

Glory was rigid and unmoving beneath his hands, but for the rise and fall of her chest as she breathed deeply. Cade held the glass to her lips again, coaxing her to drink the whiskey, and she obliged him, sipping at it, swallowing minuscule amounts as he encouraged her to cooperate.

The doctor muttered something beneath his breath, then reached for another instrument from the basin and Cade heard the click of metal on metal. Knowing it meant that one of the pellets had been found and removed, he breathed more easily, and then the doctor leaned closer to the opening in Glory's shoulder.

"Mop up this area a bit, McAllister," he said, holding out a clean piece of gauze. "I can't see what I'm looking for here."

Cade did as he asked and the man bent closer to the open wound and probed again. Glory groaned, uttering a sharp cry as the metal pincers again found a pellet and drew it forth from the bleeding flesh.

"I suspect that's it. I don't see anything else, and there were only two entrance wounds, so I think we're in the clear." He dropped his instruments into the basin and took the gauze from Cade's hand, wiping the area with care.

"I'll just stitch this up and put a bandage on it, ma'am, and we'll be done in this spot." He pulled a small sewing kit from his bag and Cade watched with eyes that threatened to weep. The doctor threaded black silk through the eye of a curved needle and looked up at Cade and nodded.

"Just a minute more and we'll be done."

Cade held Glory's head against himself, knowing that the piercing of her flesh would be painful, and he must hold her steady lest she move, hindering the medical man's stitching.

She was quiet, barely breathing, her eyes closed, only a single tear falling from beneath each eyelid as Cade held her close, whispering soft words in her ear, praising her for being brave, speaking of his pride in her and praying silently that the doctor would soon be finished.

Sooner than he'd expected, the deed was done and a bandage was applied, tape covering the area. The doctor turned his attention to the wound on Glory's upper arm. It was a simpler thing, for he only needed to wash it out thoroughly, then put carbolic salve on the long gash and finish it off with a bandage that circled her arm.

"This is gonna heal up in no time, ma'am. Won't hardly leave a scar, either," he told Glory.

"My baby?" she whispered.

He rose from the chair, sorted out his instruments and put his bag back together. "Not to worry, Missy. That baby wasn't hurt, not one little bit," he said, and then patted Glory's arm kindly.

Cade remained where he was, his handkerchief once more called into use, for Glory's tears were flowing.

"I'm sorry, Cade. I just feel real shaky inside."

"I imagine so, ma'am. You need to stay in bed and take it easy for a day or two. Don't take any chances with that baby of yours."

"I'll take care of her, Doc," Cade said, rising to usher the man from the house. He turned back to the bed and lifted a hand to Glory. "I'll be right back, sweetheart."

The sheriff had cleared all the litter out of the kitchen when Cade made his way downstairs. "Wasn't any sense in you taking a look at these three fellas, Doc. They were beyond your help, no matter how you figure it. Mrs. McAllister is a damn fine shot, I'd say. Took out two of them and it took both McAllister and me to handle the third one. I've got them loaded onto your wagon, Cade, and I'll take them into town. I washed up the floor pretty well, but I suspect your lady will want to do a better job once she's back on her feet. I'll be back out to gather up that gold right soon. I'll wire Pinkerton's that you found it."

"I'll take care of the floor," Cade said. "I know my way around the kitchen with a bucket of soap and water," Cade said.

The men left and when they'd gone, Buddy and

Essie came back in the house. "Can I go up and see Glory?" Essie asked, waiting for permission.

"If you're real quiet. Don't make any noise to wake her. All right?"

"I'll be ever so quiet. I just want to sit down by the bed and watch her."

Cade didn't have it in his heart to deny the child, so he nodded and sent her on her way.

"I'm gonna change my clothes and then I'll help with supper, Pa," Buddy said. He ran quietly up the stairs and was back within minutes, still buttoning his shirt as he came into the kitchen.

"Let's see what we can find to eat," Cade said, heading for the pantry. Buddy followed him, speaking quickly.

"Pa, there's someone here. Looks like Mrs. Bradley, the lady Glory talked to yesterday on the way back from town."

Cade met Etta Bradley at the back door. She carried a kettle in one hand, a covered pan in the other. "I thought maybe you could use some soup. I heard the racket going on over here, guns firing, and such, and Robert came in all excited over the mess you all had with those three hoodlums. There's chicken soup and some fresh cinnamon buns for the lot of you. If you need any bread, let me know and I'll send my boy over with it. I suspect your wife won't be up to cooking for a day or so, Mr. McAllister."

"I can't thank you enough, Mrs. Bradley. Glory just had a couple of pellets dug out of her shoulder and the gash on her arm bandaged, and I think she's dozing. Essie went up to keep an eye on her while Buddy and I fix supper. This will be wonderful, for I'm not much of a hand at cooking."

Etta spoke in an undertone. "Earl told me that Mr. Clark thought the world of his wife. He spoke well of her and always told Earl how lucky he was to have her here with his children."

"Well, me and Buddy are of the same mind, ma'am. Glory is the sun in our sky, sure enough."

"Ain't that a fine thing to say? She'd be right proud to hear you speak in such a way, Mr. McAllister."

Etta Bradley took her leave, reminding Cade to send for her if he was in need of anything. She climbed into the buggy she'd driven and turned her horse around, heading for home.

"She's a nice lady, Pa." Buddy peered into the pan that held the cinnamon rolls, then sniffed the chicken soup. "Smells almost as good as Glory's soup, don't it?"

"Almost," Cade agreed.

He set the kettle on the stove and added a good chunk of wood to the fire that burned within. The cinnamon rolls he put into the warming oven up top and then helped Buddy set the table for the three of them. He figured that a cookie sheet would make a good tray and after they ate, he'd take up a small bowl of soup for Glory.

"I think it would be grand to be a doctor, like Doc Stevens, don't you, Pa? I was thinking that maybe when I grow up I could help people and fix them up when they get hurt. He knew just what to do, didn't he?"

"He sure did, Buddy. He went to school for a lot of years to learn how to do the doctoring he does. It takes a long time to read all those books and learn all the things a doctor has to know."

"Do you think I'm smart enough to study like he did? Maybe go to medical school when I'm old enough?"

"I don't know why not, Buddy. You're a bright boy and there's not a reason in the world why you can't be anything you want to be. Even a doctor."

"I'd like to think about it, anyway. I'll work

real hard in school and learn everything I can, so when I'm old enough to go away to college, I can study hard and maybe one day I'll be Dr. McAllister."

"Legally your name is still Buddy Clark, you know," Cade reminded him.

"Can we change it to McAllister? I'd really like to have your name, Pa."

"We can sure find out, son. I'll speak to the judge about it the very next time he makes his rounds and visits the jailhouse in town."

"I'll bet Essie would like to be named McAllister, too. Then we'd all have the same name, me and Essie and Glory and you. We'd be a real family then. Just like the sign says—McAllister Family."

Cade felt his heart swell within his chest as the boy spoke. Never had he thought to be overwhelmed by such pride. Nor had he expected such words to come his way.

He turned to Buddy, wrapped his arm around the boy's shoulders and drew him close to himself. "You're not too old for a hug, are you, son?" he asked, trying to hide the sound of huskiness he heard in his own voice.

"I like gettin' hugged, Pa. Glory does it sometimes, too, and it makes me feel all warm inside."

"I know just what you mean, Buddy. I feel the same way when she hugs me."

"Glory really likes you, Pa, don't she? I mean, like a lady likes her husband. She liked my pa real good when he was alive, but it was like he was her father, just like he was our pa. But with you, she looks at you in a funny way sometimes, and then her eyes get all soft when you come in the house, and when you put your hand on her shoulder or touch her hand, she just looks like she's all shiny inside. Did you ever notice?"

"Yeah, I've noticed, Buddy. That's how I feel when she smiles at me, too. It's the way it's supposed to be when a man and a woman get married."

Buddy leaned closer to Cade and spoke quietly, lest he be overheard. "I think Glory loves you, Pa. I mean really, even more than she loves me and Essie. She likes lots of folks, but it's different with you, ain't it?"

Cade felt as if he was getting into deep water, but would not take the risk of hurting the boy's feelings no matter what. "There's a special link between a man and his wife, Buddy. You'll find out one day when you're older and thinking about getting a wife for yourself. When you find a woman you want in your life and decide to marry her, you'll know what I'm talking about."

"And that's how come Glory is gonna have a baby, ain't it, Pa?"

"You've got that right, Buddy. I helped Glory to make a baby, and when it's born, it'll be half Glory and half me, and all of it will be a McAllister, and will belong to you and Essie, too."

Buddy beamed. "I'm glad we talked, just the two of us, Pa. There was things I wanted to know and I think I understand a little better now."

"You can ask me anything you want to, Buddy. Always remember, I'll answer any questions you have. I'll not lie to you or make up fancy stories, but always tell you the truth."

The boy looked at him, his lips trembling as if he wanted to speak and yet held back the words. He walked to the window, turning his back on Cade and his voice trembled. "I was in my room, Pa. I saw the gold on the floor. It looked to me like it had been in the wall under the window and when that fella out in the yard shot the window out, it tore out part of the wall too. Did you know about the gold? Is that where my father hid it?"

Chapter Seventeen

Cade wished fervently that he did not have to speak the words that lay on his conscience, but he'd promised Buddy the truth and the truth was what he must give the boy.

"When I knocked out the wall to put in your window, I found the gold in leather bags, Buddy. I've been sent here to find it, son, for I'm what is known as a Pinkerton man. They hired me to find the gold and I'm afraid I came here under false pretenses. I don't know if you understand what that means, but I lied to Glory and let her think it was just an accident that I happened to be here. But, even though it was a job for me to do, I found myself falling in love with Glory and wanting to marry her. It was wrong to take her as my wife while I was living a lie, but I was afraid if I didn't tie her to me by marriage, I'd lose her when she found out who I really was and why I was here."

"Does Glory know now that you're not just a regular man, but a fella sent here to find the gold my father hid? Will she still want to be married to you when she hears why you came here?" Buddy's brow furrowed as he considered Cade's deception and the effect it would have on the whole family.

Cade placed a large hand on the boy's shoulder and his words were slow, as if he must choose them carefully. "I didn't know what to do with the gold when I found it, for I feared that the law might think that Glory knew about it, and I didn't want her blamed for it being there. And I didn't want folks to look at you and your sister, thinking that you were indeed the children of a bank robber. So I put it under the new window and sealed it up. I knew the time would come when I'd have to carry it to the sheriff and have him send it to the bank where it came from, but I wanted the timing to be right. And then all of this happened and now we have no choice, son. I told Glory who I really am, and now I'll have to depend on her to forgive me."

Buddy swallowed hard and looked up at Cade. "So my father really did steal it, didn't he?"

"Yeah, I'm afraid he was in on the bank robbery, son. Apparently the other men trusted him enough to let him take the gold and keep it for all of them. And then when they broke out of jail a few weeks back, they came after it."

"He didn't tell us it was there, not me or Glory either. And he didn't spend it either, Pa. He must have been hiding it for the men who robbed the bank."

"That's what it looks like, son. And I probably should have given it to the sheriff as soon as I found it, but I decided to wait till things quieted down. And then things really got in an uproar. Joe Lawson knows the gold is here and I'm sure he'll take care of it right soon. For now, you and I should put it into a pillowcase or a box or something and stick it under the bed."

"I'll do it after supper," Buddy offered, and Cade nodded his approval. The boy stood beside him, seeming to be deep in thought, and then he spoke again.

"I'm glad you told me about it, Pa. You said you wouldn't tell me stories or lie to me and I feel real good to know that you tried to protect

Glory by hiding the gold. I don't think Sheriff Lawson will be mad at you, do you?"

"No, he doesn't seem to be upset with us. I suspect he knows the gold will be brought to town right soon. He's not afraid we'll run off with it."

Buddy laughed. "He knows us better than that. But I don't think we should tell Essie about it, do you? She's too young to understand things like that."

"You're right there, son. We'll keep it between us for now. Glory knows, but she's not in any shape to worry about it."

"Will we be able to fix up Essie's room soon, do you think? She's fussin' over the shelf you promised her. And we'll have to fix up my room where the men shot a hole in the wall."

"I know," Cade said, aware that the child was not going to rest until he'd done as he'd promised.

The soup was steaming, sending forth an aroma that made Cade's mouth water. It had been a long time since they'd eaten, and he was more than ready for supper. Buddy had the bowls on the table and had poured milk into two glasses when Essie came down the stairs.

"Glory's sleeping and I'm hungry," she announced. She looked at her brother and frowned.

"Did you wash your hands, Buddy? Glory said we gotta always wash up before we eat."

He threw her a patient look and nodded, sitting down at his usual place at the table. Cade used Glory's ladle to dish up the soup for the children, deciding he'd wait till later to have his own meal, and concentrate instead on fixing Glory's instead, hoping he could coax her to eat a bit.

Glory opened her eyes when he went into the bedroom, her smile looking a bit ragged, but welcome nevertheless. "Did the children eat?" she asked.

Cade told her about Etta coming by and sat beside her, stirring the broth he'd brought for her. She shook her head, but he wasn't taking no for an answer, and ignored her small show of defiance.

"Come on, sweetheart. I told the children I was gonna feed you and that's what I'm going to do." He propped her up with two pillows behind her back and she winced as he lifted her to rest against the headboard.

"You're not going to be nice about this, are you?" She pouted a bit as he blew on a spoonful of soup, and he shook his head, holding a dish towel against her breast to catch any drops that might spill.

"Nope. You're going to eat. I'll feed you and pamper you, but I won't go back downstairs and tell those young'uns that their Glory wouldn't even try Mrs. Bradley's soup." The spoon approached her mouth and she opened her lips to sip at the broth.

"Can I just have the soup part, and leave the chicken and noodles for you?" she asked politely, her eyes begging him to heed her words.

"All right. If you'll sip all the broth, I'll eat the rest," he agreed, happy to find her cooperative with him.

His lips found hers several times between spoonfuls and he leaned close to whisper in her ear as he finished what she hadn't eaten, cleaning the bowl with a flourish.

"Buddy said it smelled almost as good as your soup, Glory. But you do something different than Mrs. Bradley. Don't know what it is, but yours has a better flavor. I'll bring you up one of the cinnamon rolls she brought over. How about a cup of tea to go with it?"

She grinned at him, leaning back against the pillows. "I kinda like this being an invalid and getting waited on, Mr. McAllister. I could get real used to this."

"Not much chance of that. I told Essie you'd be back in the kitchen by the end of the week. I don't think she's looking forward to my cooking."

"I'll be feeling better by morning, Cade. You can help me downstairs early on, and I'll fix something easy for breakfast. Maybe a pot of oatmeal."

"I'll bet I can slice bacon and fry it up. It can't be all that difficult, can it?"

"I'll sit in the rocking chair and give orders and you can wait on me. The doctor will probably be out in a day or so, and tell me I can get back to work."

"You're going to take it easy, sweetheart, just like he told you. You're going to have my son or daughter and I want you to feel back to normal before you start in washing and ironing and cleaning house."

"I will. Maybe Etta will come by and lend a hand for a morning." She scooted carefully down and Cade moved the pillows from behind her, placing them under her head.

"Is that better?" he asked and she nodded her thanks. He wiped her mouth with a towel he'd brought along and brushed her hair back, his hand gentle against her cheek. "Do you suppose it will be all right for me to sleep with you tonight, if I promise to be really careful not to jar you or roll over against you? I can't stand the thought of sleeping in another bed, Glory."

She smiled, her eyes looking heavy again, and he pulled the sheet up over her chest. "How about taking another little nap? Essie will want to sit with you, and I'll have her come up if you'll promise to try to sleep. The doctor left some pills for you to take for the pain, and I'll bring them up with a glass of water for you."

"I'll try," she said, covering a yawn with her right hand. "But not till I have my cinnamon roll and cup of tea."

"All right. I'll be back up in a few minutes."

She didn't argue about the pills when he brought them to her and Cade recognized that Glory was more than ready for relief from her bout of surgery. He held the cup for her and watched as she sipped tea, swallowing her pills without a fuss.

He knelt by the bedside, his head beside hers on the pillow. Glory turned her face to his. "I wasn't worried, but I feared for the baby, Cade. The doctor seems to think there's not a problem though, for he said everything sounded good when he listened with his stethoscope."

It was growing dark by the time the dishes were finished. Buddy had gathered up all the gold and packed it into a box. He took it to Cade and Glory's bedroom and stood in the doorway. "Do you want this in here?" he asked, holding the heavy box before him. Cade waved him into the room and motioned to the corner where he'd set the screen back in place.

"Put it back there, son. I'll give it to the sheriff when he comes back out."

"I'm going to bed, Pa. We got lots to do tomorrow, keeping up with our work and Glory's too."

"It'll all be fine, Buddy. Glory's going to come downstairs in the morning and tell us what to do."

"I'll help, too," Essie said from the hallway. She carried her nightgown with her and sent a coaxing look in Cade's direction. "Can I come in here and get undressed and say my prayers for Glory, Pa?"

"I don't know why not. I've put the screen back up and you can change behind it."

Essie scampered across the room and Glory

took Cade's hand. "I'm ready for bed, too, just as soon as the children are settled."

"I know you are, honey. I'll close up the house and be right back." He left the bedroom and Glory heard the doors close down below. Within minutes he was back, settling on the side of the bed as Essie came out from her corner and knelt beside him. He put his big hand on her head as she said her prayers, wiping his eyes a bit as she asked for a special blessing for Glory and then yawned widely as she rose and leaned against him.

"Good night, Pa," she said, leaning to kiss Glory's cheek. Buddy waited for her to finish with the ritual and then took her to her own bedroom. Cade heard him tell the child they'd be getting up early and then both their bedroom doors closed.

"I'll leave our door open, in case either of the children have a hard time sleeping tonight," he told Glory. "I don't want Essie to be having nightmares. I can't believe she hasn't been fussing over the fella that rode off with her. But she hasn't said much about it. I think she was more worried about you than herself, Glory."

"You may be right. She whispered in my ear

earlier that she wasn't afraid, for she knew that she'd be rescued one way or another. She's a pretty sturdy little thing, isn't she?"

Cade nodded, leaning to blow out the kerosene lamp before he got undressed for bed. His clothing dropped to the floor and he sat on the side of the bed. "Where do you want me, sweet?" he asked.

"On my right side, please. I want to put my head on your shoulder, Cade, and I can't lie on my left arm. If you're in front of me, I can lift my arm across your chest and keep it a little elevated that way. I'm afraid it's pretty sore."

"It's gonna be sore for a while, with all the digging the doc had to do to get those pellets out."

"How long do you suppose it will take before I can cuddle with you?"

"You're going to cuddle with me tonight, sweetheart."

"No, I don't mean just..." She laughed a little and he thought he caught a hint of tears in her voice.

"You mean, when can we make love?" His arm slid beneath her head and he lifted her to lie close.

"I guess that's what I meant. I don't know why I couldn't just say it the way you did."

"You're a woman, and still right next door to being an innocent, sweetheart. Men don't seem to care if they sound kinda blunt about such things, I suspect."

"But I'm your wife, Cade. I shouldn't still be shilly-shallying around, not able to speak my mind."

"You can say anything you like to me. You know that."

"Then can I ask you something? Will Joe Larson understand about the gold? Will he believe that we didn't know it was here until you found it in Buddy's wall?"

"He'll know that I was looking for it. I told you I was a Pinkerton man, Glory, don't you remember? I was hired to find the gold, but I got all caught up in you and the children and wanting to marry you, until I lost track of my reason for being here."

"It's almost a blessing that when you hid the gold again till you could talk to the sheriff about it, it came to light when that man's shotgun blasted through Buddy's wall."

"I'm glad the gold was there, Glory, for it no doubt saved your life. If the shot hadn't hit the gold, it would have hit you, full force, and might have killed you. As it is, the sheriff will get the gold and get it back to Pinkerton. He said he'd told them that it had been found, and I doubt they'll want to know all the whys and wherefores of my finding it, just that it's here and will soon be in their possession."

"I feel bad that Harvey Clark was a bank robber, for I've been thinking for years that he was a good man and a good father," Glory said quietly.

"Well, he was sure enough a crook, but that doesn't take away from him being a good father to those two kids he left you with. He had some redeeming qualities, Glory, and yet he was a criminal and was executed for his crimes."

"I'm just glad you showed up here, Cade, and ended up wanting to marry me," she told him.

"But the fact remains that the real reason I came here was because I was sent by the Pinkerton Agency to find the gold, not because I was looking to buy a farm and settled on this place by chance," Cade said, fearful that his words would hurt her more than the pellets in her arm had.

"So that's all you came here for, Cade? Just like the rest of the men who wanted to marry me in order to get rich?"

"Not for that reason, sweetheart. I came because I was hired to do a job, and in order to do it, I had to live here. It wasn't written in my orders to marry you, Glory. I married you because I fell in love with you and wanted you for my wife."

"But you lied to me and the children, didn't you?"

"I couldn't do anything else, Glory. I know it's hard for you to understand my motives, because I'm still not real sure just how pure they were. I was just doing my job and living day by day. Then I took a good long look at you and knew I was a goner. And I knew it wouldn't be any hardship to marry you. You presented a mighty fetching picture the day we met. As a Pinkerton man it was like a gift you'd given me, accepting my proposal. I could live here and look at leisure for the gold. But in all the excitement of being married and having a family, I lost track of my reasons for being here. It wasn't until I happened upon the gold in the wall where Harvey hid it that I knew I'd have to turn it over and then tell you the truth about myself. It's the hardest thing I've ever had to do, for I feared you'd not want me after you knew the truth. I decided then to put the gold back in the wall and wait to tell the sheriff.

Just admitting out loud to you that I married you under false pretenses scared me half to death. I was so afraid I'd lose you, Glory."

"But you didn't love me for real, did you, Cade? I've been holding a grudge against you for a while now. I felt like you were taking the farm away from me and making it your own. When you bought the horses and the heifers I was angry at you because I'd lost all control of things. And now I find that our whole marriage was a lie and I've been made a fool of."

"That's not true, sweetheart. You've never been made to look a fool. I knew you weren't happy about things of late, Glory, but I want you to know that my putting my cash into this place really is an investment for all of us. I wouldn't take this place away from you for the world. It'll always be your farm, yours and the children's."

"I suppose I know that now. But it hurts to think you married me and told me you loved me and you were lying to me all along," she said, tears flowing freely as she hid her face in her hands.

"Don't cry, sweetheart. I don't know how to convince you that I love you and I want us to have a life together, just as we've talked of, all along. I don't want to lose you, Glory. I won't ever lie to you again, I promise. We'll turn the gold over to the sheriff and we can make a fresh start and be a family, just like we've planned right along."

"I want to be your wife and I want us to be happy together, all four of us. No, all five of us," she added quickly and then looked up at him with real fear shimmering in her eyes. "Those shotgun pellets could have hit me and hurt our child, Cade."

"Well, they didn't. And for that I'll be forever grateful. When everything is said and done, we'll have us a new baby and a fresh start. I'm hoping Joe Larson will come out here tomorrow and pick up that box over there in the corner. I'll be glad when it's all settled and back in a safe in the bank in St. Louis."

"Well, I'm done worrying about it, Cade. I love you and in case you're still fretting about it, I've forgiven you for telling me lies when you came here. I understand that it was a part of your job, and I can't help but be thankful that Pinkerton sent you here, or I'd never have known you and had you in my life."

"You're no more thankful than I am, sweetheart. There's so much love for you within me that it kinda chokes me up sometimes when I think about it. I love Buddy and Essie and I know I'll love our baby, too, but most of all, I love the woman I married. You mean the whole world to me, Glory. I want you to know that."

"I guess I do, Cade. When you hug me and kiss me and hold me close, the warmth of your feelings just kinda surround me. I named it once as my sanctuary, and I guess that's about the best name for it. You make me feel safe and secure and loved, and you'll never know how much I yearned for just such a thing for a lot of years."

Glory was quiet for a moment, then became animated again. "I hate to change the subject, Cade, but we've got a lot to talk about. First off, we need to talk about Buddy going to school. I'll sew him some shirts and we can buy him new trousers to wear."

"Hold it right there, Glory. We'll buy his shirts. You've got enough to sew, what with a baby coming and Essie needing stuff done for her. And don't forget those wrappers. You'll be needing a couple of them right soon, I figure."

"Now for another thing. Will Buddy be all right riding back and forth to school on the black mare?"

"I don't know why not, Glory. He sure did a good job of riding back and forth to town to get the sheriff and then the doctor. I think the black mare will work out well and she's the one he's kinda partial to, so let's let it go at that. He'll have other boys along the road probably to ride with, maybe even Etta's boy next door. We'll get him new shoes at the store along with the pants and shirts and fit him out in a big way. He'll feel like a real big shot, won't he?"

"No, Buddy will never be too full of himself, Cade. He's sensible and has a good head on his shoulders."

"I was just joshing you a little, girl. Thought you knew that."

She laughed. "I did. But I always have to stick up for my children, Cade. I've been doing it for a long time now.

"There's one more thing, Cade. And I need to spit it out right quick, for I've been mulling over it for a while and we need to bring it out in the open."

"What are you fussing over now, sweetheart? I thought we had everything out in the open already."

She took a deep breath and then spoke quickly. "Just who owns this farm, Cade? Is it mine or yours?"

Chapter Eighteen

"I told you the day we got married that the place is legally mine, Glory. Nothing has changed since then. It's the law that a man holds title to anything belonging to his wife. I didn't make the law—I just live by it. As far as the deed to this place is concerned, it hasn't been changed. All we have to do is go to the bank and the gentleman in charge will fix up the deed for us."

"And what will he put on the deed, Cade? How will he change it?"

"Right now, I suspect it says Harvey Clark, and we'll have it changed to Cade and Glory McAllister, with rights of inheritance to Buddy." He looked down at her. "Is that his legal name? Just Buddy?"

Glory shook her head. "No, he's named after

his pa, Harvey Clark, but his mama called him Buddy when he was little and it just stuck."

"Well, then, we'll have it put on the deed as Harvey Clark the second, and he'll have all rights to the title when you and I are gone."

"But in the meantime, it's yours, isn't it?"

Cade shook his head. "You haven't listened to me, Glory. It belongs to all of us. That sign I put up down by the road says it all. It's the McAllister family farm. And on top of that, Buddy is wanting to make McAllister his legal name, so now that I think of it, we'll just do that first and then his name on the title will be Harvey McAllister. And Essie's will be McAllister, too. And what's her proper name, anyway? Surely Essie is just short for something else."

"Harvey said her mama named her Esther and called her Essie. The day I came here, he told me Buddy was past school age and Essie was too young to be of much use to him yet."

"What made you marry him, Glory? In fact, why did you trust him enough to stay here with him?"

She thought back and smiled, the vision alive in her mind. "It was the way he put his hand on Essie's head, like he couldn't help but touch her. I knew then that he was a good man."

"Well, we'll be sure their names are changed as soon as we can see the judge. If Buddy wants it done, I think Essie will go along with it, too."

"They love you, Cade."

He nodded. "I know that, sweetheart. And you do, too, don't you?"

"You know doggone well I love you. How could I help it? You came in this house and took over and made me love you, just like snapping your fingers at me."

"What a thing to say, Glory McAllister."

"It's true. By the time you'd pulled carrots in the garden and delivered those foals and made Buddy into a young man, I'd have been a fool not to love you. You're exactly what we needed."

"And do you need me, Glory?"

"More than I can say. I tried to tell you earlier, but I don't have the right words, Cade. I need you near me, day and night. I want you in my bed when I go to sleep and when I wake up in the morning."

"Well, that goes both ways, honey. You know that."

"I just can't seem to say the words that I want to."

"Are you wanting me to make love to you?"

She buried her face against his chest and nodded. "I just don't know if I'm able to or not." She lifted her head and her lips touched his throat. Her whisper was low, but the message was clear. And Cade understood it without any difficulty. The moon cast its light upon them and the night-birds sang in the darkness. And Cade loved his wife.... With tenderness and loving touches, he once more made her his own.

Joe Lawson made his way to the farm the next day, as Cade had predicted, and sat at the kitchen table, sorting out the questions and answers that had puzzled him. Beside him on the kitchen floor was the box of gold, brought down the stairs by Buddy just moments before.

"I suspected it was just about as you told me, Cade. I don't blame you for fearing for Glory's reputation. Although I never thought about her knowing of the gold, some of the townsfolk were suspicious. I can understand why you were concerned about bringing it out into the open."

"Will there be any problem with the bank in St. Louis? And will my name be mud as a Pinkerton man? By the way, I've got a letter ready to send them, giving them chapter and verse, mud on my name and all."

Joe laughed aloud. "Like you really care about mud on your name. You're planning on quitting that job anyway, Cade. I'd bet my last dollar on that. There's not a job in the world that could tempt you to leave Glory and these young'uns and go trotting off to earn a living as a detective. Besides, they'll be so tickled to get the gold back, they won't have a word to say. And there's a nice reward for the finding of it, too. I'd say Glory was eligible for that, wouldn't you?"

"Sounds good to me," Cade said. "Will there be enough to pay for Buddy's education, do you think?"

"I'd think so," Joe said. "I'll send a wire and find out in the morning. But first I've got to take this to the bank and have them put it in the safe till we get it returned. I think the fella in St. Louis will send out a couple of men to pick it up."

He stood to leave, putting the box on the table to tie it together with a length of twine Glory had brought from the pantry. He slid his hand into his pocket and drew forth a letter.